The horse, winded and listless in the heat, did not turn quickly; in a trice Conan was upon its rider. Instead of smiting the armored, lavender-cloaked back, the Cimmerian launched himself atop the lordling and bore him bodily from the saddle. The two plunged into a red-flowered bush and rolled there in a savage, thrashing fight, sinking from view in the greenery. The plant's pendulous blossoms continued shaking in a spastic frenzy which dwindled gradually to stillness.

At length the bush shivered once again, its twigs cracking with the burden of shifting weight. From it Conan arose, holding Jefar Sharif's red-streaked dagger in one hand. Breathing heavily, he flung the knife away into the forest and stepped from the bush. Then he turned to face another flurry of hoof-splashes approaching from the nearby field.

The Adventures of Conan
published by Tor Books

CONAN
THE HERO

LEONARD CARPENTER

A TOM DOHERTY ASSOCIATES BOOK
NEW YORK

CONAN THE HERO

Copyright © 1989 by Conan Properties, Inc.

A TOR Book
Published by Tom Doherty Associates, Inc.
49 West 24 Street
New York, NY 10010

Cover art by Ken Kelly

ISBN: 0-812-53318-6   Can. ISBN: 0-812-53319-4

Library of Congress Catalog Card Number: 88-50997

First edition: February 1989

Printed in the United States of America

0 9 8 7 6 5 4 3 2 1

To Torre and the Group

Contents

Chapter 1

The Shikhara

The jungle pond spread murky and stagnant, shaded by dense foliage. A few ripples glided across its green-scummed surface to lap against the slimy shoreline. Then, close above the black water, the tangled thicket of rushes parted and a face peered through.

Dark it was, shadowed and obscure as the muzzle of a stalking beast. Yet from its dimness glinted eyes blue as brooding northern skies, a color seldom seen in these rank jungle depths.

The pale, foreign eyes searched the tree-filtered daylight of the pond bank. Seeing no exceptional danger, the watcher parted the reeds and eased out from between them: a massive man, sword-bearing and grotesquely painted, wading thigh-deep in the stagnant water.

He moved topheavy with a sun-darkened breadth of chest and shoulder, supple as an acrobat poised for swift, forceful action. The colors on his face were muddy tones of lampblack and umber; for further concealment, his headband and lank black mane trailed fern fronds, leafy stems, and other spoor of the forest.

1

The remainder of his costume was sparse, a brief leather breech-wrap anchoring knifebelt and swordbelt crisscrossed on his bare chest and back. Except for the sheen of his fine steel weapons and their bronze-studded fittings, he might have passed for a savage child of the jungle.

He paused in the pond scum, extending the long, double-curved blade of his yataghan to redirect the course of a yellow-green water serpent away from his naked thigh. Then he glided forward, his muscle-corded legs and sandaled feet draining the slime and yellow bottom-muck of the pool. Once ashore he paused, bending to pluck red leeches from the glistening calves of his legs. Straightening, he beckoned behind him with his sword to others yet unseen.

The next man to emerge from the reeds needed no lampblack, since his skin was already dark as jungle night. His face had been daubed instead with white clay to break up its full-featured symmetry. He stood fully as large as the first warrior, armed and armored with light mail and an identical S-curved blade. And he might have moved just as gracefully through the mire, if his attention had not been taken up by others toiling behind him.

The half-dozen who followed were less grandly-sized men, with the olive skins and hawk noses of Turanians evident beneath their daubed makeup. They wore bewildering variations of Turanian military garb, with here a spiked metal cap, there a short purple tunic or chain-mail vest. In further defiance of common uniform, their outfits were threaded with jungle fronds, bright blossoms, and long, iridescent plumes of tropical birds. The blades they bristled with clanked often, and their progress through the marsh occasioned low splashes and muttered curses. These sounds invariably caused the black officer to wheel on them, hissing fiercely for silence.

Their pale-skinned scout, meanwhile, moved higher up the pond's steepening bank. He sank in places to all fours, his yataghan sheathed now on his back. From a distance, his progress was visible only by the faint play of jungle light on flexing limbs and the occasional flicker of a disturbed branch or a frightened, upward-spiraling moth. There was no larger animal life to be seen; though one might expect the dense overgrowth to be alive with the rustlings and twitterings of small creatures, a watchful silence reigned.

From the creeping warrior's own vantage, the way was by no means effortless. His course lay through clinging, dripping foliage, beneath and around slack vines whose thorns could gouge and poison the skin. Yet he dared not stop long to find his way, lest the hovering flies and blood-seeking gnats should settle on his skin to bite and suck their fill.

Near the crest above the pond, the foliage opened out. The creeper braced his hands on the littered earth to haul himself up and peer over the top. Then, with a sudden twist and a muttered oath, he wrenched his hand back and rolled away to one side. Squinting in the green dimness, he stared at what he had touched: the face of a fanged, snarling monkey carved from stone, its round head furred over with damp moss.

"Conan, are you all right?" Feather-soft, the whisper drifted up to him from where the black man crouched a few man-lengths downslope.

"Aye, Juma," the scout mouthed in response, raising a hand to silence the mutters and thrashings that were occurring along the line of men behind him. "'Tis nothing."

"Good. But Conan, thrice-curse it!" The black officer's hiss was faint but intense. "Next patrol I scout ahead, and you take charge of these unruly louts!"

Grimly smiling, Conan nodded and turned back to the

evil-looking carving. Considering it, he judged it part of a railing or a free-standing statue buried by jungle growth across the course of centuries; probably it meant that their goal was near. Renewing his grip on the carven monkey's furry pate, he dragged himself upward to peer across the brushy crest, into the leafy void beyond.

The monument rising there was too vast for even the greedy jungle to swallow completely. Hewn from solid stone, formed of what must have been a towering natural monolith, the great shrine tapered onionlike from its broad, swelling base to a slender, lofty pinnacle. Conan could see the pointed shikhara gleaming in hazy daylight high above, piercing to the sky through the many layers of dense foliage. And every cubit of the temple's surface was decorated with intricate carvings —from the wide, porched galleries overhanging the jungle cauldron where Conan lay, to delicate friezes that chased each other in bands around its distant spire.

The subject matter of those carvings was difficult to make out, even from this short remove. Seen through the screening branches, a few tangles of life-sized human shapes seemed to Conan to resemble fierce combats; other twinings of bodies looked more amorous and sensuous. He guessed that, like most sculptures he had seen, the statues depicted the diverse cruelties and pleasures of kings and humanlike gods. Tracing these forms was especially hard, because everywhere the jungle's greedy green tentacles invaded and obscured them. Many of the heroic forms looked bound or strangled by parasitic vines, and often it was impossible to tell the carved human contours from the monstrous windings and swellings of ancient roots.

But the shrine was still habitable . . . and inhabited, it would seem. Ahead and a little to one side rose a curving entry stair, weed-choked and crumbling. In the thick-pillared shadows of the terrace at its end, Conan glimpsed a single pale flicker: the play of daylight, surely, on a burnished metal blade. Peering closer, he made out above it the round paleness of a face scanning the temple's surroundings. To confirm the impression, there came to his jungle-keen nostrils a faint scent of smoke sweetened by ceremonial incense, drifting unquestionably from the direction of the shrine.

To Juma and the Turanians who crept up close behind him, Conan spoke in whispers and quick gestures. He dispatched them toward the base of the stair, indicating that they should await his signal before overcoming any guards there. Then, writhing snakelike, he was off through the roots and stems of the downward slope.

For long moments his progress was stealthy and swift, measured only by the shiver of a branch or the momentary deepening of a green shadow. Then at the base of the temple he emerged into plain view, nimbly mounting the side of the stone edifice. At first there was little challenge apparent in the climb, for the building's massive base shelved inward, with plenty of handholds and footholds in its ornamentation. But he soon enough faced the overhang of the shrine's main body, where its bulbous shape swelled out overhead. Though just as deeply carved and ribboned with vines, this outjutting face would have been judged by most men impossible to scale, the more so without a rope and in total silence.

But Conan, only pausing at the angle of the slope to tie his sandals to his belt, assaulted the overhang fearlessly. He hauled himself up monkey-like, clutching with bare toes and fingers at carved niches and elbows of vine. Often his legs thrashed in empty air as he forced himself upward hand over hand; at other times, his lithe body clung close amid sculptured shapes both sacred and profane. He appeared almost to take part in their

murderous and orgiastic writhings, as just another hero
or godling carved in paler stone and deeper relief.

At long last he mounted to the balcony rail at the
widest level of the shrine. Once there, he was free to hug
the grainy stone, panting shallowly so as not to betray
his presence by deep gasps. His climb had brought him
up a few paces from the head of the stair, with the
broad, gadrooned bulk of one ornate pillar standing
between him and the shadowy roost of the guard he had
seen.

Now he tried to verify the man's presence, first by
peering through the gaps of the thick, carved railing,
then by raising his head cautiously over its edge. From
this distance, the interior gloom was easily penetrated,
with nothing in sight but a lavishly decorated walkway
strewn with rock fragments and plant debris. He stood
up to lean inward over the rail; then, at the sound of feet
shifting restlessly within, he jerked back to his precari-
ous crouch outside. No one passed near, so Conan
judged that the lone guard still loitered in his place at
the stairhead. He stood upright, stretched himself prone
on the rail, and eased across it on his belly.

Edging around the spiral-ridged curvature of the
pillar, he spied the guard's arm, bare and muscular,
banded with colored cords at shoulder and elbow in the
style of the savage Hwong tribe. The man's bronze
cutlass was stuck in his waistband, his hands resting on
the rail as he watched the jungle.

Drawing a deep, silent breath, Conan moved up close
behind him. His massive arms were poised, knife
gripped tightly in one hand, ready to seize the sentry's
face from behind and lay open his throat. His shoulders
tightened for the gruesome deed; but instead, feeling a
sudden kinship with the simple tribesman, he turned
the knife in his hand and struck the man over the temple
with its silver hilt. Catching the collapsing body under

the chin with his free arm, he lowered the sentry quietly to the ground.

Just then a yell rang out behind him, followed by a shrill jabber of Hwong speech. Conan turned to see a second sentry come charging from an inner passage, wielding a saw-edged hardwood club. With no time to draw his sword, the northerner raised his dagger to fend off the stroke. The downswing was knocked aside, but its force drove the knife out of Conan's hand and shaved skin from his knuckles in passing.

Before the attacker could swing the club again, Conan lunged against him barehanded. Seizing him by the throat and the crotch of his brightly woven breech-clout, he lifted the man and flung him headfirst over the rail. The Hwong's cry of rage and alarm sounded lingeringly this time, to end in a faint bleat of expelled air as he struck the stone outworks below.

Cursing at the noise and at the racking pains in his knuckles, Conan found his knife and sheathed it. Drawing his yataghan from behind his back, he stepped out onto the narrow stairway and waved it high in silent summons. His companions were already halfway up, their legs racing over the small, worn steps as Juma silently waved them along with his sword. Conan turned to the inner archway, which was a narrow descending stair. No more defenders came out, but he heard a panicked jabbering below and glimpsed a face peering up at him, quickly to vanish in shadow.

Conan cast swiftly about the temple porch. The farther gallery and ascending rampways looked long-deserted and weed-choked; likely there was no benefit to be gained exploring there. It was from below that scented smoke issued; as his companions arrived on the terrace, he plunged into the downward corridor.

Conan took four or five of the tiny stairsteps with each stride. Mentally he cursed the tightness of the corridor, which was miserly in comparison with the vast outer dimensions of the monument. Its narrowness would permit only the first man in line to face the enemy, and even then it afforded no room to swing a sword. Worse, as he descended, his own bulky shadow and those of the men scuffing behind him quickly cut off the daylight. He was forced to slow his headlong rush and prod the scented darkness before him with his swordblade.

Squinting to pierce the dimness, he found himself at the base of the stair in a T-branching corridor; there, suddenly, he was attacked. An unseen club-wielder at one side beat down his extended sword, while the lurker in the other arm of the T stabbed up at his chest with a short, bronze-tipped spear. Catching sight of the razored spearpoint's glint, Conan jerked back, retaining a desperate grip on his yataghan; an instant later his blade lashed out and struck off the menacing speartip— cleanly, like severing the head of a striking serpent. Then, with his fellow-warriors pressing forward at his back, Conan leaped into the level passage to engaged the club-swinger.

Sparks flew from the stone walls as Conan drove at his half-seen enemy. Metal chimed shrilly as his blade tried to stab past the man's desperate parries. In a trice the club's deep-notched edge caught the steel blade of the yataghan, twisting it down and aside out of action. The tribesman bore down savagely on the swordblade, trying desperately to snap it . . . even as Conan's knife, plied in his free hand, buried itself to the hilt in the man's side.

The Hwong collapsed with a moan, and Conan finished him with a quick, chopping swordstroke. No more enemies stood before him in the dimness. From the rush of feet behind him, he guessed that his fellow attackers had broken through in the other direction. He stepped over the corpse and pressed forward. A yellow-ish, indirect light outlined the curving passage ahead.

With a couple of Turanians panting at his back, Conan came to the end of the corridor. It opened into a shadowy room, broad and low-ceilinged, with a fire burning on the floor at its center. About the chamber dim shapes of ancient idols, stone pillars, and human figures reflected its glow.

At the room's far end cries and weapon-blows sounded, where a pair of spearmen held the other wing of the attacking party at bay in the cramped entry; but this door was unguarded. Conan and his companions were well into the room before a youthful Hwong came pelting around the fire to face them. The young brave was attacked at once by the Turanians, giving Conan time to take in the dim scene.

Outlined by firelight was a bent figure in a stiff, flaring gown. From the cloak's bristling feathers and winking ornaments, Conan judged it to be that of a shaman or magic-maker. In the crook of his arm the wizard supported a tall wooden staff crowned by a glittering, jewel-encrusted skull, whether real or cast of shiny metal Conan could not tell, so dense was the ornamentation. Its stooped owner, busy mumbling and tossing powders into the fire, glanced briefly up, and the dim backlight showed Conan a wizened, shriveled face of unguessable age. Calmly, then, the sage turned back to continue his chant unbroken, as if unconcerned by the intrusion of armed men.

Pinioned upright beyond the fire stood another re-markable figure, a slender female much harder to ignore. Naked but for some small adornment about her neck, she displayed strikingly the almond-eyed, saffron-skinned beauty which Conan found so alluring in the women of this southern clime. Shimmering full-lit before the fire, her body wavered above it like a shapely yellow flame. At her sides, two Hwong braves held her arms, forcing her so near the embers that her skin gleamed with perspiration. Her face, dark-eyed and tight-lipped in the gloom, gazed down into the flames in desperate resignation.

Whether the fire itself was the object of her fear, Conan could not guess; yet there was certainly something odd about it. The blaze was knee-high and arm-wide, a brisk conflagration, yet no supply of fuel was visible nearby. Where stubs of burned logs should have protruded, lazy fumes and smoky tendrils wove about the base of the flames. The whole fire came, perhaps, from the glistening dust the old priest sprinkled, grains of acrid incense whose pungency filled the room. The colors of the fire were strangely bright and varied; at times its glow almost seemed to take organic shape, like the swell and clutch of a carnivorous sea-flower bathed in restless ocean tides.

In the few racing heartbeats required to take in the scene, Conan's companions struck at the lone tribesman from two directions at once. While they chopped him down with a flurry of merciless blows, Conan veered toward the captive woman. Meanwhile Juma, bellowing fierce Kushite curses, broke through the archway at the far side of the chamber. The two guards who opposed him were scattered like tossed knuckle-bones before his roaring charge.

The pair of warriors holding the yellow-skinned woman flinched back at these threats, the nearer one releasing her to draw a long, barb-bladed knife from his belt. Once, twice, it clashed against Conan's flailing yataghan, until a powerful backhanded slash laid open the man's neck and cast him sprawling into the fire. The other guard, meanwhile, had begun to drag his captive toward the shadowy rear of the chamber; now, at

Conan's instant pursuit, he hurled her to the floor and turned to dash away into the shadows himself. The northerner bent over the woman, seized her arm, and hauled to her feet. Swiftly he ascertained that her lithe, straight limbs and supple body bore no wound and no weapon. With her sweat-damp hands clutching at his arm for protection, Conan turned to face the cacophony of shouts echoing around him.

The magician had finally retreated from the fire, having disabled the two troopers who had accompanied Conan into the room. One danced weaponless, howling and slapping at several small gouts of colored flame which blazed from his tunic and even from his bare flesh; the other Turanian rolled screaming on the floor, beating at his garments, from which billows of thick smoke curled. The maker of these uncanny fires was scuttling nimbly away, dragging his skull-topped stave along with him, aided by one of the surviving guards from the far door. His trail was marked by flaming sparks of fire-dust, which still dripped from his withered hand.

"After him, Imperials! It is Mojurna! Come, you Turanian dogs, slay him!" Yell as Juma would to summon his troops in pursuit, they were slow to follow; some hung back to subdue wounded but still-fighting Hwong; others bent to help their agonized fellow warriors extinguish the gnawing flames, pinning the men down while scraping at their smoldering scars with keen knifeblades.

Conan's impulse to dash after the fleeing wizard was hampered by the grip of his liberated captive at his arm. Rather than drag an unclothed, unarmed female back into danger, he stopped to pry himself loose from her.

"By Astoreth's sacred dugs, woman," he roared at last, "let me go slay your tormentors!"

As he shook her off, he was unable to tell from her

blank stare whether she clung to him out of fear for herself, or for him, or to protect the wizard. Regardless, he broke free and lunged after Juma and a pair of less eager Turanian troopers, who dogged the Mojurna's flame-speckled track.

Their pursuit was short. As they closed with the ancient shaman, he scuttled between a grimy altar and a hulking statue of a lion-headed warrior, into a deep crevice at the back of the gallery. Juma bent nearly double to follow him into the cranny, then darted suddenly backward as a heavy, dusty scraping sounded overhead. An instant later a massive slab thudded down in the entryway, striking sulfurous sparks from the lintel where it came to rest.

A few moments' inspection showed that the trick door, whether mechanical or magical in its workings, had effectively sealed off the escape passage.

"By Otumbe and Ijo!" Juma swore fiercely, kicking the patterned face of the slab with his sandaled heel and probing at it with his sword. "The old one has escaped! 'Twas Mojurna, the rebel chieftain we sought, Conan, I am sure of it!" Squinting at the impenetrable stone in the dim, fading firelight, he shrugged and turned back to the watching soldiers. "Come on, perhaps we can pick up his trail in the forest."

"Aye." Conan turned away with him. "In any case, we should not tarry here. If the wizard can make stones fall, he may try to seal us up in this chamber."

He detoured back to his female prize, who stood watching where he had left her. Taking her by the wrist, he led her toward the entry. Still unclothed, she walked without apparent shame before the Turanian troopers. The men left off kindling torches, binding the Hwong captives, and aiding the burned troopers, turning to stare and mutter covetous remarks. Even the moaning wounded fell silent at her approach. But to the looks and gruff comments she gave no apparent heed.

Passing near the dying fire, Conan halted with his ward to gaze at the remains of the man he had knocked into it. Considering the small size of the blaze and the short time which had elapsed, the body had been consumed with uncanny totality. Only a few tarnished metal trappings and stubs of bone remained, outlining the man's shape in a sooty, sprawling X superimposed across the still-winking ashes.

"Dangerous sorcery, by Crom!" Conan muttered as he passed the incinerated remains.

"No, not by Crom, but by our ancient goddess Sigtona," the woman declared at his side in smooth, liltingly accented Turanian. "Such is the Shining One's power." She shook her stately head, averting her eyes from the smoking remains. "I am glad it was not I who fed the goddess."

Chapter 2

Mojurna's Sign

"**M**ake way! I go on the emperor's business!"

Hiking his caftan up around his knees to keep it from flapping unbecomingly, Azhar the acolyte hurried along the tiled corridor. He shoved through a company of shaven-headed, bare-chested eunuchs and silk-wrapped female slaves bearing linens and water-jugs. These yielded scant way to him, forcing him to brush against their sleek, oiled bodies as he scurried past. Behind his back they flashed ribald, ironic grins at this self-important young man, not truly of a high caste. He was, after all, the slave of mere wizards, not of a mighty king.

Azhar, meanwhile, rounded the corner at the end of the passage. He emerged onto a long, roofed balcony patterned by bright daylight beaming through the filigreed stone railings. He maintained his brisk pace, sandals slapping the intricate mosaic tile. On his left, framed by the slender, graceful pillars supporting the balcony's vaulted canopy, spread Aghrapur, capital city of Turan. Golden under noon sun, the jumble of tiled roofs and glittering domes stretched away out of sight, the view fading swiftly into a smoky, coppery haze born of ten thousand kilns, cookfires, and forges.

If not for the smothering haze, Azhar knew, the balcony would have commanded an even more breathless view of distant plains and mountains. Yet piously he reminded himself that the lord of the palace, the resplendent Emperor Yildiz of Turan, held sway over more of the earth than could possibly be glimpsed from the tallest mountaintop, even on the clearest day.

At length the porch rejoined the domed mass of the central palace. Azhar reentered cool, scented shadow, turning down a curving corridor in the direction of the emperor's apartments. Finally, before a pair of gold-inlaid doors he halted, panting. Two red-cloaked Imperial Guards barred his way, their double-bladed axes meeting at the level of his chest.

"Let me pass!" he gasped to them. "I bring word to His Resplendency from the Court of Seers. I am to tell Emperor Yildiz—"

"Enough!" The ranking guard's craggy, battle-scarred face was too stern to betray even contempt. "Go below to the common chamber and petition the eunuch, Dashibt Bey. If your business is of any merit, he can arrange an audience."

"But sir . . . I mean, Guardian! Ibn Uluthan, the chief mage, told me . . ."

Breathless and confused, the acolyte faltered. Struck then by a sudden recollection, he reached to the neck of his caftan and fished anxiously inside it. The guard waited motionless before him, showing no fear of any weapon the scrawny lad might produce.

What he brought forth from his richly embroidered garment was a heavy signet ring, a glinting golden lump on a loop of silken cord. He pinched it waveringly in the air for the guard to inspect.

"The horned conch . . . symbol of the Khitan Seers."
The guard-commander looked coolly from Azhar to his
younger comrade, who nodded understandingly. The
Guild had entry where others were denied, even into the
imperial presence.

Without further words, the officer retracted his ax.
Hooking its weighty head on a catch at his belt, he
turned to unlatch the ornate door. When one of the
portals swung slightly ajar, he passed through, with
Azhar treading cautiously at his heels. The second guard
secured the door behind them.

Azhar, following the heavy footsteps of the armored
warrior, scarcely dared crane his neck to marvel at the
sumptuousness of the royal apartments about him. A
dazzling rainbow of rugs and cushions littered the black
and white tiled floor, their lush softness strewn between
massive columns of varicolored marble and heavy tables of gold and onyx. Here and there amidst the lavish
appointments, immaculately groomed servants waited
still and silent as human furniture, with none of the
insolence of the lesser palace slaves. And this, Azhar told
himself with a thrill of awe, was only the Great One's
vestibule.

His escort halted to exchange muttered words with a
bearded slave whose splendid turban betold high rank.
Then he led the way through one of several nobly
arched doorways into a high-ceilinged room. It resembled a ballroom, except for its floor; this fell away
toward the center in broad, shallow stairsteps resem-
bling those of an arena.

Around the upper edge of the depression, adorned in
lavish silks, lounged eunuchs and courtiers of the highest rank. At the far side of the room, the Resplendent
One himself sat on a padded couch, fanned by two
kneeling servants. And yet at first, Azhar found himself

unable to lavish his eyes on the divine sight, so peculiar
was the nature of the entertainment underway in the
shallow pit.

There crouched two women, young and athletic-
looking, facing each other in bizarre combat. One was
armed with twin pairs of broad-tipped pincers, the other
with blunt horn-hooks grasped in either hand. Though
barefoot, both women wore blouses and pantaloons of
thin, gossamer-like fabric, flimsy at best and now badly
rent and ribboned by their exertions. Each, it appeared,
was trying to strip the clothing away from her opponent.

As the acolyte watched wide-eyed, the raven-haired
girl lashed out with her tongs, snatching away a stream-
er of fabric to lay bare a shapely expanse of her
red-headed rival's thigh. But the Circassian was quick to
retaliate, hooking the neck of the other's blouse and
shredding it down the front, so that half its cloth
streamed in tatters from the wearer's supple shoulder.
At this triumph, a patter of faint, polite applause passed
around the circle of watchers.

Abruptly the combat halted. Azhar, following the
obedient gaze of watchers and contestants alike, looked
to the emperor, who had snapped his fingers sharply at
his elite guard's approach. The two women, bobbing
their heads obediently, jogged and jiggled to the side of
the arena where they sat together on the bottom step.

Emperor Yildiz the Resplendent, whom the acolyte
had never been privileged to view so closely, was a
small, chubby, olive-skinned man. Azhar, as the guard
led him forward, searched in vain for some sign of
imperial distinction: certainly his silken robe and
pointed-toed slippers were of the rarest quality, his nails
and his fringe of hair well-trimmed. But his olive-
skinned face, and indeed his whole bearing, had a tame
look about them, an air of intense ordinariness quite at
odds with the grandeur Azhar had expected.

"Well, messenger?" The emperor turned his small, dark, bored eyes from the kneeling guard to the stricken-faced acolyte. "What news does the Court of Seers offer me now? Sorcerous warning of some new disaster in the southern campaign? Or just another incomprehensible wrinkle of my astrological destiny?" Yildiz examined Azhar's expressionless face with the faintest hint of annoyance.

"Oh, Resplendent One!" Lightheaded with awe and penitence for his first, blasphemous thoughts, and smitten by the great ruler's mild voice like a reed before a mighty gale, Azhar found himself collapsing to the floor to grovel on knees and elbows before the emperor's padded couch. "Great Lord, forgive this interruption!" His fingers scrabbled numbly on the patterned tile, venturing almost to touch the upcurled toes of the ruby-crusted imperial slippers. "My arcane masters bade me bring word of this morning's event . . . but I scarcely dare trouble you, Sire . . ." His voice quivered to silence, a last tremor of dread animating his hunched shoulders.

"Yes, yes, I know. And what is the news? You may rise." Yildiz gestured impatiently to the attending guard. "Help him up, will you?"

"Oh, Your Resplendency!" Struggling with his own unruly limbs and feeble voice, Azhar felt himself hauled upright by a strong hand at the scruff of his neck. "My master Ibn Uluthan is in audience with Your Splendor's military liason before the Crystal Window." He choked out the words through the constricted collar of his caftan, still not daring to meet the Great One's eyes. "Emperor, they told me to ask . . . they beg your divine presence, O Lord of all Turan!"

"Is that so?" Yildiz arose energetically to his feet. "Then they may be making some progress at last, Tarim willing! If they are, I shall be happy to see it." A golden-haired male servant came forward from the wall to place a massive, bejeweled turban on the emperor's head, which added considerably to his height and grandeur. Then he flicked a finger at Azhar and the guard officer. "Come, boy, we shall take the inner way. Meanwhile, let the combat continue for the edification of my guests."

As the warrior-girls arose to face one another again, Yildiz led Azhar forth from the room. A diminishing series of archways and double-guarded doors brought the three at last into a long, angling hallway. Windowless it was, lit by oil lamps suspended from the ceiling at the junctions of cross-corridors. Azhar knew of this nominally secret inner passage reserved for the emperor's private use, but he had not guessed its extent. It seemed to run the whole length of the vast palace, with stairways and branchings penetrating to the building's remotest wings.

Taking down a lamp from a hook to light their way, the guard led them up a long spiral stairway to a brassbound door. Here Yildiz produced from his silken garments a many-pronged key, which he plied in a concealed aperture. With a faint click, the door swung open on the broad atrium of the Court of Seers.

The high, domed chamber echoed with the shadowy, musty silence elder sages require for their meditations. The octagonal room's corners, lined with shelves of dusty fetishes and scrolls, cowered well back from the light; but its center was bright with dusty sunrays streaming down through glazed slits in the vaulted dome, within which a wooden mezzanine had been installed for stargazing.

The floor level of the room contained several arched entrances, but only one window. Before this stood two men, a senior seer and a military officer, who turned solicitously toward the open door. As Yildiz walked

forward, flanked by the bashful Azhar, the high-ranking
men offered deep, lingering bows.

"O Gracious One, welcome!" The speaker, Ibn
Uluthan, was a tall man wearing the dark burnoose of a
court sage, with the hood thrown back from his gray-
tousled head. "We requested your presence, my Lord,
because of great matters in the offing. Now Your Excel-
lency can see our spells at work."

"Indeed, O Emperor; Uluthan and his fellow magi-
cians have not misled us this time, it would seem." The
black-clad officer, General Abolhassan, nodded a grudging smile at the wizard, his strong yellow teeth gleaming
in a hawk-nosed, dark-mustached face. "It appears that
we finally have intelligence from the southern campaign." Military cordons and insignia winked from the
black mound of his turban as he wheeled toward the
bright window.

The object of his attention stood out strikingly, since
its light was a blue-green glare, strangely out of keeping
with the pale golden rays pouring from the window slits
overhead. Outlined by its eerie radiance, the newcom-
ers moved closer with an air of fascination. The prospect it looked out on they found even more surprising:
not the hazy cityscape Azhar had recently witnessed
from the terrace, but a jungle profusion of trees and
brush simmering beneath a hazy tropic sky, with
mounds and spires of ancient, crumbling architecture
looming in its midst, and human figures fleeing in its
depths.

However vast the imperial palace, it was clearly
impossible for such an immensity to be enclosed within
its walls. Even the stoic guardsman, swallowing a silent
oath, knew that he was witnessing formidable sorcery.
The window itself was nothing more than a sturdy
black-tiled ceramic casement set in a south-facing wall,
and glazed over with marvelously smooth crystal. Yet its

view opened, not on some lavish indoor garden, but on an alien place far removed from this teeming northern city.

"Fascinating, indeed! Good work, Ibn Uluthan." The emperor, moving closer to the casement, nodded at the smiling wizard. "I have but glimpsed the power of your spell before; never was it so satisfactory as this!" He pointed down to the human figures visible in the jungle depths. "The trackless jungles of Venjipur! And those, I take it, are our expeditionary troops carrying out a military operation?"

The beaming sorcerer nodded. "Yes, Your Resplendency. To achieve this effect, we simply intensified the projections of astral force we have been making for months now. As you know, we were plagued with false images caused by the enemy's mystic emanations. But this morning, for reasons that are not entirely clear to us, the Venji spell began to weaken. By following its emanations back to their fading source, we were able to pinpoint this activity."

"You don't know why the resistance stopped?"

"No, Emperor; we hope it means the death of the arch-wizard Mojurna. Without his powers, the Venji rebels can never again resist our sorceries."

As Ibn Uluthan spoke, the view from the window swept breathtakingly forward and down, making the watchers reel and clutch at the sill for support. The light wavered and dimmed, tree-fronds melting into the casement as it magically pushed through the forest. But the sense of motion was only an illusion; from Ibn Uluthan's subtle motions, it became clear that the sorcerer was varying the angle and direction of the window's view by swirling his fingers in a small bowl of black oil on a podium before him.

General Abolhassan moved close beside Yildiz, pointing down at the moving figures who were now nearer and clearer in the prospect. "Those men are Turanians, one of our elite jungle patrols. A fortnight ago I sent orders southward designating Mojurna as a target of priority; these troopers may just now have slain the old scoundrel and cleared the way for us. If this kind of contact with the Venjipur front can be maintained, as Ibn Uluthan says it can, it will relieve our command problems, quicken our responses, make possible an almost limitless expansion of our empire . . ."

"Indeed, I could direct such a war myself, with little need for your intercession, General!" Sparing but a brief glance for Abolhassan, Yildiz gazed down intently on the supernatural vista before him—which, under the wizard's deft manipulation, was following the Turanian band swiftly through jungle depths. Nearest to their aerial vantage loped the last trooper, a large, tigerish man who seemed to be purposefully lagging behind the rest, scanning the jungle for signs of pursuit.

"That giant is a northern barbarian, is he not?" Yildiz asked of no one in particular. "A Vanir, by his looks. They make such splendid figures in uniform; I wish I could recruit more of them!"

The lurking man's expectations of pursuit were soon rewarded: out of the leafy shadows flitted three dim shapes, near-naked warriors racing to encircle him. The lone trooper's blade flicked once, twice in the dimness, causing half-seen thrashings on the jungle floor; then the yataghan swept in a glinting circle, sending the third and last of the pursuers sprawling back across the writhing bodies of the other two. Scarcely pausing, the lone skirmisher turned to follow his band.

"There, you can see," Abolhassan proclaimed to the others, "these Hwong rebels are poor fighters. Our imperial troops vanquish them easily, with or without sorcerous aid! Spells like this are diverting, true—but even this window is of little use, lacking a swift means to communicate with the battlefront." He glanced at the wizard, whose eyes gleamed green in sorcerous daylight as he guided the moving window through the forest. "Carrier pigeons have served us so far; they will continue to be the best means, unless some better magic is devised."

Yildiz gave no indication whether he heard the general. He gazed intently on the jungle scene, his eyes reflecting some of the satisfaction they had shown during the entertainment in his private arena. "How wondrous it is, Ibn Uluthan, to have a direct view of the action! It strikes me that we can use this magic to involve more of our own priests and nobles in our frontier campaigns, and promote more warlike zeal at court. We need something dramatic like this to get the people's fighting spirit up!" He smiled at the others, then shrugged complacently. "Of course, we shall assert our territorial rights in Venjipur in any case; it is of no great consequence. But having this link to our successes there could help to rally the court behind us."

"Indeed, your Resplendency, an excellent idea," said General Abolhassan, sounding unconvinced. He nudged Ibn Uluthan. "Now, Mage, since this jungle detachment has done its work—and in any case, the fate of such a small unit hardly matters—can you possibly conjure us a view of the gate at Venjipur City proper, to check the trim of the imperial sentries there? Believe me, nothing reveals the morale of a fighting force better . . . but say, what is this?"

All five men turned to stare at the glowing window, as from the edges of the casement wisps of pale mist intruded on the jungle greenery. Spreading rapidly, the fog not only obscured the scene, but seemed actively to eat away and dissolve the slowing images of branches and drooping jungle vines. Before their eyes, the entire view soon melted to a formless void of white shot through diagonally with indistinct, sleeting droplets.

In the misty center of this limbo something small and gray appeared. Clarifying and growing swiftly, it seemed to hurtle toward them.

Just as the acolyte Azhar scuttled back, and the others gathered themselves to spring away, the projectile halted. It now filled most of the window: a brightly ornamented skull, cast or plated in purest silver and lavishly inlaid with crystals and precious stone. Its teeth were chisel-pointed diamonds and its sinister eye-sparks smoldering rubies, while green jade and yellow topaz framed the hard, fleshless planes of its face.

"Bismillah!" The wizard Ibn Uluthan, giving vent to the oath, left off fumbling in his mortar of black liquid. "That skull is Mojurna's emblem, his personal fetish, may Tarim wither him! Emperor Yildiz, my deepest apologies!"

"Hmm . . . does that mean our enemy is back in control of the sorcerous aether, Mage? And so soon?" Yildiz glanced from window to wizard with an air of mild disappointment.

The sorcerer hesitated, watching Yildiz. All present knew that the emperor's disappointment, though understated, could easily prove fatal in one commanding such vast power.

Azhar the acolyte, who had been yearning to speak, finally dared to anticipate his master. "It is a strong spell, Your Resplendency, cast either by Mojurna or some very formidable apprentice of his, I would say."

"Probably the warlock himself," Ibn Uluthan added, "since he is known to be jealous and unsharing of his powers. The general's detachment must have failed to kill him."

"Damn your insinuations, wizard!" Abolhassan, by

contrast with the emperor's mildness, lashed out suddenly. "There is no reason to assume that my troops failed; anyway, is your power so feeble that a toothless old witch-man scattering parched herbs and moth-wings can overmaster you anytime it doesn't happen to slip his doddering mind?"

"You speak too hastily, General!" Ibn Uluthan, still standing by his podium, glanced apologetically over his shoulder at the garish skullface. "Remember, the Gulf of Tarqheba is far, far south of Aghrapur. Our mystical powers are rooted here, in our people's faith in the god Tarim, the holy temples and imperial relics we worship, even in the sacred stones of this palace. Those powers are vast, but not absolute. Each mile further from Turan, across the Colchian Mountains and into the southern jungles, our own power weakens and our enemy's grows stronger!"

"Fah, lame excuses!" The general shot a self-righteous glance at Yildiz, then turned again to upbraid the sorcerer. "You have been given all the wealth and authority you requested, Ibn Uluthan . . . and more, against the counsel of some of us. That should enable you to do your part! Are you saying that the mightiest empire in the world cannot impose its mystic will on a band of jungle savages and ignorant rice-puddlers?"

"General Abolhassan." Yildiz's voice, soft but resonant, restrained the warrior. "It ill befits you to be so wroth when I, your emperor, am not. Surely we are well on our way to victory in Venjipur in any case? All my counselors have assured me of this, including you." The emperor nodded at the seer, then turned toward the door. "When I see fit to administer a rebuke to Ibn Uluthan, I will do so. Meanwhile, I hope that he will continue his most able efforts."

"Certainly, Your Resplendency!" Scowling, the general nodded curtly at the sorcerer, then turned to follow Yildiz and his guard to the inner passage. Azhar and Ibn Uluthan watched them depart. As they left, their backs were lit by the window's surreal glow and the jeweled skull's eerie, radiant smile.

Chapter 3

Fort Sikander

As the tropic sun climbed higher its hot weight increased; the ruthless orb mounted the sky like the sweaty bulk of a wrestler, slowly strangling his opponent and forcing him down to the hot, dry earth.

Since his arrival in Venjipur, Conan had often wondered at the sharpness of the contrast between steaming jungle miasmas and the parched heat of the compounds. Here, where the invaders had cleared away trees and vines to build an encircling palisade, the bare earth was ridged into furrows and stump-holes, baked rock-hard by sun . . . at least until afternoon, when rain squalls off the Gulf of Tarqheba would surely melt them back to slimy mud.

As noon approached, even the sunrays reflecting off the yellow earth were scorchingly hot; Conan shifted back underneath the frayed awning of the mess tent to avoid them. Jostling inward among huddled, muttering soldiers and sloe-eyed Venji camp girls, he nevertheless lingered near enough to the entry to have an unobstructed view of the staff officers' compound across the yard. Leaning against a tentpost, he endured the flat taste of his beaker of kvass and the smelly companionship of the field canteen.

Juma edged close up beside him, grumbling as was the universal custom. "Small thanks Captain Murad gave us for raiding the demon temple! Conan, you were too honest, telling them the old wizard escaped!" The black trooper smiled, his teeth and eyes glinting yellow-ish in the shadows. "We should have taken off the head of his ugliest warrior and kicked it a few leagues through the jungle. Then we could have passed it off as Mojurna's, and they would have granted us a week's leave in the capital!"

Conan shook his head, laying a good-natured hand on Juma's shoulder. "Nay, fellow, that old lizard-splitter is too dangerous a foe to trifle with. If our commanders thought him dead, 'twould make them all the more lax and reckless. And who bears the brunt of their half-hatched schemes?" He drained his cup of sour beer, grimacing. "By all the gods of the snowy mountains, Venjipur is a vile place! I joined this war because southern duty sounded easy; now I count myself lucky to survive another day!"

"Aye, Conan, too true. Remember when the Venji campaign seemed a good chance to make rank?" Juma's grin flashed again, wistfully. "But here all the commissioned officers are eagle-beaked aristocrats born to command." He scowled morosely. "If they never expose themselves to danger, how will vacancies occur? Aii, it is too dismal to think about!" The Kushite gazed moodily around at the troopers loitering near them. Settling on the largest one, who overtopped even himself and Conan, he confronted him and asked, "What of you, Orvad? How did you find your way here to Fort Sikander?"

The trooper he addressed was truly a massive man, so tall that his straggling hair brushed the grubby canvas overhead. The lank black strands hung unnaturally close to his skull on one side, denoting the loss of an ear—probably on some northern battlefield or civic maimer's block; none had ever dared ask him where. His remaining facial features, though overlarge and hideously battered, identified him as a native of Turan or Hyrkania. He was slow to speech, knitting his scar-seamed forehead and peering at Juma a long time before answering.

"I killed a tavern-keeper in Sultanapur," he rumbled finally. "The fellow tried to drug my wine and steal my pay. Then I killed some of the taverner's kin, and a few city guards." Orvad frowned thoughtfully. "When I went back to the garrison, the commandant called me before him. He said if I enjoyed killing so much, Venjipur was the place for me. So I came here." The giant lowered his eyes, shaking his head in childish disappointment. "But the commandant didn't tell me I'd only be killing Hwong, these little jungle monkeys! That's not the same as killing men!"

His observation was greeted by guffaws from the others in the tent. The gruff male outburst was soon joined by shriller female tones, as troopers translated the joke for the camp slatterns. Orvad looked around at them all, his brow knitting in suspicion at their levity, his big fists slowly knotting—until Juma ventured near enough to lay a hand on his shoulder. "Yes, Orvad, you are certainly right! Everyone here feels the same! Luckily the Hwong are not easy to kill, so that gives us all some sport."

At Orvad's slow smile and nod, the watchers laughed heartily again. Juma, after placating the giant further and ordering him another drink, returned to Conan's side. The Cimmerian, somewhat detached from the merriment, was gazing out from under the pavilion at a log-walled, canvas-roofed building opposite.

"Even dull-witted Orvad is not content!" Juma muttered at his side. "Was there ever a soldier so dim that he enjoyed serving in Venjipur?"

"Maybe." Conan nodded at a corner of the pavilion where a cluster of rough-looking troopers sucked vapors out of long, yellow-fuming pipes. "Remember, for lovers of lotus, this land is paradise," he observed to his friend. "All the old Venji hands develop the taste eventually, they say, making them useless for other kinds of service. Someday you and I, Juma, may learn to love Venjipur too!"

A level, earnest voice joined in from beside them. "Ofttimes, brothers, I think that we are here only because of the lotus trade." The lean, desert-brown soldier, known to Conan as Babrak, joined them with easy familiarity. "The red and purple lotus extracts command vast prices in the Hyborian lands. Together with the other narcotic strains, the vile stuff is one of Turan's prime trade-goods. A shameful thing for a land that professes to follow Tarim's law!"

"Aye, truly." Conan kept his gaze trained outside the pavilion, over the other troopers' heads. "My own encounters with lotus have been mostly unwilling, and some of them near-fatal. I put no trust in that kind of city-bred slackness."

"Nor I," Juma assured them, though his good-natured smile may have held an ironic glint. "In my native Kush, the black lotus was tabu. But that did not keep foreign mystics and wizards from risking their lives in the deep jungle to gather it."

"A sad thing," Babrak assured them. "As you may know, true followers of the prophet disdain all narcotics and unmanly indulgences." He waved in one hand a pocket-scroll he had been holding at his side. "In a heathen land like this, it is essential to have a strong faith to protect one's spirit from decay. If ever you wish to learn Tarim's way—"

"Aye, 'tis a good way, a way of fierce fighters," Juma answered quickly. "Would that you could persuade more of your fellow Turanians to follow it—including our soft-bellied officers. For myself, I still pray and swear by the gods of my ancestors."

"And you, Hyborian?" Babrak's cool gray eyes fixed on Conan. "What god do you follow?"

"My oaths are to Crom and his fierce, frosty cousins," Conan answered shortly. "But hold, I must go; they have ended the interrogation!"

The others followed his intent gaze across the compound, where two spike-helmeted officers stood outside one of the tent barracks. As Conan pushed forward out of the pavilion, his two friends edged after him. Others drifted in their wake, sensing a diversion to speed the dreary morning.

Outside under the baking sun, a pair of native troops dragged forth two scrawny, blood-smeared bodies, recognizable in their dusky nakedness as the Hwong captives from the jungle shrine. As the Venjis tossed the victims onto a cart behind a slack-eared mule, their torturer and slayer emerged—a thick-muscled, copper-skinned man with dark tattoos patterning his cheeks and the shaven top of his head. Conan knew him as Sool, one of the eunuchs of the local warlord Phang Loon.

From the shadows of the tent Sool dragged forth a slender arm, around which his blunt fingers were clamped, followed by a shapely shoulder and the staggering form of the woman Sariya. She wore a cotton shift her captors had given her to cover her nakedness; but it proved scanty enough as Sool propelled her violently forward, to stagger onto one bare knee in the dirt of the compound. As she arose, blinking in the sun's brightness and trying to dust off her shift, the beauty of her long, straight limbs and fine-boned face drew low comments and hisses from the watching men. The slave Sool paid the girl no further heed, turning to join the departing Turanians.

Sariya seemed well in control of herself. She did not appear to have been tortured—as indeed, she had assured Conan she would not be because of her rank. Obviously the interrogators had finished with her, and to Conan's relief, none of the staff officers seemed to take a personal interest. He strode swiftly forward, calling out, "Sariya! Come, girl, I'll find you a place."

But as she raised her dark eyes to him, another figure interposed—a tall, lean trooper, brown and hard beneath sweat-stained leather field-vest and breeches. Dark hair straggled from beneath his grimy turban, fringing a seamed, sun-toughened face. A long, curved dagger hung sheathed at his belt, and the coil of red cord tucked beside it marked him as one of an elite corps of lone killers, whose duty took them on long forays into enemy territory.

Conan did not know the man, but the reputation of his unit was all anyone needed to know. He took another firm step forward, and the trooper moved between him and Sariya. "Why so eager, petty officer? Have you not learned that, excepting only the Emperor and his High Counselors, we Red Garrotes get first pick of all the women?" The man's drawl was ironic and confident, his face dangerously calm as he sized up Conan's height and fitness.

"Be warned, fellow." The Cimmerian's voice grated low but clear as he moved near his challenger. "I took this captive yesterday, and she remains in my charge. I will brook no interference."

"Is that an order, northling? Think twice before you move to enforce it! My rank is the equal of yours—and

my manhood the greater." The lean assassin flashed a
look at the growing straggle of onlookers, who laughed
appreciatively. "You must be the raw foreigner I heard
of, Captain Murad's newest petty—if so, Sergeant, be
warned that your men despise you! 'Tis said you run a
suicide squad at the gray one's bidding; learn your
place, or you'll not last long in Venjipur."

Reaching behind him, the garroter laid a brown, wiry
hand on the unflinching Sariya's saffron shoulder, caressing her under Conan's eyes. Most of the watchers
laughed at the spectacle, eager to see the comeuppance
of an officer, and a barbarian at that. The boldest moved
up beside the challenger to leer at Conan.

"Do not worry about the girl, Cimmerian," a voice
called from their ranks. "In time she will go among the
camp followers; then you too can have your turn!"

A murmur of laughter following this remark, and in
its midst Conan moved. His action was too swift to be
traced by the eye, except as a change from utter stillness
to utter speed, traced by a single flash of steel. His lunge
carried him between Sariya and the elite trooper,
sending the unprepared woman staggering with the
glancing force of his rush. In the shocked stillness
ensuing, amidst the puff of hanging yellow dust, every
eye peered blinking to assess the damage, and count the
toll of the dead. All marveled to see that, swift as the
attack had been, it had not been swift enough.

Conan crouched in a fighting stance, hands poised
ready in air. One held steel, the other, blood—and not
his adversary's. Rather the red drops marking the dust
of the compound fell from his own palm, slashed open
by the curved dagger clutched in his opponent's raised
hand.

"So you see, northling, things happen swiftly in these
tropical lands. The hooded snake strikes fast, the mongoose faster yet! Had you watched patiently and learned,

you might have lived to acquire the necessary quickness yourself." The garroter leered at his audience. "Now, alas, 'tis too late for you to gain wisdom."

His speech had served the purpose of covering his actions as he raised first one foot, then the other in front of him, deftly inserting something into the toe of each sandal. Foot-knives, Conan realized, too late to do anything about it. There would be no choice but to fight on the enemy's terms.

Conan had heard of these weapons, flat-handled blades inserted between the ball of the foot and the sole of the sandal, with narrow necks to be gripped by the first and second toes. Their use was a deadly art of the southern lands. Those glinting from his opponent's feet were of bronze, leaf-bladed and deeply grooved. Conan did not doubt that they were poisoned.

The watchers formed a tight circle in anticipation of the duel, some murmuring together in groups and presumably laying bets. Conan noticed that Juma and Babrak took up protective stances on either side of Sariya, slapping their hilts menacingly at any who edged too near her. Vowing silent thanks to them, he turned to meet the red strangler's rush.

The jungle trooper had unsheathed a second curved dagger from behind his back, providing him a steel fang on each limb. Bending suddenly like a bow, he launched himself at Conan in a gleaming pinwheel of death. He kicked out first one foot, then the other, then spun forward, his daggers slashing high and low simultaneously. While fighting he ceased his taunts, intent on the intricate motions, his brown-knotted throat issuing only sharp gasps and grunts of exertion.

The Cimmerian, with points flying at him from a dozen angles in blinding succession, gave way generously before his foe. In the human dust-devil's whirling, slicing course it was virtually impossible to see the next deadly stroke coming. Swiftly he fell back and aside, letting his foe measure the ground with acrobatic leaps and prancings. The moves were flamboyant, more likely perfected in taverns and alleys than in any jungle fight.

Conan thought of letting his attacker tire himself out—but an oddly narcotic gleam in the man's eye warned that his wiry vitality might endure, even increase over the course of the fight, depending on his drug of preference. So he set out to balk the man's attacks in small ways, shifting sidewise at intervals and striking gingerly at the metal-scything limbs as they flashed by. Each rush brought them closer to the chanting, jeering line of watchers.

A change in the jungle-fighter's rhythm caught Conan off-balance; desperately he dropped to all fours as a midair leap sent his attacker scything straight over him, daggers and toe-knives whizzing past his ears and kidneys. This raised lusty shouts from the spectators; yet the blood they bayed for did not spurt or trickle. The only wound, made earlier to Conan's hand, had ceased flowing, clenched inside his massive, dusty fist.

But as the lithe assassin instantly renewed his attack, that same gory fist flew open to dash blinding, red-spattered dust into his face. A simultaneous kick of Conan's sandal struck the back of the Red Garrote's hurtling thigh, amplifying his spin and sending him careening into the shouting onlookers.

As he disentangled himself roughly from two victims, one cursing, the other yelping with wounds, Conan saluted the crowd with a raised dagger, winning a lusty cheer from Juma—and from the others, feverish murmurs of bets being revised.

The two fighters squared off again, both panting this time, with no inessential flourishes or feints. Their grim intensity hinted that the match might be settled in one more swift, deadly pass. In the blinding noon sun their

shadows made two hovering knots on the earth, each
extending a curved talon toward the other. These dark
blots gave the only real contrast to the sunwashed scene,
blacker than the weathered hues of either man's harness, deeper than the tan of dusty, sun-browned limbs.

In a pulse the black shadows rushed together, tan-
gling indistinguishably, the red strangler's kicking assault blocked by Conan's forward lunge. Blades scraped
harshly and bodies met crosswise, tight inside the
vicious orbit of hand- and foot-driven knives. The duel
closed to a tight grapple marked by short, sharp stabs
and desperate kicks. In this earth-rooted struggle, body
to body and hand to throat, the warrior whose straining
toes were encumbered by metal knife-hasps discovered
a disadvantage.

The fighters strained together, crouching low over the
ground, and a pair of crescent daggers fell to earth.
Slowly, inexorably the red assassin's slimmer torso was
borne uppermost in the knot of striving flesh, arching
skyward even as it bent sharply back on itself. A surge of
effort tightened the human knot, and a pair of brittle
snaps sounded, loud as whipcracks across the dwindling circle of onlookers. There followed a flurry of
directionless kicks and twitches, then the strangler's
body flopped to earth, rebounding there with unnatural
limpness. A black shadow fell across its lifeless disarray
as Conan flexed upright, panting and bleeding, scanning
the crowd for any other ill-wishers.

The soldiers' frenzied excitement at the fight's out-
come threatened to cause a brawl or draw high-ranking
attention; as they stood milling and haggling over bets,
Conan shook off the lingering pain of the fight and
moved deliberately. Striding to Sariya, he clasped an
arm across her sun-warm back and pressed a long,
probing kiss on her upturned mouth, marking her
publicly as his own. Whoops and catcalls from the

onlookers told him that his claim had been duly noted. Sweeping the crowd with his defiant gaze, Conan drew the slender girl alongside him. Flanked by his friends, they started away.

"Go carefully from this hour, Conan." Babrak's warning was low and grim in his ear. "You have not finished your business with the Red Garrotes; they would slay any outsider to avenge even the least-regarded member of their band."

"Aye, Conan." Juma shook his head in mock consternation. "Did you really have to kill him in public like that? Now I hardly feel safe strolling with you."

Conan led them around the end of a barrack where, out of the mob's sight, they quickened their pace. "The fight was necessary to serve notice. That fool's death bought Sariya's life. Now any who covet her know they must answer to me first." He led the group toward the timber gate of the inner palisade. "We can take a hut in the village compound, where the officers live with their women." He kept Sariya close by his side as they walked. "Like it or not, girl, we are together—but I swear I will not force myself on you."

She was inspecting his injured palm, cradling it between her slim hands. Her accent was as exotic and lilting as he recalled. "My poor, great mongoose, we must be sure that this heals well!" She met his eyes with a frank look. "In all Venjipur there could be no better champion, Conan. I will show you my gratitude."

Chapter 4

The Silver Pool

The gong sent ripples of brazen sound shimmering from the mosaic vaultings of the imperial chamber. The armed guard who had struck it waited until he saw the emperor's perfunctory wave of dismissal, then turned and vanished outside the curtained archway. General Abolhassan, whom the still-chiming stroke had heralded, stepped reluctantly forward.

"Your Resplendency, the news I have is not of surpassing urgency. I did not realize that you were . . . occupied. If it pleases, I can attend you later—"

"Nay, not at all, General! I bid you stay." Yildiz addressed his visitor from his bed at the center of the chamber, where he lay disporting with harem concubines. "Step forward and state your business."

"Lord, I wished only to furnish you the latest intelligence from Venjipur; it confirms our suppositions in the matter of the wizard Ibn Uluthan's recent failure. 'Tis of no great timeliness, and could easily be postponed. . . ." As he moved nearer, casting reluctant eyes on his emperor's lush relaxations, his voice trailed off indecisively.

41

The imperial bed was a thin velvet bolster afloat on a
broad, marble-curbed pool of quicksilver. The shining
metal lay smooth and unsullied, supporting Yildiz's
considerable weight evenly and without so much as a
ripple. It bore with equal ease the pair of dark-haired,
dark-eyed houris lying alongside and atop the emperor.
These two carried on their leisurely caresses as if the
high-turbaned, black-clad general had not entered the
room at all. Plump they were, veiled by mere vestiges of
their customarily scant harem garb. The emperor himself, mercifully, was mostly clad, and partly draped by a
silken coverlet.

"Do not worry, Abolhassan; I am not the least indis-
posed to your presence here." Yildiz craned his neck
slightly so as to address the general from his reclining
posture. "The demands of leadership sometimes force
me to entertain a number of projects at once—equally
true of yourself, no doubt." Yildiz reached across the
ruffled edge of his mattress with one pudgy arm. "Just
be seated and help yourself to wine, if you wish." So
saying, he shoved toward Abolhassan a metal-borne
golden tray containing crystal cups and an ewer. It
skated across the silver liquid, to bump lightly against
the curb and float there, spinning slowly.

"I thank you, Sire." Abolhassan seated himself on the
edge of a marble bench at the poolside, not deigning to
reach for the wine-ewer. "To be brief, O Emperor: Fort
Sikander confirms that our raiding party did not succeed in killing the Arch-Mage Mojurna. They interrupted some dark ritual he was performing in an
ancient Venji temple, but the wretch escaped, whether
by cunning or by means of his spells." As he spoke, the
general forced his eyes discreetly to trace the intrica-
cies of the tiled floor. "Unfortunately, Sire, it is therefore
to be expected that his mystic emanations will continue, and that the poison of mutiny against your Resplen-

dency's righteous rule will persist in Venjipur. A regrettable state of affairs, Sire! Many thanks for your attention."

Abolhassan arose to leave, only to be halted by his emperor's voice. "The raiding party, then . . . was it the one we spied through Uluthan's magic window?"

Reluctantly the general turned back and nodded. "Indeed, Resplendency. Commanded by two petty field officers, Juma and Conan." He found it awkward to speak, noting that one of the imperial houris was regarding him speculatively from kohl-darkened eyes while she nuzzled and nibbled at her emperor's stout, hairy belly. "That was my error, Sire," he added distractedly. "I should have specified that the command be given to someone of noble rank."

"Conan, yes—a Vanir name, that. Probably the oversized trooper we saw in the magic window." Yildiz shifted beneath and between his servants like a sow rearranging itself among shoats in a crowded pen. "Truly, that glimpse of military valor was stirring! We need more of that kind of savagery here at court, to inspire new interest in the foreign war. As you may know, General, I often feel that the eunuchs, as a whole, do not faithfully support our southern enterprise. Do you not share that impression? And some of the sharifs and their senior wives have spoken out forthrightly in opposition to the war! What can one say about such a lack of spirit?"

"Might I suggest, Resplendency, that since your power is absolute, you simply compel them to change their views?" Detained unwillingly before his master, Abolhassan felt irritated at having to say the obvious. "A few high-placed exiles, floggings, lopped heads, or a dance or two with the strappado can work wonders for a country's fighting spirit!"

Although his harem girls did not visibly flinch at such

violent talk, Yildiz stirred impatiently. "Yes, of course, that is so, Abolhassan. But I would rather have things continue running smoothly here at court. We do depend on the eunuchs as administrators, you know; any disruption in their ranks would sow dissatisfaction in diverse quarters." Yildiz rolled onto his belly, positioning his back to be kneaded by two pairs of scarlet-nailed hands. "And the nobles too have their rightful powers and prerogatives. I certainly do not want a larger war in my capital than the one in Venjipur." He grunted, adjusting his posture before his captive audience. "If I am indeed all-powerful, then does it not behoove me all the more to prevail by reason?"

"By reason, Sire, or by any other means, as you wish! Now, if you have no further need of me . . ."

"Nay, Abolhassan, linger a moment or two more. My dear General, I apologize for my thoughtlessness in taking my pleasure before you without offering you similar diversion. Just be seated, man, and feel free to call for any refreshment you may desire." From his prone position on the floating mattress, with a snap of his fingers and a flick of his wrist, Yildiz brought a harem-girl scurrying from a curtained alcove to the bench at Abolhassan's side. She was younger and slimmer than the emperor's two companions, barefoot in filmy pantaloons and a brief, jeweled-embroidered vest. Her ruby lips and antimony eyes were half-concealed by auburn curls clasped in a circlet of purest gold. She seated herself beside Abolhassan, lavishing on him a lingering caress, which he shook off uncomfortably.

Meanwhile Yildiz cleared his throat. "Now, General, back to business! In my efforts to explain and justify the southern war, I have come up against certain complaints which you, in your military expertise, might help me to address." Although his handmaidens lavished careful affections on every part of his portly frame,

Yildiz seemed to have no difficulty organizing his thoughts; in fact his concentration was quite remarkable. "One such quibble," he began, "is an allegation of graft: that the bulk of money and provisions dispatched to Venjipur never even find their way there—or else, once they arrive, are diverted to profiteering and high living by unscrupulous functionaries in my service. Of course, you and I know that there is always a certain amount of graft necessary to keep the wheels of any state enterprise turning. I have tried to explain that, yet the critics seem to feel that substantially more is involved here."

"Outrageous, Sire! Who dares make such irresponsible charges? The lying traitor should be broken on the wheel! I can personally guarantee that no such abuses take place. But I will launch an investigation—" The general found himself momentarily interrupted as the harem-maid, sidling next to him, blew into his ear, fondling the short hairs at the back of his turban. Valiantly he pushed her off, continuing, "If such things are taking place, I shall have the offenders remanded for the harshest penalties."

"Excellent, General! Henceforth I will speak with more assurance on the subject. Another vexing charge —a related one, perhaps—regards the nature of the diplomatic ties we have formed in Venjipur. It is said that the factions we sponsor there are shallow opportunists or downright criminals, careless of our interests, who will be incapable of ruling the district competently once we secure it for them. What is your analysis of that?"

"Impossible, Sire!" Abolhassan was still fending off his persistent bench-mate; finally he elicited a smothered sob from the girl by means of a remorseless pinch to the flesh of her upper arm. "I myself, of course, have never been to Venjipur. But I can vouch that our allies there are impeccably chosen. They are the land's hereditary warlords, descendants of past conquerors, embodying the same sound principles of aristocracy and autarchy by which Your Resplendency rules our sacred empire."

"Very good, Abolhassan! I will remember that argument." Supine under the intensifying ministrations of his harem women, Yildiz twisted around to flash the general an approving glance. "But I see that you do not avail yourself of the fleshly comforts I have offered—is the wench unsatisfactory? Shall I send her off and fetch you a woman of fuller shape, perhaps, or of more worldly experience?"

"No, Sire!" Abolhassan arose from the bench, flushed with irritation at the shameless questioning. "It is only that I am accustomed to harsh military regimen, Sire—a hard, narrow bed, as they say, and pleasure taken only rarely, in a caravanserai on the eve of battle, or amid the flames and ruins of a conquered city."

"I see." Yildiz nodded understandingly. "You would prefer a boy, then?" Observing his general's pale, clenching face, the emperor resumed swiftly, "Very well, Abolhassan, please yourself." He gestured the cringing maidservant out of the room and continued speaking.

"The last and most farfetched rumor whispered by my informants is that the entire Venji campaign is an unwarranted distraction, a mere excuse of self-seeking officers to strengthen their hand at the expense of more homely needs—roads, canals, and so forth. The implication seems to be that this heightened military power is somehow to be used to weaken my reign." Yildiz paused a moment to redirect the efforts of his browsing concubines. "Of course, the devotion of my staff officers is unquestioned. Therefore, I am puzzled; can you tell me how such a misconception might have arisen? Could it

have anything to do with the foreign regiments we have
taken into our ranks in the course of imperial expansion? Or with regional rivalries, perhaps? Are there
rumblings of revolt in any of the home provinces?''

Abolhassan, standing pike-straight, glared down at his
supine inquisitor. ''Naturally, Emperor, such damaging
allegations are too serious to be regarded lightly, or
dismissed in a single interview! I give you my sacred
oath to explore any hint of these offenses further and, if
there is truth to them, take the necessary action. I thank
my gracious commander for raising this concern, along
with the other problems we discussed. I bid milord good
day!'' The general spun on his heels, heading for the exit
with strides whose tremors set the mercury pool shimmering, and whose velocity scarcely allowed for a
further recall.

As it happened, Yildiz's voice drifted after the departing general in offhanded farewell. ''Good day, General.
Oh, and Abolhassan, keep me apprised of the fortunes of
that young foreigner Conan! He seems the sort who
might someday be put to a higher use.''

That same night the general attended another audience, this one in less lavish surroundings. It was in a
small, anonymous chamber buried somewhere in the
vast warren of the palace, lacking windows, pillars, or
hangings—notable, indeed, for its bare functionality
and absence of any concealment for prying eyes and
ears. There were only the dark blue-plastered walls, a
single door, smooth-paneled and tightly bolted, a low
table, cushions, an oil lamp. Yet the words spoken here
were at first so low and guarded, and the sidelong
glances so furtive and frequent, that the room might as
well have been the earhole of Emperor Yildiz himself;
such was the rumor-bearing reputation of the Imperial
Court at Aghrapur.

The monarch of the scene, by his size and splendor if not by rank, was the eunuch, Dashibt Bey. He sat by necessity at the center of one long face of the rectangular table, nearly spanning its length with his own breadth, spreading his bulk across two of the thick cushions. Golden lamplight picked out highlights in the numerous gems and clasps of his costume; it played along the iridescent folds of silken turban, sash, and cummerbund, making their wearer seem a greater source of light than the feeble, wavering flame itself. Though the great functionary would doubtless have preferred a full meal, the privacy and secrecy of the gathering had restricted him to bringing along only a gilded basket, from which he periodically plucked ripe fruit to devour while he listened to General Abolhassan's low-voiced tirade.

"The vile imp! The pudgy, bespangled vulgarian! There he lay, making me wait attendance on him while he was stroked by his fat trollops—I, his ablest general, reduced to the status of a mere towel-boy! Worse, he then tried to foist off his stable of pawed-over strumpets on me! A good thing his downfall is imminent; otherwise I might have been moved to drown him in the mercury pool of his sybaritic bed!"

Dashibt Bey stirred in place, sending refracted highlights dancing about the walls. "Sometimes Yildiz seeks to outrage his supplicants in the hope of throwing them off guard. That tactic never worked with me, because I am unmoved by the carnal passions." The eunuch belched discreetly, tossing aside a gnawed fruit-pit. "But tell me, General, what was the tone of his interrogation? Do his suspicions come even remotely near the truth?"

Abolhassan stroked his sharp-stubbled chin, preened his black mustache, and shook his head. "Nay, I cannot think it! He made one insinuation which took me aback at first, about my entertaining more than one purpose at

a time. But I must conclude that he is pathetically
ignorant, chattering just to hear the sound of his own
voice. Court gossips have ingratiated themselves with
him by pointing out the obvious; now he tries to
overawe me by throwing it back in my face. He struts
and postures to make it appear that he is in control,
when in truth all know he is not."

"Aye, General," a rasping voice added, "great Tarim
knows, the complaints which the hated one mouths are
the selfsame moanings of the effete noble faction at
court—those who would parcel out the rule of empire
and shackle the power of the True Faith!" The brown-
robed speaker, bald and waxy-pale, was the high priest
Tammuraz, known to all as a fanatic, yet secure as the
emperor himself in the church's time-honored hierar-
chy. "All such quibblers will be justly dealt with," the
holy man continued, "once righteousness is enthroned
again in Aghrapur. Yildiz is weak because he places
more trust in courtiers, soothsayers, and black magi-
cians than in the Shining Prophet himself!"

"Truly, the nobles and courtiers of Aghrapur are not
to be feared," Dashibt Bey said, taking a pomegranate
from his basket, "except to the extent they can enlist
Yildiz's aid. Their household troops are weak, and the
real allegiance of city and army alike is to the church."

"And to the eunuchs," Abolhassan added with an
ironic smile. "Do not forget your own ubiquitous sect,
Dashibt Bey! That pompous fool Yildiz was most em-
phatic about not offending your brothers and disrupting
the smooth running of his empire."

"He is right to that extent only, in saying the real
power lies with us." Smiling, the courtier tore the
dark-rubied flesh of the pomegranate, twisting its innards outward with his beringed, stubby-fingered
hands. "Fortunately, I can guarantee that my brethren
will follow my lead staunchly, with only the standard

amount of haggling and intriguing among ourselves. I defer to you, General, because even deft administrators need a plausible figurehead. The hour is not yet ripe for us eunuchs to raise up our own champion and follow him to mastery of the empire."

Dashibt Bey's declaration was received by the others as a bold jest, with condescending laughter all around. Smiling, Abolhassan proceeded to list the various military units that could be counted on to shift their loyalty to him, ticking off factions on the dusky fingers of one hand: the southern and eastern expeditionary legions, the Aghrapur city garrison, most of the civil guard, the armies of the rural shahs, and miscellaneous troops under arms in the Ilbarsi province and Hyrkania. He finished by hooking his thumb back with a forefinger, displaying to the others a broad, battle-scarred hand capable of considerable grasp. "That leaves us to face the sharifs of Aghrapur, the Imperial Honor Guard, a few deluded loyalists and courtly fops—no one of consequence. And yet, regrettably, our forces are scattered, and mobilization for civil war is always chancy. It will require careful planning."

"Is it realistic, then, to think that the land will be ripe for revolt in the near future?" This question was posed by a richly arrayed nobleman, Philander by name.

"Without a doubt!" Abolhassan replied, looking dangerously ruffled. "Time favors us in that wise. Remember, the same colonial wars and uprisings which strengthen our military hand in the provinces make conditions gradually worse here at home. Yildiz takes the blame for levying more troops and taxes, and being a greedy ruler or an inept one, while we reap the bounty in men and equipment."

"Truly, 'tis so," the priest Tammuraz chimed in, "or so my agents tell me! Only pray to Tarim that this war drags on longer, and that Yildiz continues to sustain it."

"Have no fear; he dotes on these petty wars, especially the Venjipur campaign!" Rubbing his hands together, Abolhassan smiled triumphantly around at the group. "He justifies us to his critics, blandly denying our treacheries and iniquities. Most recently he has grown enamored of one of the troopers he saw in Ibn Uluthan's window—a hulking northern oaf called Conan. My plan is to cultivate this barbarian, feed Yildiz stories of his prowess, false or true, and so play on his weaknesses, until our plans have ripened sufficiently. If we are careful, if we remain sly, we can lead the fatuous tyrant to his doom!"

Chapter 5

Court at Arms

"Did it ever enter your thick northern skull that you were sent here to kill your emperor's sworn enemies, not your fellow Turanian officers?"

Pacing beneath the palm-leaf awning of the staff barrack, Jefar Sharif halted abruptly to keep within the limit of the shade. He pivoted to glare at Conan, who stood waiting in the open yard. Beyond the young sharif loomed Conan's immediate superior, Captain Murad, gray and motionless in the dark doorway.

Sharif resumed his stalking. "And all in a fight over a woman, one of these low Venji slatterns. Three days past—you were lucky I was away when it happened! And thank your birth-stars that you are of officer rank, and so cannot be flogged!" The hereditary officer's golden spurs scraped the hard earth, his rolled cavalry gloves slapping the leg of his riding-breeches as he paced. His thin-mustached lip curled up in a sneer. "I have always said that, because of ill habits like this brawling, foreign troops should not be allowed rank in Turanian units. A shameful incident!" He wheeled on

Conan again. "Well, fellow, have you anything to say for yourself?"

Conan, standing in the hot sun, with murderous impulses surging the length of his sword-arm, searched for some way to translate them into civil speech. When first summoned to this dressing-down, he had not been disarmed by Jefar's subalterns; now the two guards stood at separate corners of the barrack, too far away to intervene if he should decide to take personal offense. And yet, he reminded himself, he was a military officer.

The Cimmerian, with his yataghan hanging heavy at his side, decided at last that this foppish sharif could hardly understand what danger his curt language placed him in. Conan forced his rebellious gaze down to dusty earth. "I killed the swi . . . the trooper, in my own defense, Sharif." He managed to speak acceptably, ending with the officer's correct title, though it nearly gagged him.

"You did, did you? Well, at least I can see that you are repentant." Ceasing to pace, Jefar flashed a righteous look from the older, wary-eyed Murad back to Conan. "But tell me, did it ever pass through your dim barbarian consciousness that—"

"Sergeant, what is your age?" Stepping forward from the deeper shadow, the captain came to Conan's rescue —or, perhaps, to his rash commander's. Murad's gray-bearded face crinkled in a hard squint beneath his weathered gray-green turban. "And where do you hail from?"

A hot, airless moment passed in the courtyard as Conan fought down his ill-temper and resorted to hasty mental calculations. "Nineteen winters, by my reckoning, sir. I am Cimmerian."

"Nineteen, a mere boy!" exclaimed Jefar Sharif, who had at best a year or two more than that to his own earthly sum.

"And already warranted an officer," Murad continued purposefully. "Most unusual! I see that you survived this duel with but slight damage." His eye moved to Conan's injured hand, poulticed and bound with long, fibrous leaves of a medicinal jungle plant. "How else, Sergeant, have you distinguished yourself under Turanian arms?"

Conan leveled blue eyes at his questioner, speaking with careful frankness. "Captain, I was the last survivor of the battle of Yaralet. I saw the rebellious satrap Munthassem Khan destroyed by his own sorcerous dabblings, and the city restored to Turan's rule."

"So I heard." Murad stroked his sleet-tinged beard. "Yaralet—a bloody encounter, was it not, with thousands slain in both hosts?"

"True, good Captain, perhaps!" Jefar Sharif silenced his elder subordinate with a wave of an imperious hand. "But if this northerner was really the sole survivor— why, then, we have only his account of the affair. A trooper who manages to outlive all his comrades can safely be adjudged one of two things: a fighter of exceptional prowess, or else a slinking, sneaking—"

"Whatever the case, he volunteered for Venjipur duty," Murad said, sharply interrupting his commander, flashing a warning look at the scowling Cimmerian. "And until this incident, he struck me as a capable soldier. Understand me, Conan: A good officer is a valuable item, a piece of property the Turanian Army would rather not see wasted in brawls and agonizing punishments. Nor in insubordination and mutiny." This last he said with a pointed glance at Conan's side—and in response, the Cimmerian's hand reluctantly, longingly relinquished its grip on his yataghan's flared hilt. "We need men like you alive in the field, Sergeant," the captain finished, "ready to slaughter the enemy!"

"Aye, fellow!" Jefar Sharif still, apparently, felt it necessary to add his counsel. "If this affair had been somewhat more dignified—say, a duel between noble officers, or a summary execution in the heat of battle, intended to prevent desertion or bolster morale—why, that would be another matter! There is seldom any problem with the killing of an enlisted man, or even a noble, if one is of creditable birth oneself. But a brother warrant officer of an elite unit . . . you must learn to be more careful of appearances, Sergeant!" Jefar concluded, bestowing on Conan a fatherly look that ill befit his stripling age.

"Enough—I mean excellent, Sharif. Now remain here a moment, Sergeant, while we decide the disposition of your case." Murad turned with the young noble to step inside the shaded doorway. Conan waited in sweltering heat, feeling the tropic sun scorching through his thin-shirted shoulders all the way to his gizzard, or so it seemed.

The only sound in the midafternoon doldrums was the swishing of palm leaves in the nearby stables, where Venji servants fanned the Turanian officers' steeds. The desert-bred beasts had to be ventilated to survive the damp noon heat, and even so they performed sluggishly on the mildest of days. But the half-dozen staff officers, cavalrymen all, continued to regard horses as necessary appurtenances of command, practically a part of their uniform.

The captain and Jefar Sharif, nodding together and stepping back outside, regarded Conan solemnly. "Sergeant, here is our finding," Murad announced at last. "Your punishment will be reflected in a harsher schedule of duties, beginning with a hill patrol tomorrow morning. That will benefit not only our beloved emperor but also, perhaps, your own unruly spirit."

The sharif would not allow Murad the last word. "We would levy a harsher penalty on you, Sergeant, if we thought it could possibly satisfy the wrath of those you have offended by this ill-advised murder. But the Red Garrotes will seek vengeance regardless of our verdict. And I wager you'll find their methods more discreet; learn from them if you can."

"Jefar Sharif is right, Conan." Murad nodded gravely from the porch. "We will issue a stern warning to the stranglers, but I cannot guarantee their obedience. Now go forth, give sober thought to the responsibilities of your command, and watch your back!"

With a nod and grunt of salute, Conan turned to exit the staff compound. The punishment had, indeed, been fiendishly cruel; at his side he felt his sword fist slowly unclenching. Passing the guard dozing at the gate, he slowed to take stock of those waiting outside.

There were loungers aplenty, ubiquitous idlers who guaranteed the fast spread of news through the fort. Gossip was the coin of the invading army, and betting was its commerce. As Conan watched, a pair of troopers detached themselves from fence-rails and strode off in opposite directions, doubtless to spread the word of his release. Others eyed him speculatively, whispering between themselves and probably setting stiff odds against his longevity. To Conan, the most welcome watcher proved to be Juma, who strode from beneath an awning, hailing him loudly and fearlessly before the watchers. In his enthusiasm, the black giant dragged along a couple of half-willing troopers to meet him.

"Conan! Well, Sergeant, how went the court-martial?" He relinquished one of his companions' necks to clap Conan's shoulder resoundingly. "If Sergeant is still your rank, after this affair?"

"Aye, it is." Conan grinned back at him. "Extra duty and a few hill patrols, Murad has decreed. Nothing severe—at least not yet."

"Sergeant, sir." One of the troopers, a fresh-faced boy, interrupted them. "Will they really transfer you back to Aghrapur for punishment, as Sergeant Juma was telling us?"

Conan laughed resoundingly. "Nay, Hakim!—and do not spread that false rumor, lest half the garrison murder the other half in hope of suffering the same penalty!"

Their noisy gesticulating gathered a few more watchers to them, some even offering Conan guarded congratulations. But most seemed to shun him, aware that he now possessed dangerous enemies. And after a few moments of banter, the Cimmerian took his leave, drawing Juma along and promptly asking him about Sariya.

"I left her at the hut with Babrak, Conan. I came because there is surely more danger to you than to her. Now we must go back, so the child of Tarim can return to his camp duties."

Together they headed for the main gate of the fort. Conan insisted on going by way of the mess tent, braving baleful stares and ironic whispers for the sake of openly advertising his freedom. They walked on to the main formation of troopers' tents, stopping by the campfire of Conan's detachment. Announcing the next morning's patrol, he was greeted by anonymous groans and curses from beneath the bleaching canvas canopies. But it was not his practice to try to enforce morale. He and Juma passed on out the gate of the compound, heading for the unfortified village and the scatter of makeshift dwellings along the jungle's fringe.

Two days of grumbling exertion by Conan's and Juma's troopers, aided and bullied by their sergeants' burly arms, had raised a good-sized bungalow at the edge of the trees. Split hardwood timbers borrowed from the fort's supply squared up its corners; the walls were lattices of bamboo and bough, interlaced with tough palm fronds. A frame of elbow-thick bamboo trunks formed a basis for the shaggy, palm-thatched roof. Sariya's graceful fingers taught the resting troopers to weave mats of split bamboo for the floor; her simple jests and childish laughter even made them enjoy it.

While gathering bamboo in the jungle, the warriors scared up a wild pig. At cost of a deep gore to one man's thigh, the raging sow was speared to provide a feast for the night of the hut's completion. The wounded soldier, doctored and pampered by Sariya, lived to share the animal's succulent flesh with the others; she made him eat its heart, so that its vengeful spirit would not haunt him and sicken his wound. Now the grimacing, razor-tusked skull bleached atop the roof-peak of the bungalow, warding off ghosts and other evils.

Beneath its protection, they found Babrak studying one of his many scrolls of Tarim's teachings. As Conan and Juma approached from the fort road, they could see him lounging in the shade of the open porch, which was already more lived in than either of the hut's two rooms. Sariya, wrapped in a length of blue cloth from the village market, knelt over a smoking fire in the middle of the yard. She arose to greet her protectors with eager embraces. Upon Conan she lavished kisses, but no questions.

"You walk proudly, and I see no stripes of the lash. Well enough, then!" Babrak, leaving the porch, pressed up beside Sariya to administer a stiff, formal embrace to Conan, though his field-green turban barely brushed the taller man's chin. "You have weathered your court-martial well, by grace of the One God."

"And by sufferance of them all, it would seem." Conan returned his friend's clasp wholeheartedly, making Babrak grunt. "My officers have resolved to leave my punishment to the Red Garrotes."

"Fear not, Conan," Babrak told him. "If need be, I

will stand with you against a whole regiment of those assassins! Tarim teaches us to protect the righteous."

"I do not ask it. I can protect myself." Conan moved with them into the shade of the porch. "But if aught happens to me, I leave it to you, my friends, to care for Sariya. She has no family and no other home than this, so she tells me."

"Is that so, lass?" Juma asked, showing frank concern. "What of your tribe and your clan?"

"I have none." The maid seated herself beside the hut's bamboo door, doubling her trim knees on the rough matting before her. "Since earliest memory, I have been raised in jungle camps of Mojurna's devotees. Mere months ago I learned, to my horror, that I was destined for sacrifice." She told the story with affecting frankness. "Now that I have escaped my ordained fate, my old teachers and sister acolytes would only mock or revile me."

"Even so," Conan said, "'tis a good thing you were spared." He settled down beside her, his bandaged hand finding its way around her waist.

"Oh, yes, Conan! It is far better to live!" She twined against him, pressing a kiss on the side of his neck. "I have seen so little of life! There is much more I want to see, much good that I can do." She fell silent abruptly, glancing at the fire; then she arose and left the porch, kneeling to tend the covered copper and clay pots steaming on smokeless coals.

"A fine girl," Juma said, gazing after her with the others.

"Truly, she must have put an enchantment on me," Conan whispered earnestly. "Already she has emptied my purse, and I do not even mind! The trifles she buys for the hut are of use, or at least pretty. She has a way of making life comfortable."

"Aye, yours is a house blest by heaven, I can see." Babrak arose from his cross-legged crouch. "But forgive me, I must return to my duty. The half-bell struck long since, and I dare not be late for drill. I leave you to your repast." He turned away, smiling. "I trust you will enjoy it, or at least pretend to your woman that you do." With a passing farewell to Sariya, he left the yard.

Conan, reaching for an earthen decanter and sloshing it to gauge its reserve of date wine, raised it to his lips and swigged deeply of the syrupy liquid. "We are lucky Babrak sought us out," he said, passing the flask to Juma. "I wonder what he sees in us."

"Who can say? Perhaps that we accept his faith, yet do not proclaim it hollowly ourselves. He is a good man." Juma drank, then handed the decanter back to Conan. "Too good a man for Venjipur."

By the time Sariya called out that the meal was ready, the buzzing of the forest insects seemed distinctly louder in the men's ears. The graded clay floor of the porch did not seem so level either; Conan reeled slightly as he arose to go to the fire. He burned his fingers carrying a hot kettle back to the house between dry palm fans, but did not drop it or reveal his discomfort to the others. They set the pots on a thick mat in the hut's front room, and Sariya opened them, releasing pungent steam clouds that rose like djinni of the eastern deserts.

"A fine feast!" Juma proclaimed. "Looks like something from my boyhood hearth in Kush."

Even so, Conan thought the black warrior eyed the food a little dubiously. "Smells sweeter than the boiled mule-meat and groats they serve us in the fort," he said heartily, himself kneeling down unsteadily at the mat. "What is it made of, girl?"

"The meat is marinated eel from the village market. Here are baked tsudu root and boiled swamp-thistle."

Sariya plied a bamboo spoon as she spoke, scooping the viands onto fresh banyan leaves. "And stuffed, steamed locusts! Very fresh, I bought them alive this morning."

"Mmm . . . unusual." Conan accepted a dripping, burdened leaf from his smiling housemate and set it down gingerly in front of him, to be observed awhile from a distance. "Are these all native foods of Venjipur?"

"Yes, part of the bounty of Mother Jungle. And very good for you. The eel-meat gives you the strength of the eel, and the locusts are an aid to"—she blushed slightly, averting her eyes—"male vigor."

"Well, then, I cannot pass them up," Juma proclaimed good-naturedly. Accepting his own heaped banyan leaf and laying it on the mat before him, the Kushite reached into its midst to pluck forth one of the gray-green, bristling lumps. With a flash of eyes and teeth that bespoke either good humor or rash courage, he popped it into his mouth. "Mmm—umf." A moment later, he was gulping steaming-hot tea from a clay cup. "Well-spiced, I will say, Sariya!" he coughed. "But tasty, girl, tasty."

"A rare treat it is, doubtless." Not to be outdone, Conan took up one of the pink-filled insects. He perused it just closely enough to see that the largest, toughest legs had been trimmed off. Then, shutting his eyes, he shoveled it into his mouth and chewed. The crunchy flesh reassuringly resembled Vilayet Sea shrimp, only sweeter; but the filling was peppery, seasoned with some jungle herb or hot radish. Tears sprang to his eyes as he swallowed the morsel half-chewed, rinsing his mouth with wine that only seemed to scorch his tongue the more.

Sariya, meanwhile, had commenced eating in a methodical way, daintily spooning up her food with a small bamboo scoop. Conan and Juma imitated her, finding the other dishes more palatable. The eel was tender and candy-sweet, the vegetables soft-cooked and mildly flavored. Conan even crunched more of his deviled locusts, squeezing out their hot stuffing first into an inconspicuous fold of his leaf-plate.

"Good, coarse, wholesome food," was Juma's comment. "Very like that of my home village on the seacoast of Kush, which I left so many years ago."

"Aye. Wild food was what we ate in Cimmeria." Conan sniffed the pungent fumes of his tea, sipping it tentatively. "Our Venji armies would be more mobile if they could live off the land and barter with the natives, instead of relying on unwieldy elephant trains for supplies."

"True, the supply lines are vulnerable to attack." Juma plucked a thistle-stem from between his teeth. "But just try, sometime, to make these northerners eat swamp-rice, the local mainstay—'tis a hopeless task. Some spew it up or sicken on it; all revile it. I have no objection to it myself." He scraped up mashed yellow root-pulp from his wrinkled plate and sucked it from his bamboo spoon. "The main trouble is, these desert folk do not belong here in Venjipur. Their horses grow sluggish and sickly in the heat, their steel blades rot with rust, and they themselves fall and rave every summer with the quaking chills."

"Aye. And not only the weapons rust." Conan sweetened his tea with wine before sipping more of it. "Men's toes drop off from wet-rot and leprosy, even without a festering wound to poison them. An arrow-nick alone is enough to do for a man in this clime. Lucky am I that this scratch of mine heals so well." He waved his poulticed hand before his companions. "This devil-blighted heat, rain, and mud sap a man's strength as surely as the sucking flies do! By the time he has been here two seasons, a civilized northerner is dull and slow-witted, unable to feel a thumb-sized yellow ant gnawing his neck."

"And what of you, Conan?" Juma asked him. "Will you still be hard and keen after two years of Venjipur?" The Kushite eyed him bemusedly. "What is your plan to preserve yourself from these dangers? A fast camel west to Iranistan?"

Conan laughed. "Nay, Juma, you and I will flourish here. Do you not see, the ills we have spoken of, each and every one, are equally our chances for betterment! The more amiss with this campaign, the more opportunity to advance oneself by setting it right." He crumpled his near-empty leaf plate and tucked it into one of the scraped, gaping pots. "What is needed here are bold, clear-sighted officers not too bound up in Turanian imperial claptrap—men like ourselves to take hold of things, thrash out victories, and gain rank and fame by them. That is what a war like this is all about, is it not?"

"So . . . suppose it is?" Juma belched amply and stroked his full belly, all the while eyeing his host with the cool skepticism of a career officer. "What would you do to improve the running of the war?"

"What would I do? Why, many things!" Warming to his subject, Conan waved his cup airily beside his head, spattering tiny drops on his guest. "As we were just now saying, I would use local foods in the army mess to make our force self-sufficient. Get the best native cooks, like Sariya here—and local healers, to find out how the Hwongs avoid the ills that beset our troops. Change the uniforms, first of all, and the drill! What place do cavalry tactics have in swamp and jungle, I ask you?" The Cimmerian knit his broad brow in a nearly comic attitude of concentration. "We could create a force that would not only win the war, but stay on afterward to enforce the peace, and even enjoy doing it! But those changes would only be a small part—"

It was Juma's turn to laugh, and he did so hear[ ] "Stop, Conan. Can you hear what you are saying? H[ ] would you work these wonders, with every trooper an[ ] officer fighting you with all the ferocity they spare the[ ] Hwong? Not a one of them but has interests and prejudices running the other way! The food, for instance—what Turanian would touch the meal we have eaten tonight? They would call it unclean and spit on it—no offense to you, Sariya, but it is so." He flashed an apologetic look at his hostess, who sat at ease beside them, watching and listening with an attitude of interest.

"Nay, Conan," Juma continued, "there are some bad things in this world that can only make themselves worse. I fear this campaign is one of them. Instead of seeking fame, I caution you to be as small and invisible as you can while in Venjipur. Obey the rules and, less zealously, your orders. Never take chances, never volunteer." The Kushite faced his host earnestly. "This is the sum of my experience here; now you have seen some of the cost of calling attention to yourself." He shook his head. "Of all things, the worst thing to be in this war is a hero!"

Conan laughed, shaking his head good-naturedly. "Juma, Juma! If I thought that you yourself could live one moment by those craven rules, I would love you the less for it! But I know it is not so—and you know it, even though you mean me well in saying it." He reached around the mat to lean heavily and confidingly on his friend's shoulder. "For men like us, Juma, there are no limits. Tell me, have you ever played imperial draughts as the Stygians do?" He winked intimately at his fellow trooper. "In their version of the game, a pawn can advance to become a king!"

"Conan, I do not jest." Juma glanced uneasily at the open doorway. "You know the danger of even speaking

that way, so let us talk of other things. Do you not see
that Venjipur's hunger for human suffering is greater
than all the armies of Yildiz can satisfy? We must take
care not to be swallowed along with the others."

They continued their conversation, failing to resolve
many greater and lesser topics. During their talk, the
afternoon rain fell. They laid their pans out in the yard
to be scoured by heavy, pelting drops. They sat out on
the porch enclosed by a dripping, transparent liquid
curtain, watching rain-pitted water running and pool-
ing across the yellow clay.

At length the shower retreated into a mountainous
jumble of misty cloud, pink-tinged in sunset over the
Gulf. Juma took leave of them and returned to the fort,
treading on flat stones spaced across the muddy yard.
Conan, passing inside the hut, bolted the tough bamboo
door, then turned to follow Sariya through the curtained inner archway.

Their sleeping-room was bedecked with flowers.
Twined into the palm thatching of the walls, braided
between the rafters, gathered in clusters on the mat
floor, the blossoms shone almost luminous in the dimming light of the bamboo-framed window. Their fragrance hung heavily in air already rich with the smell of
rain-soaked earth. Conan knew that some of the flowers,
like the drooping pink lotuses wound into the lashings
of the room's broad hammock, gave off fumes that were
mildly narcotic. Their effect only increased the faint
swimming of his senses as he watched Sariya unpin and
unwind herself alluringly from her dusky-blue garment.
Her body shone amber in the dusk, more radiant than
the blossoms all around her, graceful as the slenderest
lily.

When he moved to embrace her, she turned her face
up to his. He saw that she had twined a pink lotus in her
black tresses, above one delicate ear. The flower's heady

aroma mingled with her own subtle scent as he caressed her, then lifted her bodily onto the yielding canvas of the hammock. The swaying of the airborne bed merely added to the plunging, reeling exhilaration of his own senses, as the two joined in a consuming rush of passion.

Sariya, for her part, abandoned herself to the arduous labors and equally arduous pleasures of her new existence. Though little-traveled, secluded from the world throughout her youth, she guessed that no man could make her feel the fullness of life's simple round better than Conan. She cherished their time together, using her well-learned skills to reward him and make things better, for however long it might last.

There were dangers, of course; but Sariya believed that Conan could cope with the immediate, tangible ones. She knew that by night in their hammock, even after exhausting bouts of lovemaking, he slept no more deeply than any panther draped across a forest limb. She often heard him waken in response to faint noises outside the hut, sometimes slipping from beside her and out the window with inhuman stealth and silence.

Once, on his return, she saw a gleam of steel as he wiped his dagger-blade clean, and smelled the coppery scent of blood when he crept back to her side. She sensed that his savage devotion would save her, or else it would call down forces too violent for either of them to control. Either way, she loved him.

Chapter 6

The Elephant Patrol

Wet foliage slapped the riders' faces, rubbery leaves shedding tepid drops that gathered in rivulets down the men's necks and torsos. The wetness tickled like insect-tracks, unscratchable beneath breast and scapular armor; otherwise it scarcely mattered, for it neither cooled nor warmed their skin in the stifling jungle heat.

Meanwhile, beneath the troopers' folded legs, the elephant's thinly padded back rolled and rippled patiently like a living sea. From time to time the beast's sinuous trunk snaked upward among the branches to tear off a tasty-looking limb, shaking the riven tree and showering brackish droplets on the passengers.

"Driver, more room overhead!" Irritably, Conan prodded the hunched shoulder of the elephant-guide Than. The small man sat low astride the elephant's neck, and so he scarcely felt the turmoil of thrashing branches. "Steer the brute wider around the trees," Conan admonished him, "or I'll brain you!"

Just possibly, the northerner's guttural rendering of the singsong Venji dialect was understood by the guide. If so, he showed it only by a shrug of his diminutive shoulders and a wave of his bronze-hooked elephant goad. The ponderous rhythm of the beast continued inexorably under them, and foliage continued to lash past their ears without any noticable improvement.

"There is little hope of change, Sergeant." The archer Kalak, sitting beside Conan in the low-rimmed howdah, spoke in deep, well-modulated Turanian. "The elephants rove beneath the trees to cool themselves and to forage leaves for their ravenous bellies." Peering from under bushy brows, he gazed knowingly at his commander. "Their drivers can scarcely change their ways; the venerable creatures have minds of their own."

Conan scowled, peering ahead. "Good for them, but what about the enemy? How will we ever see their traps and ambushes?" He raised an arm to protect his face against lashing green fronds. "I would expect these all-knowing elephants to be concerned about that too!"

"They?" Kalak arched his black eyebrows. "Why, they pay no more heed to human strife than they do to wars waged by fleas across their leathery backs!" He laughed immoderately at his own fancy, with a third trooper, Muimur, joining in from the rear of the howdah. Gradually Kalak resumed his straight-faced demeanor. "Truly, Sergeant, traps are not to be feared here. As I said, the elephant has a mind of his own."

Conan grunted acknowledgment, fixing a sidelong glance on the warrior. He respected Kalak, yet he knew the man to be a chewer of lotus-root. Sensing that some of the fellow's levity was at his expense, he nevertheless saw little to be done about it, short of heaving the crack archer down their elephant's steaming flank. So he settled back to watching the jungle, enduring the tension and discomfort of the journey.

The men wore a minimum in the heat, offering bare arms and legs to mercies of sting-flies and enemy darts, all for the sake of coolness and mobility. They trusted to helmets and chest armor to protect their vitals, relying too on the lofty bulk of their mammoth steed to intimidate the Hwong. Mounted at either side of the howdah were pivots for crossbows, which could be cocked and fired swiftly by means of long, overslung levers. Ivory clips kept the arrows from slipping out of their nock, so that the weapons might be pointed sharply downward to wreak death at ground level.

Their giant war-elephant was the first and largest of three, followed by Conan's twoscore spear and sword-wielders slogging along on foot, followed in turn by four couriers leading horses probably half-dead by now with heat. If they encountered a sizeable enemy force, the plan was to hem them in with elephants and pin them down with infantry. Meanwhile, the horsemen would gallop back to Fort Sikander for reinforcements that would probably decide the battle.

But even the elephant riders, squatting behind the low wooden bastions of the howdahs and hedged in by points of sheathed spears and bundles of arrows, could scarcely feel safe. Conan briefly caught himself hoping that the enemy would not find them, and that no battle would be joined on these bizarre, unequal terms— particularly since there was no clear purpose to be served by it. A small body of Hwong might be slain or routed, true; but any small group of rebels could almost certainly elude them. The real function of this middling force was to scout the hills and show off the emperor's strength in a few remote villages. Conan doubted even elephants' ability to surround and pin down savage Hwong in a forest; rather, he feared the kind of sniping, strike-and-run attack that this ill-planned maneuver exposed them to.

And yet so far the jungle had shown them no hostility. Forested hillsides and stream-gushing hollows rolled steadily beneath their steed's trundling stumps. The blinding smother of bamboo, brush, and tree-fronds occasionally parted to reveal steamy jungle vistas, flower-carpeted galleries ablaze with sloping sunrays. The patrol passed villages too—clusters of straw shanties dozing amid rice-fields in the marshy valleys. The yellow-brown farm folk observed their passing with sullen stares from beneath their wide-tented straw hats.

The troopers had been directed to follow a network of jungle trails in a curving radius north of the fort. Lacking bearings, Conan trusted his elephant driver to find the way, occasionally and vainly checking a scrolled map furnished by the captain. At times he could discern a trodden path winding ahead of them through the jungle; at other times not. At one place, he peered downward to see the inlaid stones of an ancient, overgrown highway passing underfoot; ahead in the brush, grouped like blind sentinels, stood crumbling columns of ancient statuary. Conan glanced around suspiciously, reassuring himself that this was nowhere near the jungle temple he had previously assaulted.

As the column arrived at a turning in the antique road, the foremost elephant halted. Its long trunk probed at a carved monolith heavily shrouded by vines. The driver made no effort to goad the beast forward, but sat patiently; meanwhile the second elephant in the column drew up behind them, glowering like a jungle demon in its giant mask of quilted, copper-bossed armor. Its pink nostrils craned forward to probe curiously at the lead animal's hindquarters.

"What are these creatures up to? Why have we stopped?" Casting around suspiciously, Conan switched his guttural queries from the Turanian tongue to the Venji one. Meanwhile, the lead elephant brushed aside pendulous vines to reveal symbols graven deeply in the weathered stone of the monolith. The Cimmerian watched as the moist finger at the end of the trunk carefully traced one of the carvings, a looping, three-lobed figure with down-trailing ends.

"Remember, Sergeant, this beast is probably many times older than you or I," Kalak's voice whispered solemnly at Conan's side, without apparent irony. "The elephant folk too have their gods, and they remember the ways of past dwellers in this forest. Best to let them pay their ancient homages."

Uncertain whether he was being made a fool of, Conan posed no further questions. In a while, his elephant turned to shuffle onward along the ancient track—if such it still was, for the pavement was no longer visible. Conan glanced back to see the next elephant take its place before the pillar, raising its trunk to snuffle at the same carved sign.

He bade his driver stop their beast and wait, lest the column be dangerously scattered by the delay. He knew his foot soldiers would welcome the rest, for the elephants, even heavily armed and armored, set a brisk pace. He stood up in the padded howdah to stretch his own cramped limbs—and with instant watchfulness saw motion ahead: a line of burdened Venji natives winding toward them, their heads and pack-baskets barely visible a hundred paces further up the jungle path.

Instantly Conan clasped each of his companions on the shoulder in silent warning and commenced whispering orders. He sent Muimur clambering down the elephant's armored side, with orders for the other pachyderms to move forward on both flanks of the trail, and for the spear phalanx to fill in the center. Muimur's final order would be to the horsemen, dispatching two of them to alert the fort. The others would follow as closely behind the elephants as their skittish steeds might be induced to go, awaiting further messages.

Kalak mounted and primed the crossbows, while

Conan kept up a tense vigil forward; he urged Than to trundle their beast off the trail, closer underneath the damp, concealing foliage. But it did little good—for even as the front of the approaching party came into open view, the crashing of the elephants in the jungle on either hand alerted them.

Rebels they were—naked Hwong tribesmen guiding armed peasants in jungle-green jerkins. With surprised shouts they threw down their burdens and drew weapons, falling back along the trail in practiced order. At their rear sounded the fluting of a shrill-toned pipe, doubtless a warning signal.

"Forward, men of Turan! Kill our enemies!" Conan's shouts were cut off by foliage lashing in his face as Than urged the elephant ahead; nevertheless the spearmen along the trail heard and broke into a charge, answering with spirited cries. Goaded by their drivers, the striding elephants began to trumpet with deafening effect. The brassy tones vibrated palpably under Conan's doubled knees and ripped through jungle galleries, the very trees seeming to wilt and tremble in their blast. At the shock of the din, many of the retreating bearers dropped their weapons and began to claw away through the forest in panic.

Now Conan's elephant reached the abandoned cargo, its trunklike limbs bursting and scattering rice-sacks and bales of green cloth. The Turanian spearmen, unable to match the animal's ponderous gait, lagged well behind. Soon the beast overtook the first of the staggering, stumbling fugitives, a farm lad in green jerkin and pantaloons; the peasant's brief scream ended in a thudding yelp as he vanished beneath scuffing, trundling limbs. Just beyond him the central group of rebels ran and staggered, to be scythed aside and flung headlong by bronze-sheathed tusks, or else snatched up by the massive, nimble trunk and dashed against trees.

In the thick of the slaughter the behemoth trumpeted again, its deafening bellow transforming the screams of its victims to dumb, terror-stricken pantomimes. All the while, astride the neck of this vast engine of death sat the diminutive Than with his comically sloping shoulders, guiding the beast gently and murmuring singsong encouragements into its leathery ears.

Through all the carnage, Conan drifted as on a racing cloud, high above jungle shrubs and the scattering rebels, surging past curtains of flowered vines and gnarled, garlanded tree-boles. The supple smoothness of the giant animal's movements barely tossed its passengers, though the creature ramped and slaughtered madly. Time and again Conan tried to bring his crossbow to bear, only to see his chosen target trodden under or flung aside by the greedy brute.

"Better to use the side-mount for your bow, Sergeant," Kalak said, waiting patiently next to him. "Aiming forward, you risk shooting our beast's trunk or its flapping ears—and our driver."

"Aye, 'tis so." The Cimmerian, bracing his knees against the roll of the howdah's padded floor, eased his weapon down on its metal-capped pivot. "In any event we shall soon have targets aplenty."

He was looking ahead to where the enemy column thickened into a double file of half-naked Hwong warriors. These troops appeared to lack either the room or the inclination to fall back on their fellows. Armed with spears, bronze axes, and quivers of darts, they deployed smoothly into the greenery on either side of the trail; unlike their surprised forward party, they showed no great aspect of fear.

"Seasoned fighters, these," Conan added. "We had best order a concerted attack." Conan's elephant, although slowed by the carnage, was nevertheless closer to the enemy than the other two now lumbering up noisily on the flanks. At the Cimmerian's command, Than halted the panting beast, allowing the spearmen running along the trail to catch up. Obeying their commander's arm-signals, the other behemoths stopped and waited as well.

"Now, men—for Tarim and Yildiz, attack!" With the spearmen fanning into the low greenery behind him, Conan bellowed the order and felt his own massive steed lurch forward. This time enemies were sheltered at either side of the trail; Conan heard Kalak's crossbow twang an instant before his own released. The two arrows drove forcefully into the bright foliage, shearing off stems to strike with audible impact, but not before Conan was levering back the taut cord and nocking a new projectile into the hardwood groove. His second shot sent a Hwong rolling out from behind a tree, coughing and clutching at a shaft embedded in his ribs.

A dozen and more times swift, twanging death rained out from the turrets of the converging elephants. Then, just as suddenly, the battle became too desperately close for arrow-play. Long spears began to jab up from the bushes at the elephants' trunks and armored faces, to be splintered and hurled back at their wielders by the impatient, snorting beasts, and Conan's foot soldiers pressed forward on either hand, making projectile fire too risky. Than drove their trumpeting mount relentlessly forward along the trail to avoid crushing friendly troops, and all at once they were among milling foes.

Abandoning their crossbows, Conan and Kalak arose to their feet and plied long spears, stabbing relentlessly to keep Hwongs and armed peasants from scaling the elephant's sides or hacking with their bolos at its soft underparts. Axes and darts were thrown high, to clash against their breastplates or go whizzing past their ears. At the fore, Than clubbed attackers with his elephant goad, while his frenzied beast used one rebel's limp body as a flail to belabor others. Yelling Turanians pressed forward from behind, fighting to surround the beast and protect its vulnerable hamstrings.

Hemmed in partway by their adversaries, the rebels did not break and run; some regrouped in a denser hedge of spears blocking the trail, while others faded back into the jungle to harry the ends of the attackers' line.

"Bismillah!" Kalak exclaimed. "I have never seen such hordes of the accursed monkeys!" Conan followed his pointing finger to see heads and shoulders bobbing among the ferns, those of several hundred more rebels streaming along the trail toward the fray.

"Crom! We must have blundered into a massing army." Conan turned to look for his second. "Muimur, dispatch the remaining couriers to the fort—have them tell the captain we need all of his cavalry, and more elephants—infantry too, since it may be a long fight."

Muimur, following a line of skirmishers to the side of the embattled elephant, shouted up to his commander. "The horsemen are already gone, Sergeant! They rode in accordance with the sharif's standing order for cavalry, to depart as soon as we met strong resistance."

"Asura's gnawing devils! Those worthless hay-chompers . . . then send back runners!" Availing himself of an assuredly temporary lull in the battle-tide, Conan laid down his spear across the howdah's rim. "Find men who know the shortest path to Sikander. Make sure they tell Murad we are engaging a thousand Hwong at least."

"Aye, Sergeant!" Muimur turned away. Before Conan could watch him carry out the order, a new hedge of enemy spears pressed near. He turned back to the fight, stabbing and parrying at the mobs of foemen who managed to circumvent the elephant's flailing trunk and tusks.

The battle on the ground was even fiercer, with the advantages of Turanian drill and maneuver virtually canceled out by tree-trunks and thorny shrubs. Hwong skirmishers had a way of falling back into brush, waiting for the oncoming line to split around an obstacle, then lashing out savagely with spears and bolo-knives at the exposed troopers, massing several fighters against one. The northerners' armor usually saved them, but inevitably one was cut down from time to time; and the rebels seemed careless of losing several casualties to their opponents' one.

Conan watched three of his men charge beneath a pink-flowered tree, spears shaking, and only two come staggering back out. "By Mitra, we must support the attack!" he told Kalak, who was steadfastly recharging his bow. "These elephants are no good at retreating. They would rout and trample our own men, once the cursed Hwong start pricking their nether parts with spears. We must push forward!"

"Aye, that was the plan." Kalak sped his arrow into a milling mob of enemies, then reached forward to ply the crossbow's lever. "But these monkeys refuse to scatter! They rally and fight as never before, Tarim wither their yellow hides!"

"Their closeness may yet cost them dearly," Conan answered grimly. Laying aside his spear, he leaned forward to address the driver Than carefully in the Venji dialect. "Guide, we are stalled here while the enemy mounts an attack. Can you drive this beast into their midst?"

Turning in his seat with a cryptic smile, the scrawny driver reached to the front bulwark of the broad timber elephant-saddle. He loosened a pair of lashing-cords, then pulled down a canvas cover to expose a broad-bladed bronze weapon whose presence there Conan had not even suspected. Reaching forward with his hooked goad, Than guided his elephant's massive trunk around and back over its shoulder; the supple limb snaked though a velvet-padded ring at one end of the weapon, grasped its long, leather-bound haft, and raised the flashing blade up high into the air. A murmur of surprise sounded from onlookers on both sides of the skirmish line. The great beast bellowed, lumbering forward beyond its screen of friendly troops.

The rebels might have scattered at the sudden onslaught, but they found they had no room. Hwongs and armed peasants pressed up the trail, blocking their backward impulse. Straight at them the elephant drove, raising its new weapon.

The press of men and spears was thick, yet the first rank was thinned easily by a swipe of the great battle-ax. Long as a tall man, its broad double blades standing wide apart as a warrior's cocked elbows, the implement cut through limbs and spearshafts as smoothly as a scythe through straw. Its first stroke sundered men and set their comrades screaming in fountains of blood. Before the rest could react the brute was atop them, trundling over dead and living alike, hacking and threshing the survivors with its crimsoned, gargantuan blade.

Meanwhile, from their swaying perch on the monster's back, its riders stabbed wildly with their long, unwieldy spears, piercing victim after victim, like frenzied fishers spearing salmon from a barge. In all the dreadful carnage, hardly a weapon was raised against them. Meanwhile over the din could be heard fainter cries as the other elephants closed in, threshing the jungle with angry tusks.

"We must break free of this press!" Panting, Conan abandoned a spear which had become too deeply lodged in human sinew and gristle. He lunged back to extract another from its sheath along the elephant's

side. "If we keep the elephants circling ahead of the
infantry line, the enemy will not reform, and our men
can cut them down."

As he spoke, the ambling elephant beneath him slid
and stumbled across a pile of gory bodies. Lurching
forward among fleeing men, it staggered head-first
against a small tree, which nearly gave way with the
force of the collision. Exhausted, the animal dropped its
heavy ax to stand over the half-uprooted trunk, its great
flanks heaving and trembling, its frontal armor a gruesome, red-dripping mask. Before them the central mass
of rebels continued to fall away, those on the trail
streaming backward or aside into the jungle even as the
Turanian phalanx marched chanting up from the rear.

"We cannot use the trail until the forest alongside it is
clear of rebels," Conan announced to those on the
ground. "When this brave beast is rested, we will scatter
the enemy ahead of you, crossing and recrossing the
trail as you advance. Beware of enemy counterattacks; it
may be a long fight before reinforcements find us!"

Hours later Conan watched Muimur die, pierced
through by a spear driven in sidewise between his
breastplate and backplate. Kalak was already dead, shot
in the eye by one of the short, unreliable Hwong
arrows—probably a poisoned shaft. Tossing the bodies
overside, Conan continued alone with Than atop the
plodding elephant, leading a directionless assault, ex-
pending his last, precious arrows on shapes that flitted
darkly and anonymously among the tree-shadows.

He knew not how many men he had slain this
day—scores, hundreds perhaps, using the strength of
his own hand, without trying to count the elephant's
vast depredations. His troopers' tight, disciplined line
had shrunk rapidly, and at least one of the other two
elephants had fallen to spears. There was no safe

defensive ground nearby, nor enough men and beasts
left to fortify a camp. Perhaps, he told himself numbly,
the time had come to form a square with the remaining
elephants at the center, and wait for nightfall.

For the dozenth time that day, his weary steed paused
to drink at a shallow stream. It sucked up water noisily,
seemingly by the barrel. Then the beast hooked its trunk
high in the air and emitted a thick spray, drenching itself
and Conan with a sudden, forceful downpour. Amidst
the blinding torrent, he saw Than suddenly driven from
the neck of the elephant by the sweep of a long spear.

With a shout, he seized his sword and leaped from the
howdah after the driver, only to meet the point of a
second spear thrusting upward in midair. Hard-driven,
the blade pierced his thigh, scraping agonizingly against
bone before it sliced out through the back of his leg.

At the bottom of his fall, his yataghan clove the face of
the spear-wielder. An instant later he struck hard earth,
shrieking in agony as the grounded spearshaft pushed
and twisted in his leg. While he writhed in the jungle
filth, he was dimly aware of the elephant spewing out
the last of its water and trundling after one of the
attackers with an angry scream, to catch him up and
dangle him from a bulging, furiously knotted trunk. Of
Than he saw no more. He could spare little heed, for
pain clutched him, gnawing at him as a snarling,
ravening wolf gnaws a hapless hare caught in its jaws.

Pain overmastered his every impulse, surging and
swelling like hot acid in his veins and venting from his
throat in racking, moaning gasps. He fought to regain
control, dragging his paralytic frame through mud and
leaf-litter in an effort to ease the torturing pressure of
the spearshaft in his riven flesh.

Fighting oblivion, he managed to sit up and brace the
spear across the dead or dying body of his attacker. A
dozen pain-wracked blows of his yataghan were enough

to hack through the tough bamboo pole. That left him free to topple onto his back with a cubit of the knuckled green shaft, cord-wound and bronze-tipped, still transfixing his leg. He hesitated at trying to draw it out through the wound, lest it increase his blood's steady trickle to a spurting torrent. Fumbling at his waist, he undid his swordbelt and looped it around his blood-slimed thigh.

He passed the end of the strap through the buckle-loop and cinched it tight, then tighter yet, knotting it clumsily when he began to feel light-headed with pain. Then, reaching around his half-bent leg with both hands, he laid hold of the corded shaft just behind the spearpoint. He pulled mightily, hearing a grating moan escape his own taut lips as he did so. Under steady pressure the spear-haft gradually shifted, its last flaring bamboo joint slipping deeper into the swollen, gory lips of his wound. Then black pain billowed up from the center of Conan's being, obscuring his vision as he plunged out of the conscious realm.

Jefar Sharif waited restlessly beside the parapet, watching the dark fringe of jungle grow even dimmer and more impenetrable under the purpling sky. He would have paced to and fro, had there been adequate room on the uneven bamboo treadings over the gate. But there was not, so he vented his nervousness in idle comments to Murad at his side.

"No movement out there, friendly or otherwise. And no more couriers." He glanced at his elder subordinate, looming gray and still in the twilight. "Perhaps we should dispatch an elephant battery mounted with torches, to seek out any lost troops and guide them back?"

"I would not recommend it. Such a small force would be prey to ambush." The captain's voice, though low and discreet, scraped with weary exasperation in the evening stillness. "'Tis an ill practice to send forth units piecemeal; better we had sent our main force out at noontide to support the embattled patrol, as I counseled."

"That would have been over-reacting, I still say!" The young sharif shook his head stubbornly, his crimson turban bobbing darkly in the gloom. "Our returning couriers advised us of no such need. The thirty fresh horsemen we sent were surely enough to defeat any foe the barbarian's patrol blundered into."

"Perhaps—assuming they managed to find him in the jungle." Murad spoke restrainedly, without inflection. "But what of the runner who staggered up to the gate bleeding, telling us that Conan's band faced five thousand Hwong?"

"Nonsense! The fellow was maddened by the same arrow-poison that killed him! Yet even so, that insubordinate black officer—Juma is it?—insisted on marching his whole troop off to their aid. I should not have permitted it." The sharif did not bother to pitch his self-justifications in a low voice. "Remember, Captain, we face other dangers than jungle ambushes! This skirmishing may only be a ruse to draw our strength out of the fort."

"How could there be a ruse, when you yourself did not fix the route of the patrol until this very morning?" Murad shook his head in long-suffering exasperation. "Do you not understand the virtue of a fort, that a few troops may defend it against many? You should have backed up your probe with full regimental force, as planned. Likely they met a Hwong army there in the jungle and were wiped out, along with the few cavalry and infantry you sent. 'Tis poor strategy to do things by half-measures."

Jefar Sharif turned a supercilious eye on the captain.

"You display even less sound strategy, Captain, by addressing your superior officer thus. True, you have gained a certain fitness through long experience. But my fitness is greater, I remind you, for it comes as the natural result of my noble birth!" He posed arrogantly before the older man, confident in large part because the captain's solemn gray stare was obscured by gathering dusk.

A moment later, appeased by the lack of any further response from his minion, the sharif turned back to the rail. "At any rate, supposing the brawling brute and his handful of troops are dead, with a few elephants to boot—small risk, small loss! You yourself told me that an officer must learn to spend lives freely."

The captain nodded, watching Jefar solemnly. "True enough. And what of the secret orders that arrived today?"

Frowning, Jefar lowered his tone to a rueful laugh. "Could you have imagined it? We are instructed to take special care of the barbarian, because of some unlikely interest he commands at court! I ask you, could a despatch be more astonishing, or more ill-timed?" He cleared his throat raggedly. "Still, 'tis no great loss. We can tell Abolhassan that his exotic pet died a hero. It makes me feel safer, indeed; I would have hated to show that unwashed savage special consideration. But say, what moves yonder?" He turned his gaze across the adzed tops of the palisade's timbers. "Halt, there, you! Stand and declare yourself!"

At the sharif's nervous hail, men stirred atop the watchtowers. Likewise came shouts and bustlings from within the fort enclosure; the garrison had been kept alert for a siege all afternoon, with the villagers and camp followers summoned inside. In moments, Jefar and Murad were joined from below by torch-bearing sentries, whose lights revealed an armored elephant approaching in the gloom. Ragged and blood-spattered, it shambled forward with steps that thudded slackly on the packed earth, shaking the parapet underfoot.

"It is our beast," Murad announced, "unless the rebels have draped one of their own in Imperial trappings. I see no driver, so beware of tricks and sorcery. Bring your ballistas to bear on the animal, but keep watching the jungle rim all the same!"

From somewhere beyond the elephant a deep, resonant voice hailed the wall. "Captain, do not shoot!" The watchers began to discern another figure approaching, whose black skin matched the jungle gloom.

"Who comes?" a dozen sentries cried, leveling their crossbows.

"Sergeant Juma, sir! With my troop, plus survivors of the battle." His voice was broken by panting, his weapons clanking as he slowed his trot. "We met the beast in the forest and followed it back here, though we were never able to halt it." As the black man approached, other dim, turbaned figures became visible in a straggling line behind him. "It saved us from being lost in the jungle by night."

"Sire, men are riding in the howdah!" cried a sentry on the palisade, looking down on the animal as it trundled to a stop before the gate. "Two of them. Dead, by the look of them."

Jefar's voice grated sharply over the murmurs which immediately arose. "You, Sergeant—if such you really are! Form up your companions there in the torchlight. Then we can decide whether or not to admit you."

In a matter of minutes the gate had been thrown open and the survivors brought inside. The elephant was calmed by a guide and induced to kneel beside a cargo ramp in the entry-yard. Jefar and Murad supervised as the bodies were lifted out and laid on the wooden dock, to be inspected under brilliant torchlight.

"This is the driver, Than, one of our best." Somberly Murad tilted up the sallow face. "Pierced through the chest by a spear, as you can see. The beasts are loyal; they often pick up their fallen drivers and try to rescue them. And here"—the captain reached out to brush lank black hair aside from a death-pale face—"here is Conan, the patrol officer himself! Bled dry by this wound in his thigh, perhaps—or more likely, poisoned by it. He must have died in his place of command on the howdah."

"A sad loss." Jefar Sharif moved up beside the dock to face the troopers gathered around. "And yet, I am told, it was in the course of a fierce fight, resulting in the slaughter of a small but spirited enemy force. A harsh price, yet not too much to pay for the greater glory of—"

"Wretched slacker . . . coward!" A sepulchral voice arose eerily behind the sharif. Suddenly it took tangible form—a pale hand clutching at his shoulder.

"You promised to relieve us! We fought the day through . . . I watched my men die!"

Those nearest stood stunned, seeing the terror-stricken sharif dragged back against the platform. The spectral handgrip doubled abruptly, shifting to his neck; meanwhile, a skull-white face, scarcely recognizable as human, snarled into his ear. "Where were our reinforcements, rogue? Why did you betray us?"

"Enough! Restrain him at once!" Murad leaped to Jefar Sharif's side, gesturing troopers up onto the dock to lay hold of the vengeful, undead sergeant and pry his hands from his gasping commander. One of them was Juma, who murmured urgent, soothing phrases to the half-delirious Conan while forcing him back onto the planks.

"Hold him down, and shut up his raving!" Murad supported the red-faced sharif, slapping his back to help him draw breath. "The man is wild with spear-poison! Tend to him; save him if he can be saved."

"Aye, we will try," Juma said, clasping Conan's shoulders.

"Aarghhauh!" Waving an arm, Jefar tried to shout in wrath or fear from a throat still too constricted to form sounds.

"Take him to the infirmary—the Cimmerian, not the sharif," Murad added, keeping hold of his frenzied superior officer. "And guard him carefully. Though doubtless he will lose that leg!"

Chapter 7

Wizard's War

"So, Ibn Uluthan, how go your divinations?" General Abolhassan strode officiously among the chests and tables cluttering the star-patterned tiles of the Court of Seers. "The eunuchs say that the Venji magic still defies your best efforts." Stopping at the center of the echoing dome, the black-turbaned warrior folded his arms across his chest in an imperious, mocking pose. "Can you and your apprentices yet foresee a day when you will be of any real value to the war effort?"

Azhar and the lesser acolytes, meekly apprehensive, kept their heads bent over scrolls and magical paraphernalia. But their master, Ibn Uluthan, looked up with an air of irritated righteousness from his carved lectern and the sheaf of yellowed pages on it.

"No, Abolhassan, I confess that we have made negligible progress, to your lord and land's regret." Pale and hollow-eyed from his nightlong vigils, the mage squinted skeptically at his military visitor, whom he equaled in height if not in robustness. "Although we, unlike some, labor selflessly and whole-spiritedly for our emperor's aims, using every conceivable means"

89

—Uluthan swept one arm wide, indicating the array of materials and workbenches assembled to deal with the Venji riddle—"I cannot always claim that our exertions are blessed with quick or easy success. Nor do I see why our misfortune, and your emperor's, should be a source of noxious levity."

"Nay, Wizard, I meant you no insult." Smiling, Abolhassan shifted his broad, black-draped shoulders easily without actually changing position. "Even if at times I have said the support of our imperial treasury for your arcane tampering may be . . . excessive . . . still, I would not want you to think that I question your sincerity." The general's smile became placid, tolerant. "I meant only to express my surprise that a seer as illustrious as yourself could fail to triumph over old-fashioned jungle taboos and dried lizard fetishes!"

"My good General." Ibn Uluthan's reply was patient. "Age can hardly be said to weaken a religion or a spell. And the Venji have possessed powerful empires of their own, as their temple ruins clearly show. In the remote past, some of their dynasties may even have rivaled or exceeded our modern Turanian splendor." The sage shook his turbaned head. "But these influences have faded; our great obstacle is still Venjipur's distance from here."

Drawn once again to consider the problem, he spoke thoughtfully. "Supreme as our power is in Aghrapur, it scarcely bears exportation to a wild land of few folk and fewer Faithful, lacking true shrines or relics, and never even traversed by the holy feet of our mystics. A savage place it is, gripped by degraded, elemental deities, with foul Mojurna as their croaking prophet.

"Of course, such a pagan cult poses little danger to us here; you see no jungle demons prowling the streets of Aghrapur. Our star-castings have a high rate of accuracy, and our various prognostications within the settled empire are of unquestioned value. Our power, in fact, remains unchallenged—except when we try to channel it southward to the devil-plagued Tarqheban coast!"

The sorcerer's gaze, leaving the general's ironic face, wandered absently across the room to the tall, black-silled window, where hung gloom relieved by only the palest radiance. Through the casement, if one peered deep into the dim obscurity, could be seen the faint, half-illusory image of a jewel-bedecked skull.

"Very well, Ibn Uluthan," Abolhassan said in his deep, faintly amused voice. "I thank you for rendering me a more thorough accounting than I could have wished. I only wondered whether Mojurna's magic has been overcome—whether it will soon be possible, as you once showed us, for our beloved Emperor Yildiz to stand in this chamber and see with his own eyes the events transpiring in far-off Venjipur."

"In answer to your question: no." Ibn Uluthan turned a sullen shoulder to his visitor, moving back behind his lectern. "But with the blessings of Tarim and gracious Emperor Yildiz, our efforts will continue. Some aspect of the problem must inevitably yield to our scrutiny, and in time you may expect a breakthrough. But for the moment, no."

"Thank you, Mage. I expected as much." Showing no great dissatisfaction, Abolhassan spun on his heel and left the hall.

Of course, he told himself as he crossed the outer balconies, the spells would have been a convenience. Oversight of the battlefront, even direct command, would benefit all concerned with the campaign, especially that detestable busybody Yildiz. But the present situation, with all its delays and indirections, afforded advantages he was in a unique position to exploit.

Leaving the shade of a filigreed trellis, Abolhassan strode through blazing sun to a gilded, onion-pointed archway. The cool, perfumed halls of the palace swallowed him again, its smoothly descending rampways taking him to the judicial galleries.

There murmured and echoed the business of state, proceeding as it did every day and late into the night. Merchant squabbles, family vendettas, pleadings of law, tax, and troth—those interminable questions, nominally the domain of the emperor, were now adjudged and enforced by eunuchs.

Abolhassan was careful to skirt the public corridors with their mad assortment of chained felons, unkept clans of litigating goatherds, and clusters of dicing advocates. There a general's noble garb and exalted bearing would be met by fatuous looks or cries of beseechment. Happily, the meeting for which he was now overdue lay in the Court of Protocols, a large inner gallery reserved for ceremonies involving His Resplendency and His highest satraps.

A pair of household guards at the Court's double doors bowed him through. Once inside, he was surprised by the strident tone of the interview already underway.

"You beguile our sons and brothers into your armies, or else impress them outright! You send them to die far away from their homes and families! You teach them to murder and pillage, so that their hearts can never be at peace in the grace of Tarim!" The speaker, holding forth at full pitch, was female, a comely woman expensively garbed. From her head waved an unruly banner of pale yellow hair which Abolhassan thought he recognized from previous petitionings and civil delegations. The target of her diatribe, sitting alone on a stool and looking distinctly ill-at-ease, was the medium-sized, pudgy Emperor Yildiz.

Seemingly heedless of his divinity, the woman railed on. "I ask you, Resplendency, is any thought given to the cost of these excursions to savage lands like Venjipur? Not only the cost in lives, but in suffering and ill-will here at home? And what of the public works that are set aside, the temples and roads that go unbuilt? Are these crying needs less important, I wonder, than horsy heroics in some far-off wilderness?"

Her pale hair had always been striking, Abolhassan remembered; it shone now in bright contrast to the prim black and brown tresses of the five other court wives seated by the speaker. Irilya's youthful form, erect and mobile in her blue silk gown and gold-threaded shawl, both emphasized and softened the force of her arguments. As he watched, the general felt a stirring deep within his breast, and began to regard this young woman in a new light. He examined her with attentive, intimately interested hatred.

"But wait, milady—ah, General, at last you come!" Yildiz turned in his seat, leaning toward Abolhassan in obvious, pathetic relief. "I have been trying to assure the Lady Irilya here of the wisdom, and indeed, the long-term necessity of our southern policy. She and these other court wives are deeply concerned. Knowledgable too, I must say." The emperor laughed nervously, with a hint of thankfulness at seeing Irilya sink back down onto her cushioned stool. "I was explaining to them the hydraulics of empire, that the tides of conquest must always either flow or ebb. The mighty ocean never rests between its rocky shores, I told them, nor do we! We keep up our momentum, not just to gain fresh territory but to maintain our toughness and fighting spirit here at home, in the very fiber of our staunch Turanian hearts."

"I see no lack of fighting spirit here." Abolhassan, with a smooth bow and a measuring gaze at Irilya, took his place beside the emperor. "But what these gentle ladies may not fully appreciate, through their finely cultured understanding of world events, is the continual, pervasive threat that faces us, the menace of barbarism! Those who have not made a lifelong study of map-reading can scarcely appreciate the hazard of Turan's position in the world." The general's gray eyes flashed from Irilya's to those of her delegation with a sober, warning glint. "On every side, ladies, are barbarous hordes who eagerly await a first sign of our weakness, the smallest chink in our imperial armor. All the great empires of history, once they have forgotten this menace, have been overrun—their cities broken, their temples profaned, their thrones and altars besquatted by vile, hairy hides! If we do not keep up unrelenting pressure against this eternal threat, why, even the sacred virtue of Turanian womanhood will be imperiled—"

"Enough, General! I have heard this speech before." Irilya, rising up again on her silk-slippered feet, showed none of the fluttery nervousness of her courtly sisters at the officer's remarks. "Myself, I do not need to look so far for a threat to our welfare; I worry about the growing power of the military caste in our own land." Her eyes and Abolhassan's met with a nearly audible clash, like blades ringing together in air. "So far as foreigners are concerned, is there not a danger that one of these petty wars will bring us into conflict with a hungrier or fiercer race, provoking their greed and inviting Turan's own downfall? Such also has befallen great, rapacious empires of the past."

Abolhassan smiled coldly. "All the more need for Turanians to hone their fighting skills and test them in war, milady! That way we ensure that no enemy can stand against us."

"Ladies," Emperor Yildiz announced, "you are the favorite wives of some of my principal shahs; I beg you, heed me." His smooth, ingratiating tone seemed well calculated to capture their attention. "You are all knowledgeable in statecraft, offering vital and trusted assistance to your mates. Lady Irilya's husband, Shah Faharazendra, is eminent in rulership and commerce alike, leading rich fleets and caravans forth to spread Turan's fame across the world. Would that he were here now, Irilya, to . . . console you in your concerns about state affairs."

Yellow-hair pursed her berry-stained lips skeptically at this comment, yet remained silent. The emperor smiled confidingly, leaning nearer the court wives.

"Since you understand the high aims of rulership, you will appreciate a story I have to relate." Yildiz rested a hand on the pantalooned knee of one of the women, whose comely olive complexion deepened in a blush at this lofty honor. "Of those who serve their emperor in provinces like Venjipur, some, as you say, are your noble kinsmen, others mere humble subjects. A few sacrifice greatly for their beloved god and homeland; others gain as greatly in strength and wisdom, winning the high regard of their fellows, or even advancing to the status of heroes!" His eyes searched the women's earnestly, causing all but Irilya to turn their gazes demurely down. "An empire needs heroes if it is to survive," he assured the bold-eyed girl with a steady, kingly glance.

"One such soldier in Venjipur has recently come to my attention . . . an obscure sergeant in one of the outlying forts, commanding a troop of frontier-hardened infantry. Conan, they call him." Yildiz shrugged eloquently. "Not even a native Turanian, but a foreign enlistee. A Vanir, I am told."

"Tarim's grace!" Irilya interrupted, arching her pale brows at Yildiz and Abolhassan in feigned astonishment. "Can this be one of those fierce barbarian plunderers we have been warned about?"

"Truly, milady," the general parried smoothly, "but when such can be persuaded to follow the true faith, there are no better fighters. That is why we say, send barbarians to fight barbarians!"

"Indeed," Yildiz picked up the thread briskly, "this man first came to my attention not long ago, during the rebellion of our key outpost, Yaralet." He shook his head in sad recollection. "Word came that our entire relieving force had been wiped out, not by honest combat but by some heinous heathen sorcery. Soon afterward, a messenger arrived from the northern marches, saying that one unnamed trooper had survived the battle and, practically singlehanded, had returned the city of Yaralet to my rule. That man, I now know, was Conan. Before long he had been transferred at his own insistence to the southern front."

The emperor shook his head in frank admiration, kindling faint responsive gleams in the eyes of the court women. "No surprise that, since men like Conan need an arena, a bold undertaking in which to unleash their talents." Sitting well forward in his chair, Yildiz patted the knees of several of his smiling listeners as he spoke—not including Irilya, who kept well out of his reach. "Of such human material, skillfully shaped and tempered, is a strong empire forged."

"Most impressive." Level-eyed, Irilya feigned the same credulity her companions showed. "With one such warrior, capable of defeating whole armies, you will hardly need more legions to conquer Venjipur! Doubtless his exploits there have been of equal magnitude?"

"Aye, they have," Yildiz nodded, unruffled. "Of late he led a force of hand picked raiders in storming a vital enemy outpost, a heathen temple. In the fight he himself came near to slaying Mojurna, the witch-man who is prime instigator of the Venji rebellion." The emperor beamed into the wide eyes of his dark-haired listeners, his beringed hands busy patting and stroking where they could. "But that is not all; I am told that we received, just today, news of a further exploit, which General Abolhassan has joined us here to relate."

"With pleasure, Your Resplendency." The general, already edgy from his clashes with Irilya, watched Yildiz's physical communion with the other court wives in growing discomfiture. In his mind lingered a germ of doubt whether this casual patting and handholding might not at any moment blossom into the shameful kind of scene Yildiz was fond of subjecting him to in the imperial bedchamber. With an effort, he forced his thoughts to the business at hand.

"We have just received word of a successful action by a territorial elephant brigade, backed by massed cavalry and Imperial regulars. Our force overran an enemy camp, destroying approximately ten thousand rebels and routing the survivors, with negligible losses to our own side. The officer Conan spearheaded the attack— and himself suffered a grave wound from which his recovery is unlikely." Abolhassan shook his head soberly. "In all, the battle represents a signal victory for Turan."

"Truly, General!" Irilya said archly. "I am amazed that any rebels are left, since their army, by your accounts, was always so small and scattered."

"Indeed, milady," Abolhassan assured her with a venomous smile. "We have anticipated and blunted their main stroke against us. The end of the campaign cannot be far off now."

"Wonderful news, surely." Yildiz sat with brow knit beneath his jeweled turban, his hands for once idle at the sides of his chair. "Yet I worry about my officer

Conan; he is the best man to come out of the frontier marches in years, possibly ever. Can you send a swift message southward to guarantee him the best of care?"

"Certainly, Your Resplendency." After listening thoughtfully to his seated ruler, the general nodded his smiling assent. "Assuming that he still lives, I will direct that he receive very special treatment."

"Excellent!" Yildiz clapped his hands on his silk-wrapped thighs. "Now, ladies, if there are no further points to be discussed, I suggest that we end our interview. This latest news from the front is so significant, I intend to take the dispatch into the map-room and study the details." Leaning forward in his chair, he patted several rounded knees in farewell. "Be assured that your proposals have been heard and that your emperor will use every suitable means to address them. I look forward to having another meeting with you soon . . . perhaps a more convivial gathering in my chambers, with a small feast set forth? When it is arranged, I will summon you. It has been a great pleasure."

Arising with the emperor, Irilya stepped forward to grip his hand firmly in both of hers. "Resplendency, the concerns I voiced will not cease of themselves. I warn you to weigh my words carefully against the counsel of others in your court." Her glance at Abolhassan was expressive, but Yildiz's attention was already diverted by the other wives' more simpering farewells.

"Thank you all, ladies! We are pleased to have this opportunity to elucidate our imperial aims. Tarim bless and provide you!"

The door-guards moved near to assist Yildiz in shooing away the covey of silk-decked, spangled women. Meanwhile Abolhassan bowed deeply to the emperor, holding forth his rolled copy of the Venji dispatch. "Here it is, Resplendency. Most inspired, the way you handled those biddies"—he glanced aside to be sure that they were gone—"but I would beware that insolent, pale-haired one. Remember my past warnings on that score, sire; you may yet have need for the strap and the knife to gain compliance with your wishes." He bowed perfunctorily once more, backing away. "I shall be eager to discuss these matters with you further, Lord, after a nagging afternoon engagement of which my secretary only lately informed me. Thank you, Resplendency. Good day!"

Leaving Yildiz to devour the preposterous Venji dispatch, Abolhassan made his way quickly through back corridors to yet another quarter of the vast palace, the eunuchs' apartments. Here, the general was soon sickened by the scents of patchouli and sandalwood hanging heavy in the air. Yet he steeled his eagle-hooked nostrils, dismissing the odors as just another pathetic overindulgence by those who had treacherously been denied life's greatest overindulgence.

Even the gilded door which he sought out was ornate to the point of offense. Yet it did not repel him so much as what lay beyond.

"Greetings, General. You are late." The eunuch Dashibt Bey squatted on a tasseled cushion behind a low, lacquered table strewn with remnants of his midafternoon meal. The obese figure squatted at the center of a vast carpet, whose patterns blazed arabesque in the yellow lamplight, effectively concealing any food morsels and wine-stains scattered by the feast. "I would have bidden you partake also—but now, it appears, there is nothing left!" He surveyed the desolation of smeared platters, gnawed bones, nutshells, and gouged crusts. "Unless, of course you want some fruit," he added with a belch, pushing his omnipresent gilded basket to the center of the table with one stubby hand.

"No, Dashibt Bey. I come straight from Yildiz, and I

must presently return to him." Abolhassan shut the door tightly behind him. "Frankly, I do not cherish this meeting; I thought we agreed to avoid such needless risks. What business can be so pressing as to require my presence here?"

"Why, General, are not high treason and royal usurpation pressing matters? The bedazzlement of an emperor and the theft of an empire?" Dashibt Bey laughed deeply, his fingers fumbling among table crumbs. "Nay, General, do not gape so fearfully! There are no windows here, no spyholes or lip-readers in my private dining-chamber. We are alone and safe from prying eyes and ears. We may speak frankly, without the need to deceive Yildiz, or, more subtly, our fellow conspirators." His smile was evil, his beady eyes glinting from the gleaming expanse of his face. "There are some matters which need to be discussed openly, between equals."

"Equals." Abolhassan took a long moment to swallow the word, his face imperfectly concealing the effort. "Of course we are equals, Dashibt Bey! Equal partners, sharing equal risks. Though I daresay, should our conspiracy fail, you will be cut up into more and larger pieces than I!"

"You reassure me, General! You jest!" The eunuch laughed. "You lie!" His eyes did not leave Abolhassan's face. "But you lie cleverly, as skillfully as anyone like myself could wish, whose ambitions also hinge on your powers of deceit." Dashibt Bey shook his head broadly, ignoring his guest's scowl of insult.

"But do not think for one moment, General, that I am deceived! Do not imagine that I, like the others, heed your talk of ruling councils and shared powers. You will predominate; you are a natural leader of the common herd and, more significantly, of their herders, the cavalry." Dashibt Bey nodded approvingly. "Your personal ascendancy will be the last fact many fools learn in their shortened lives. The seizure of the throne will be only the start of the bloodbath." Complacency shone from his round, oily features.

"But as you are pruning the top of the slender, lofty tree of state, lopping off limbs and heads"—here the eunuch fumbled in a jade bowl, mopping up the last smear of pink sauce with a shred of crust—"do not think to dissever me! My position is too strong to allow it, and my function too vital, whether you appreciate it or not." He popped the smeared crust into his mouth, chewing in undisguised satisfaction.

"Very well, Dashibt Bey." The general hovered before the table, gazing down on the eunuch with only the faintest flare of his nostrils hinting his distaste. "I shall ignore your insults, for the time. Of course I need you, conciliating and expediting, keeping the court functioning smoothly. With you to ease the transfer of power, we can proceed quickly from this simple rebellion to greater military triumphs—"

"That is what I mean, General," Dashibt Bey interrupted. "If you think that Turan is a military state, to be led by a general into war against Hyborian nations, you err sadly. As a militarist, you ignore our predominance in commerce, diplomacy, politics—in graft, as well." The eunuch shook his head patiently on its thick padding of neck. "Why, real war would deprive our country of its best advantages! Rather, Turan's greatness requires that you act as figurehead only. Oppress the realm, by all means! Defend it, and chip away at its borders. But defer to me in all important things, especially international ones." He scowled. "And let there be no more whispers in the city garrison of a red night of slaughtering eunuchs."

The administrator, showing no reaction to the officer's surprise, continued. "Yes, I know of that scheme, General. Its instigators, by the way, have already received their transfer orders and taken ship for the Hyrkanian wilds. My eunuchs, my children—nay, do not laugh, General—my eunuch-children tell me of all that transpires in Aghrapur. We are the real power in Turan. Thus it has always been under Yildiz, and thus it shall continue. Be thankful that I have warned you; another time might have been . . . too late."

The immense man turned his head a little aside, yawning. "But you see, it is not so bad. Every king must compromise. I offer you sole rulership, after all, with as much sway as Yildiz, and considerably more. No ruler ever realizes the full, overweening scope of his dreams . . . luckily for the world and its inhabitants."

Abolhassan moved back and forth before the table, shuffling listlessly as he digested what he had heard. A long silence ensued. When he turned back to Dashibt Bey, a gray deadness was in his face. "What, then, of the arms caravan Yildiz ordered for Venjipur? Has it been processed?"

The eunuch nodded. "Half of it dispatched southward by river, the other half laid aside in warehouses south of the docks. It will be ready at our day of need." He glanced up at his guest. "General Abolhassan, you must not take this so hard. I know it is trying for you. Here, have a piece of fruit." He reached out and nudged the heaped basket forward again.

"Thank you, I will." Abolhassan bent over the choice globes and ovals, taking some time to select one for size and firmness. He chose a ripe mango, its leathery skin shading from green through yellow into blazing scarlet, like a tropical sunset. Wordless, then, he strode up onto the table and across it, kicking dishes aside roughly with his cavalry boots. Dropping on both knees onto Dashibt Bey's broad chest, he crammed the oval fruit into his interviewer's startled, wide-open mouth. With one hand clutching the back of the eunuch's neck, he forced the slimy, rupturing fruit down between the man's distended jaws until its wide, sharp stone lodged in the capacious throat. There he held it with an iron grip.

"Aagahh—ahk!" Dashibt Bey made faint utterances as his scrabbling fingers shifted ineffectually from his dagger-bearing cummerbund to Abolhassan's clenched arm, thence to his own fast-purpling throat. A series of upheavals began as his massive legs kicked at the table, flipping it upward in the air, and then scuffed at the tiled floor. His convulsions propelled him lurching backward off his silken cushion, his huge body spasming amid the shattered debris of the meal. The general inched forward along with him, his powerful arms clenched in a vengeful grip, maintaining his hold until he was sure the fruit would not be expelled. Then he shrugged free, stepping back from his victim's final convulsions just in time to hear a latch rattle and see the gilded door swing inward.

It was Euranthus, Dashibt Bey's eager second administrator. The sleek youth came running around the inverted table to kneel at his master's side. "I heard the dreadful crashing—General, what happened?"

"The poor man choked to death on a fruit-pit," Abolhassan said, his hand drifting to the dagger concealed in his own sash. "Now you will have to take his place at court, I fear, and in his numerous other profitable pursuits." Abolhassan knew that Euranthus was privy to the conspiracy; how much the eunuch might have heard outside the door, he could only guess.

"Yes, it is so!" Though Dashibt Bey's outflung limbs still clutched and shivered futilely, his junior stared down at his clogged, blue-black face as if he were already dead, not daring or deigning to offer help. "What a tragedy . . . an untimely accident!" Damp-faced and trembling with warring feelings, Euranthus grimaced up at Abolhassan. "Lucky that I am here to carry on his work!"

"'Tis by Tarim's grace that you are fit for the task, Euranthus! Pray, do not worry, I will assist and direct you in it." Abolhassan let his hand slip away from his dagger-hilt. "Perhaps, after all, this was inevitable; the fellow's greedy appetites were too large for his own good."

"Carefully, Azhar! Balance the mirror on edge to follow the motion of the sun smoothly." Ibn Uluthan looked up from his sorcerous preparations, scowling across a low table set before the tall, black-covered window in the south wall of the Court of Seers.

"I pray that I can support its weight, Master!" The thin young man wrestled heroically with the oblong mirror, whose height overtopped his own. "The frame is massive, Sire, and lapped with heavy gold."

"Indeed! When we asked for the emperor's largest mirror, his eunuchs served us lavishly." The chief mage nodded over his worktable in satisfaction. "It proves that we still have His Resplendency's favor in some matters, at least!" Looking up again, he exhorted his acolyte, "Fear not, Azhar! I know you can manage this simple task. You merely need to reflect the solar rays straight into the window at the proper time . . . in just a few moments now, when that patch of sun enters the court's centermost circle."

The turbaned wizard pointed near his acolyte's feet, amid the broad tile outline of a white pentagram enclosed in a black pentagon, girdled in turn by a white circle. "I am sure that my measurements were correct." For the hundredth time he squinted up at the curvature of the dome, where workers had widened one of the star-viewing slits, crudely, by means of crowbars. Sunlight, in volumes unprecedented in these arcane precincts, now poured down in a broad, dusty beam to the polished floor. "It should require only a few moments of celestial radiance to achieve our ends."

Azhar rested the mirror on its flat bottom-edge. "Again, Sire, what exactly are we going to achieve by this irradiation?"

Ibn Uluthan smiled sallowly from beneath the gray circles of his eyes. "Why, Azhar, I shall overwhelm our enemy and destroy Mojurna's devilish emblem, thus clearing our path of power to far-off Venjipur. His skull-face may melt away to mist, or it may explode into a million brittle shards!" With one hand he patted the folds of heavy black curtain covering the mystic window. "After all, we have the greater strength here in Turan; our prayers and talismans are vastly enriched by the fullness of our faith and the godly might of our land."

Bending to his worktable, he took up the object he had been ritually preparing. "Here is our most potent holy symbol, the sacred Hawk of Tarim." He turned the heavy golden statuette so that its outspread wings flared wide as a man's shoulders, its tawny head craning sidewise in heroic profile. "The writhing snake clasped in its beak represents the foul Cult of Set, so the priests say; but its power should serve just as well against rude jungle witchery." The mage glanced behind him, to where the bird's dim shadow struck the curtain. "When this noble silhouette is cast through the window by the full, pure light of northern day, it will be more than enough to vanquish our enemy's foul token.

"Mojurna's skull-symbol is tenuous and tenebrous, remember: a mere concentrated illusion. Have no doubt, our enemy is poised as intently on this contest as

we are, this test of sorcerous will—but over a much
shorter range, since he is far, far weaker. He is pressed
already to the limit of his feeble endurance, and this will
overwhelm him." Ibn Uluthan shook his head in weary
triumph. "Mere hours ago I conceived of this means of
projection, and already we are poised to put it into
effect. Using the strength of Tarim's blessed sun, we
shall superimpose our magical pattern over Mojurna's
weaker one, even as mighty Turan imposes its national
will on puny Venjipur!"

Braced against his heavy mirror, Azhar nodded duti-
fully. "'Twill be a noteworthy thing, Master, to see our
wizardly foe defeated with mirrors!"

Ibn Uluthan smiled. "Aye, such was ever the magician's way. But look lively, lad, the sun pierces the inner
circle!"

Squinting into the dusty light for long, patient minutes, the two watched the jagged patch of radiance
slowly light up one corner of the pentagram with its
brilliance. As its main part bypassed the gleaming white
tiles of the circle, Azhar began inching his mirror into
the light. The intense, reflected beam flashed crazily at
first over the walls and pillars of the domed court,
brightening them with stark, fleeting daylight. Finally it
settled on the curtain, wavering full-length in the
arched outline of the mirror, making the black fabric
blaze white in contrast with the chamber's interior
gloom.

"Excellent, Azhar!" The chief mage adjusted the hawk
effigy on the low table, making its spreadeagled shadow
play full against the curtain. "Be sure to follow the
sunray with the mirror as it moves; I will stand here and
follow with the sacred emblem. Now there remains
only . . . the unveiling!" As he spoke, he reached beside
him to a knotted cord and pulled it, causing the black

curtains to jerk apart and reveal the silvery crystal of the far-seeing window.

The skull was there, maintaining its unceasing vigil on the far side of the pane. The light cast by the mirror picked out its hideous visage in livid detail, kindling sparks in the many-colored gems of its brows and cheekbones and making them blaze in their polished settings. The shadow of the Hawk of Tarim was somehow difficult to trace, lost in the many-faceted and disturbingly massive physiognomy of the evil talisman. For a moment, it almost seemed to Azhar that the jeweled visage was the *source* of the light, beaming its blinding intensity back through his mirror and up into heaven.

Then, as he watched, the skull grew larger—or nearer, he realized an instant later when his accustomed sense of isolation from things beyond the window was suddenly and horribly violated. For the skull-face pushed in through the glass with a rending crash, scattering silver shards and splintering the tile casement as its jewel-crusted jaws gaped wide. The giant face, radiant in sun-pierced gloom, drove onto Ibn Uluthan like the prow of a vast, grounding ship, smashing his golden idol and seizing him by one hip in its grinning, diamond-toothed bite.

Amid the sorcerer's screams, with the light from Azhar's unsteady mirror veering and darting wildly over the scene, the greedy skull retreated, dragging its struggling victim back through the window and beyond the rightful confines of the Court of Seers. Clouds of dust, debris, and arcane papers flurried after them, lashed by unnatural winds. Inward through the anomalous breech in the wall flapped likewise the black, desolate billows of the ragged curtains. Ibn Uluthan's shrieks dwindled rapidly across an echoless abyss of distance, then were cut off, leaving the dust to settle lazily before the bare stone wall where the window had stood.

Azhar the acolyte, staggering under the weight of his toppling mirror, was flung backward as it finally fell and splintered. He struck his head against the base of a pillar, there to lie motionless and senseless.

Chapter 8

City of Iniquity

"Come, you parched desert dogs! This is no time to collapse in a stinking hostel." Conan halted on the worn threshold of the inn where the cart had deposited its passengers and their meager traps. Clamping hamlike hands on the shoulders of his two friends, he drew them back out into the teeming street. "The city of Venjipur awaits us in all its wicked glory!"

"What say you!" Juma turned to Conan, straightening up from the crouch he had assumed in order to pass beneath the low lintel. "You were fool enough to risk the cart ride here from Sikander with your injured leg; now you want to rove the alleys of Venjipur by night?" Scanning the twilit street, he stood above the dusky currents of its dwellers like a black snag in a swirling yellow river.

On all sides the city crowded close, its ancient stone buildings crumbling behind their gaudy, ramshackle facades. Awnings, lean-tos, cupolas, and false minarets, all had been added to seduce free-spending troops and catch the inflow of foreign coinage. Now, in the fading light, the street's odd angles and gaudy trappings lured the eye. In spite of Juma's denials, his ebony features barely concealed his yearning. "Nay, Conan, 'tis out of the question. You are still too lame."

"Aye. Hence the need for exercise." Conan yoked his friend's burly, leather-vested shoulders under a heavy forearm. "I must stretch the scar-flesh and keep the limb from growing stiff." He gathered in the half-willing Babrak on his other side. "And our devout friend here . . . surely he must experience at least one night of carousing, so that his repentances before Tarim will have weight later on!"

"Nay, truly, Conan, I would be poor company on such an excursion!" Babrak braced himself upright under the burden of the Cimmerian's arm. "Anyway, the kvass they serve in the street taverns is no less sour than what is poured in this hostelry."

"He is right, Conan." Glumly Juma watched the jostling, shoulder-high streams of walkers passing in the street. "Remember, this is Venjipur! You know the countless snares and dangers that lurk here."

Conan, leaning on the tall black man so as to pry him further from the inn door, spoke intensely in his ear. "Surely I do, Juma, and I crave them. As would you, if you had just spent an eternity on your back watching lizards gulp flies on the ceiling! Weeks of that recreation, then a full day of lying prone in a jolting elephant cart—and now you expect me to go flop into some moldy hostel bed?"

Conan's argument had its desired effect, forcing Juma several steps further along the stone paves. Babrak had little choice but to move along with his larger, grappling companions against the hurrying tide of pedestrians.

"As for danger—why, man, we came to this country to tweak danger! I am in a foul mood, as you may have noticed. I will be in a worse one if I do not crack some heads together or otherwise disport myself by tomorrow sunrise."

Cleaving to the others more for compulsion than support, Conan moved with them down the grimy street. Peddlers, handcarts, furtive citizens, and feral-eyed urchins flowed around them in a torrent seldom topping the larger men's shoulders. The only other things tall enough to stand out above it were slave-drawn chair-coaches and the pointy, helmeted heads of other northern troopers. These were conspicuous as well by their disheveled uniforms decked with souvenir beads, garters, and silk scarves, and their noisy, drunken aimlessness.

In all the bustle, the three companions traveled only a dozen steps before ducking through the odiferous, brightly lamplit doorway of a crowded kvass-house.

"Jugboy! A pitcher of mule-milk and three noggins here! Hey, jambee! Run up three totees kumish quick-quick!" Conan's gruff rendering of the local pidgin was adequate, within moments, to quench their thirst. But when Juma slapped down a silver ounce on the narrow table, the aproned serving-boy pocketed it and turned away, nodding and grinning idiotically. The Kushite had to grab and shake him like a weasel's prey to get him to render up change.

The establishment was crowded with knee-high tables and ankle-high stools. Around them stood or squatted patrons of widely varying races. The dim, red-lit air bore scents of sandalwood incense and headier perfumes, doubtless intended to cover the reek of the near-rancid kumiss, among other smells.

Not savored locally, the fermented mare's milk was imported or counterfeited to please the occupying horse-troops, and the beverage did not thrive well in the tropic heat. Nevertheless, it served its purpose; after a few beakers, the heads and stomachs of the three friends were awash in its queasy tide. One of its effects was frankness.

"You are lucky, Conan," Babrak observed, "to be on your feet so soon." He pursed his lips to belch discreetly. "Of the stragglers from the jungle fight, fully half those with lesser wounds have perished of the blood-rot. And many of your troop's survivors will be missing limbs and other valued parts."

"Aye, my friend." Conan nodded solemnly, gazing into his tankard. "Crom bless the both of you dogs for taking me out of that stinking infirmary and into Sariya's care, back at our hut. That bone-chopping Imperial surgeon should be turned loose against the enemy, curse his foul breath! But Sariya . . ." He shook his head profoundly. "The woman has a way about her . . . I was weak unto death, but she nursed me to life."

"Weak is not the word I would have used, Conan." Juma looked ruefully to Babrak. "We know, because it took all our strength as well as Sariya's to hold you down during your raging fevers."

"Indeed," the smaller man nodded. "You refought all your battles then, with foes both earthly and unearthly!"

"She is an angel. I would doubt our wisdom in leaving her at Sikander." Ignoring them, Conan frowned over his foamy cup. "But she wished a rest. The village folk all befriend her now, and the guards I assigned are able men."

"Aye, righteous pillars of Tarim, every one! Do not worry, Conan." Babrak nodded with a smile of utter confidence. "Lucky we are, indeed, to be given so many privileges lately. Rumor around camp has it that your exploits gain you lofty favor, perhaps among the officer staff in Aghrapur!" He laughed easily, scanning the crowded room. "That is what made it possible for us to nursemaid you, you know; we now get extra rations, abbreviated duties, even furloughs like this one!" A spangled Venji girl-trollop minced past them to a nearby table, and the youth averted his eyes chastely. "Not that it means much to a strict follower of Tarim's law," he added resolutely.

"Indeed, Conan," Juma said with a sterner look. "You should be careful of this curious favor that has descended on you. We must not leave Sariya alone more than a day or so. Having known the pains and perils of the hero's game, you now enjoy its rewards . . . but beware." The Kushite glanced narrow-eyed around the room, then leaned closer to his friend. "Know you, these very enjoyments mark you and set you apart. They goad jealousy in dangerous quarters, and are seldom as benign and freely given as one thinks." He pursed leathery black lips in a frown. "Heed me in this, Conan: I have known more dead heroes than live ones."

Before the Cimmerian could dispute his friend's dismal outlook, all three troopers were distracted. A youthful Venji, pockmarked and crooked-toothed, bowed before their table in his tight uniform and began extolling the virtues of his alleged sister. She posed at his side: a red-lipped, sloe-eyed, smoldering girl-child, sheathed in a green silk gown slit almost to her armpits. At their trio of stares she settled back against one of the tiny tables, spreading her knees and seeming almost ready to offer them an immediate sampling of her talents.

"I think not," Juma announced to his friends with a broad grin. "The fruit looks a bit underripe to me. Babrak, now, he needs a more motherly type to initiate him into the conjugal mysteries. And Conan . . . but of course, you have Sariya as your consort."

The Cimmerian shifted his thick shoulders restlessly. "Now, now, Juma, I am not wed to the wench! I am still my own man. Nevertheless, I do not relish this stripling, whose vital places probably have hair pasted on! Nor do I care for her grinning tout—be off, you two!"

Feigning anger at the insult, the Venji youth jabbered threats in pidgin, demanding payment for damages. Finally he had to be propelled away by an armlock and a boot in his scrawny buttocks. The tart spat copiously at her tormentors' feet before flouncing off after him.

"They will be at us again if we get drunk enough in this place, rely on it!" Conan refilled his companions' battered cups. "And beware, fellows—even that raw fillet of monkey-meat may begin to look tempting after a few more pitchers of this swill! That is why it is always wise to move on."

The entertainment in the house had so far been limited to a bored, bead-draped girl twitching on a dais at the end of the room, accompanied by the incessant chiming and tweeting that passed thereabouts as music. Now a more elaborate show commenced, with an older, buxom actress directing and assisting in vulgar tricks performed by trained, silk-costumed jungle apes. The time was ripe for departure, so the troopers passed out into the street, which was dimmer now and less thronged. The ancient pavement and stone doorposts were also less obviously filthy, with paper lanterns and glowing, bead-curtained windows and doors giving the shopfronts a festive look.

Conan, striding with a limp he could almost conceal, led the way down a narrow side-passage. After some turns and branchings, it took them to a tavern whose low-arched entry spilled an inviting puddle of light on the pavement and the wall opposite. Just outside its healthy glow, a pair of Venji civilians stood muttering. As the three troopers approached, one of the loiterers leaned forward, revealing a long knife-scar on one pockmarked cheek.

"Lotusss!" he whispered sibilantly. "Banghee Palace have many good kind of lotus. Good girls too!" He rolled his yellow eyes suggestively. "We send you and girls to happy jade paradise."

"Ignore him, Conan," muttered Juma into his friend's other ear. "His palace is doubtless some riverside tent, and his girls really crones or ill-shaven boys. To a real lotus-lover, such details matter not at all. Duck in here, and we will be rid of them . . . but wait!"

Upon his failure to detain Conan and Juma, the scarred man accosted Babrak more insistently, seizing his arm and tugging at it. Meanwhile, the second loiterer could be seen edging around behind the Turanian—for a grab at his belt-purse, possibly, or at his weapons, or for worse mischief. The two troopers turned swiftly to their friend's aid.

Conan arrived in time to see the brass butt of Babrak's dagger sweep upward, to glance from the scarred man's chin; a low blow from his own balled fist sent the second loiterer rebounding, grunting, from the stone wall. Juma moved in with a kick to the staggering lotus-seller's ribs; a moment later the two toughs were scuttling away down the silent alley.

"Huzzah! The night has begun at last!" Juma grinned broadly, spreading his pale palms wide to clap his companions' backs. "We will raise your glum spirits yet, Conan! Good roughhousing!"

"Our friend Babrak here is not tardy with his knife," Conan observed, turned back toward the lit doorway. "He had no real need of us, except as his audience! Tavern brawling must not be one of the vices barred by Tarim's holy law."

The interior of this second tavern was broader and lower, with bamboo tables and wickerwork seats that a northerner could almost fit into. Food, as well as drink, was in evidence here; after conferring with an elderly male taverner, the three called for portions of a safe-sounding stew of fish, vegetables, and swamp-rice.

"Those alley toughs are a good reason to watch our backs tonight," Juma said, making his wicker stool strain and creak under his rangy weight. "If they were Phang Loon's bullies, they can always summon more of their kind."

"What—those gutter-snipes?" Conan's laugh faltered slightly as he felt the arm of his chair break loose from the seat due to a careless twist of his hips.

"'Tis true, Conan." Juma's shift in his own seat was accompanied by a symphony of bending, straining wicker. "The lotus trade hereabouts is controlled by Phang Loon—except, naturally, that sold by the rebels. The warlord is more powerful than any northern monarch, though he lacks the blessing of church or dynasty. That is one true cause of the strife in Venjipur—and if you ask me, we Turanians have made it worse, by uniforming his private army as the Venji Imperial Guard!"

"Not the best ones to have at your back in a fight, I am told." Babrak frowned over his stew bowl. "Juma is right, though; Phang Loon is not a man to cross." His speech trailed off with an air of distraction, his brown eyes flitting across the room toward the right-angled counter where drink was dispensed.

The focus of his gaze, the others soon determined, was a woman: a trim Venji matron clad in expensive imitation of northern female garb. Her sheath of dark blue silk, unbroken from ankle to neck, showed her off less immodestly in the smoky lamplight than did the shreds and bangles worn by the tavern-girls who flitted between tables. Iridescent silk was gathered loosely about her shoulders and bosom, revealing only the smallest sliver of bodice, while a high, stiff collar enfolded her black tresses and all but concealed her face from either side. Her slim hands languished in loose sleeves, their red-lacquered fingertips toying with a dainty, steaming teacup as she sat surveying the room.

"A man of lofty taste, our Babrak," Juma declared after a moment's appreciation. "He has chosen a noblewoman as the object of his desire." Reaching across the table to the limit of his chair's protesting tolerance, he jostled Conan to redirect his attention.

The Cimmerian, busy raking stew from his platter to his lips with the thin sticks provided for this purpose, put down the mess at his friend's behest. "Hmmm. From her modest garb, there is no guessing her age or nimbleness. Yet from the cost of her finery and her regal bearing, I would judge her owner of this place, and its madam as well!"

Babrak's olive face darkened in a blush as he lowered his gaze to the woven tabletop. "You need not chide me," he protested faintly. "I merely find it refreshing to see a Venji woman showing public decorum for once—"

"Yes." Juma chortled wisely. "And now, no doubt, you would like to learn what her private decorum consists of!" His grin flashed brightly in the dimness. "But Babrak, old friend, we do not mean to scold you! On the contrary, we support your enterprise, and we swear to do all we can to advance it! Do we not, Conan?" he asked, to the Cimmerian's answering grin.

"Nay, nonsense." The Turanian youth shook his head in embarrassed irresolution. Yet he was unable to resist a further glance at the stately woman, who may or may not have been returning their looks. "I have no enterprise in mind; my interest was purely aesthetic. As I have told you, I abide by Tarim's strictures for warriors of the True Faith."

"Now, now, Babrak," Conan said in the flustered youth's other ear, "if you follow those rules too strictly, there will be no more knights to carry on the faith."

"Aye, lad," Juma chimed in gaily. "If Tarim wanted his followers to remain totally pure, he would have preached only to eunuchs!"

"Kushite, curb your reckless tongue!" At Babrak's indignant straightening and quick-flashing gaze, the blue-clad woman across the room could be seen to stir on her high-backed stool and glance their way with what might have been interest.

"Now, now, Babrak, he spoke in jest." Conan leaned coolly in from his side of the table, keeping the Turanian off balance. "Yet there may be substance in all this . . . for I ask you, is it not true that those same fleshly pleasures that True Believers swear to forgo in this life are promised as rewards to the Faithful in the next?"

Babrak nodded dubiously, his eyes straying inevitably back across the room. "Yes, that is so."

"Then tell me, disciple." Conan spoke slowly and reasoningly. "If you never sample the delights of paradise, how are you to reckon their true value in the next world? How can they spur you to full zeal in serving your god?" His questions drew no immediate response from the youth's poised lips or his unblinking, distracted eyes. "If you obey the holy laws too narrowly, will your feet not be the less swift for it, your sword less keen in defense of the faith? Should you not first savor the bounties promised by Tarim, so that you can hold paradise clearly in view forever after?"

This argument Babrak obviously found compelling, for he turned his eyes to Conan with a light of comprehension in them. That was enough—indeed, more than enough for his two friends. At the first hint of assent in the youth's manner, they were on their feet, linking their arms in his, shoving aside the flimsy straw table and marching him across the room toward the wicker throne and its resplendent occupant.

"Greetings, your ladyship." Juma was first to address

the stately woman, speaking Turanian with a formal salute and exaggerated bow—without, however, unlinking his arm from that of the half-resisting Babrak. "Ma'am, we could not help noticing . . . our friend, here, wishes to express his admiration for your exquisite grooming and most refined bearing."

At this, the woman did not answer; she merely shifted her gaze to her other two besiegers. Her dark-red lips pursed demurely, neither frowning nor smiling. Upon her brow there may have been faint lines of maturity; but if so, they were carefully smoothed and powdered over. Her eyes, dark-rimmed and almond-shaped, had a force of penetration, and her face held austere symmetry in its Eastern cast. Furthermore, to Conan's critical inspection, the glimpses of cleavage and ankle-trim that her dress allowed gave sufficiently lush promise.

"Truly, milady," the Cimmerian said to cover Babrak's embarrassed silence, "for us battered fighters, the sight of such beauty is enough to fire our blood and . . . send us back to war boldly, to cleave and rend the enemy!" Unused to polite conversation, he looked aside at Babrak for help. But the lad stood silent with downcast eyes, visibly blushing.

"Of course, madam," Juma volunteered again, "there is no telling what miracle of rejuvenation a soldier might gain from a longer sojourn within the compass of your charms." He flashed a near-wink at Conan, who stood marveling at the Kushite's unguessed power of flattery.

The mysterious woman too blinked. "Sirs, you are very kind and . . . very bold to address me thus." At the firmness of her voice, pitched clearly in gracefully accented Turanian, Conan felt Babrak at his side brace up slightly and renew his furtive stare at the exotic woman.

"Happily for you," she continued with narrowed

eyelids, "I am not averse to taking company this evening." This statement may have been meant less for Babrak and his companions than for the several scowling Venji cooks and servants who had moved near on both sides of the counter; at their mistress's discreet glance, they began to ease away. "But I beg you, sirs"—her lips pursed in a smile whose seductive curve was experienced—"the attentions of all three of you warriors are far too kind for my humble self." She glanced from Conan to Juma with exquisitely polite disinterest. "I would hope to entertain one of you, no more."

"Why, then, that would be our young friend here," Juma said unhesitatingly, shoving Babrak forward. "For though we are a loyal band, traveling under one another's protection"—this with a glance around at the servants still lurking within earshot—"we desire most of all that each of us enjoy an agreeable tour of leave! We would not stand in each other's way. Is that not so, friend?" He nudged the mute Babrak.

"Mmm-ah, yes. It is." The Turanian's croak barely evolved into speech, after which he stood dumb and gaping within the woman's spell.

"Very good," she said, having waited in vain for further words to complement the youth's frank gaze. "That leaves only the question of price."

Juma nodded, taking this too in stride. "No doubt we can arrive at a sum that is not too excessive."

"No matter, I am not impoverished," the woman said levelly. "How much do you require?"

At this, it was Juma's turn to gape. Conan's sense of insult was for once slow to blossom; but he saw Babrak stiffen in consternation.

"Madam, you mistake me! I am not . . . ! That is, I meant . . . " Anger and embarrassment warred in the

youth, ennobling his features even as he stood tongue-
tied in their midst.

"No, be not wrathful, trooper! Compose yourself.
There will be no price." The woman, calm in the face of
his turbulence, renewed the force of her attraction with
the faintest of smiles. "I merely intended a jest, to bring
you to life and . . . to let us be as equals."

Babrak stood uncertain; but Juma, as always, came to
his aid. "Only a jest, a mere misunderstanding! Here,
now, you see—all this beauty, and wit too! Your taste is
impeccable, fellow!" Moving closer, the Kushite deftly
pushed Babrak down into a chair brought forward by
one of the manservants. "There, take a seat and become
better acquainted! We shall watch for you later, here or
back at the inn. My heartiest congratulations, and may
you both have a festive night!"

Withdrawing to their table, Conan and Babrak
watched ongoing events in the tavern, which swiftly
became uninteresting. Babrak and his patroness conversed earnestly, leaning ever closer together, ignoring
their drinks. When the woman arose to lead their friend
through a bead-curtained doorway at the back of the
house, it came as no surprise.

They had switched to drinking kvass, a sour beer
which, while more palatable than the fermented mare's
milk kumiss, made their minds reel less drolly. Nevertheless, the effects were cumulative, and the ripening
evening brought more life into the establishment, which
had begun to seem sedate. The obligatory chiming and
tweeting struck up somewhere in back, with twanging
added in for good measure. War followers, both Turanian and Venji, crawled through the place in search of
pleasure and profit. Past the troopers' table paraded a
string of underfed whores of assorted sexes and talents;
enthusiastic offers of lotus distillates to be chewed,

sucked, inhaled, sipped, or smeared in shallow gashes on the skin; and one grinning merchant offering strings of shriveled, blackened human ears for sale as proof of the buyer's fictitious prowess in jungle combat.

Many of these panderers were tripped or booted out of the two foreigners' sight, and all were subjected to insults of increasing coarseness and hilarity. Retaliation was discouraged by the subtly favored treatment the two now received from the tavern's staff, as well as by their size and obvious roughness. Yet oddly enough, chaos, when it did come, erupted around someone even larger and more rugged than themselves.

Juma and Conan recognized Orvad, the giant northern trooper, when he lumbered in to slouch over the bar. They did not hail him because they had no need of his dull wit to furnish amusement this gala night, and because to both men he was an unpleasant reminder of the garrison duty they had temporarily escaped. Perhaps they should have foreseen something; yet his bellow of outrage from across the room came as a surprise.

They looked up to see Orvad's gap-toothed mouth twisting in a snarl, his bushy eyebrows meeting above his beady eyes in anger, one hand fumbling amid the straggling black hairs at the side of his head, retracing a too-well-remembered vacancy; then he seized hold of his foe.

It was the unlucky vendor of ears, a wiry middle-aged man. They saw him lifted above the crowd's shoulders, shaken and twisted in air, then slammed neck-first against a stout wooden pillar where it supported the ceiling. Severed ears sprinkled the tavern like a light snowfall. Orvad immediately became the center of a knot of struggling bodies, a shouting swarm that fought itself in the process of sorting itself out between attackers and escapers. With a swift, mutual nod of agreement, Conan and Juma rushed to their fellow trooper's aid.

In deference to their friend Babrak and his kind hostess, they did not draw knives. That meant dodging the blades wielded by panicked fugitives, or else fending them off with raised stools. Conan quickly learned the reason for the wicker furniture: it could not effectively be used to club an opponent to death. Shouldering into the core of brawlers who were busy fighting Orvad and one another, he was forced to hurl men aside or smite at them with his fists. And these slight Venjis refused to stand solidly before a blow as a northerner would; instead they staggered back scarcely harmed, dodged aside, or tried to cling to his fists. In all, he found it unsatisfying, like battling children in a room full of cushions.

Orvad was more successful, hurling foes bodily against walls and ceiling, using unconsious ones as clubs to smite down others. In fact, he was rapidly clearing the room, and scarcely in need of help from two more veterans nearly his own size. Seeing this as they fought their way to his side, Juma and Conan exchanged fresh glances of assent. Promptly they undertook the more difficult task of calming the giant.

This was hazardous because Orvad, never very submissive to reason in his daily life, was far beyond it now. Their friendly grips on his shoulders he shook off with savage jabs of his elbows, sending them staggering and gasping like two of his lesser foes. To Conan's exhortations, shouted earnestly in his face, he responded with a bear hug, roaring and gnashing his teeth in an effort to bite off the Cimmerian's nose. Fortunately, an earthenware kumiss-jar applied to the back of his neck by Juma had a timely soothing effect. Blows and kicks to his midsection and nether regions produced further calm, as did elbow-strokes to his temples, once he bent low enough for that method of persuasion to be possible.

In time, crouching and moaning, he grew placid enough to be led to a bench near the door; or at any rate he seemed so. Unfortunately, before Conan and Juma could force him to sit, he fell prey to another bout of unreason, flinging his rescuers over tables and bolting out the doorway like a bull fleeing the slaughter-pen.

His friends picked themselves up from a plank floor awash in stale drink and blood, mutually dismissing the idea of pursuit. They eyed the Venjis remaining in the place, unsure whether to expect profuse thanks or a fresh assault; but the servants were busy dragging out bodies and righting furniture as if nothing had happened. The two troopers finished their kvass, taking time enough to show their unconcern and allow Orvad a healthy lead; then they departed.

"Otumbe and Ijo!" Juma stopped just outside the light of the tavern entry. "That Orvad is a mountain of muscle! And he knows some nasty tricks." The black man rubbed his neck with one big hand as he glanced up and down the lane for signs of danger. "If only there was a brain driving it all, he could be as considerable a fighter as you, Conan, or I!" His grin flashed bright in the alley shadows.

"Ahum. I am less a man than I was an hour ago." Conan shifted ungracefully on the cobblestones, cautious of the pain plucking at the deepest fibers of his thigh. "Methinks it was too soon to use my leg as a bludgeon on that hulking moron's scalp! Crom, it pains so much, I misdoubt I can hide it!"

"Here, let me bear some of your weight." Juma moved to the Cimmerian's affected side, offering his shoulder. "Go ahead, lean as heavily as you want. Pretend you are drunk—if you need to pretend!" They started back toward the main street, managing a fairly swift gait between the two of them. "The best thing for you now is your bed at the inn—a quiet, solitary bed if I have anything to say about it!"

"Nay, the night is only begun." Conan's speech was punctuated by soft gasps in the same rhythm as his steps. "I was craving just another pitcher or two, to lighten the pain—"

"Another pitcher! Precisely what I had in mind!" The unexpected voice and shadow loomed ahead of them so suddenly in the darkness, they had to stumble to a halt to avert a collision. "I would gladly buy the drink, just to gain a chance of talking with the hero Conan and his boon friend, Sergeant Juma." The speech was in native Turanian, firm and hearty without any noticeable slur of intoxication.

"I think you have the advantage, fellow," Juma answered guardedly, edging back and aside from Conan to clear their weapon-arms. "Do we know you?"

"Know me? Not by face or name, I would think . . . only as a fellow fighter in a holy cause. And as one whose offered drink it might profit you to imbibe."

As the stranger spoke, Conan strained his eyes to make out some detail of the silhouette that diminished the wedge of light from the street ahead. He swore he recalled this murky stretch of alley as being lit by an oil lamp when first they passed here. Could it have burned out, or its owner removed it? He remembered branchings of the way as well, which now seemed subtly confirmed by alley echoes and the faint loom of light overhead. The Turanian had almost certainly intercepted them from a side-passage; yet his prompt recognition of them could hardly be explained by keen eyesight.

"Well, man . . ." Juma's voice was ragged with the last shreds of his patience. "If you have a name, speak it, and pray that it is not on the long roll of my enemies! Be warned, I find it hard to believe that any well-wisher would detain us in this dark, treacherous place."

Over Juma's sharp utterances, Conan thought he detected faint sounds in the darkness. The scrape of a weapon, perhaps . . . or the grinding of broken glass underfoot: a shattered lamp-chimney? The noise seemed to come from behind, though Conan was certain that no shape had moved in the faint tavern-light at their backs.

"Well, fellow: as for a name, mine is Rabak." The shadow's voice rang loud and self-conscious in the darkness—drawling, perhaps to cover the advance of unseen allies. "As for this place, I agree with you most heartily. I would suggest that you accompany me to a more hospitable site down this side-avenue . . ."

Conan's eyes, sharpened by desperation, finally picked out a detail of the blocking figure he could recognize: a faint tracery of starlight reflected on steely metal unmasked by fabric. Silently Conan reached a hand aside to Juma, tracing the pattern on the trim, unarmored flesh of his friend's shirtwaist. A quick clasp of the Kushite's hand over his wrist told him that the signal was recognized: a tight, coiled circle of wire, emblem of the Imperial shock troops known as Red Garrotes.

". . . a house where heroes like yourselves are known and welcomed . . . yes, even coddled a bit," the unseen trooper proclaimed at undue length. "I have a proposition that would be well worth talking about—"

"Rather, talk about it with your ancestors in Hell!" Conan's sword leaped into his hand, then lashed forth into the deeper darkness. An agile side-twist by his target did not prevent the stranger from taking half the blade through his abdomen. His dying scream heralded an onrush of feet from several sides; swiftly Conan shook the collapsing victim off his blade, turning to face the half-seen attackers.

"Juma, we are circled! Backs together!" As he spoke, Conan heard the hiss of steel, a crunch, and a moan as the Kushite's sword came into play. An instant later a rushing body caromed into his, spinning him half around; he realized he had lost track of his friend in the clatter and stamp of warring feet. He struck out among shadows, meeting elusive resistance at best, and at once began pulling his strokes for fear of hitting the Kushite. His favored tactic of a howling charge was ruled out by his leg, which wobbled weakly beneath him from the strain of the paltry fighting done so far. His recent pain was gone, washed out of his veins by the heady wine of combat.

"Juma, I am here! Do not call out!" He knew that his friend may have been stalking foes in the dark, a tactic for which his black skin suited him well. But his own outcry brought such a rush of attackers that he vowed not to repeat it. A blade came slashing down at neck-level, too sudden to duck and almost too swift to parry; then a muffled shape struck him, bearing his weapon aside and down. Finally something whipped over his head from behind, scraping his nose and chin painfully—a wire loop. Luckily it encircled one wrist as well as his neck; even so it drew cruelly tight at once.

By Crom, at least these phantoms were known enemies! Stabbing and hacking one assailant back out of his way, he turned the point of his yataghan up to saw at the garrote, risking cuts to his own face and his imprisoned arm. His sword failed to sever the wire; however, a desperate backward thrust pierced its owner's hand or face, eliciting a yelping cry. The noose slipped free, but at once more bodies struck Conan's, driving him back against a hard stone wall and bearing down on his limbs with their ruthless weight.

He felt a ragged groan escaping his throat as his unsteady leg twisted beneath him and gave way. He toppled, feeling a shock to his head that turned blackness into blossomings of vivid color.

And yet paralytic, pain-burdened consciousness clung to him, sharpened by the prick of a cold, razor-edged knife at his throat. Someone had unmasked a lamp; now its yellow beams wavered demonically on a constellation of gloating faces that hovered close before his eyes. Most were twisted in spiteful, cynical leers, the scarred, leathern visages of jungle and gutter killers—garroters and street toughs.

He felt the steel bite his neck more deeply and lovingly. Then he saw one impassive face, the largest of them all, rolling ponderously in denial like a vast planet. It was—dimly, impossibly—a countenance he recognized: that of Sool, the hulking torturer oft seen at Fort Sikander. From beneath the vast face, a round, massive hand drifted forward to ease the pressure of the blade against Conan's neck.

As he watched helpless, the thick, frowning lips parted to form sounds—two deep, resonant words only: "Phang Loon."

Chapter 9

Castle of the Warlord

Reality was a single throbbing note, pulsing faintly at first, then expanding rapidly to a vast, unimaginable volume. Abruptly it burst and flew apart into flocks of scattering echoes. Some of the shards tangibly grazed Conan's head, flurrying past him and fluttering around his ears like soft-bristled bats.

Groaning, enmired in silky, yielding cushions, Conan raised his arms to ward off the disturbance. Groggily he blinked open his sleep-encrusted eyes. Before him in an arching, lacquered frame hung a brazen gong, man-high and still shimmering with concentric waves of diminishing sound. Before it stood the stocky torturer Sool, just setting down a pair of velvet-covered hammers. He turned. Acknowledging Conan's stare with a tight, contemptuous smile, he folded his arms and waited in silent attendance beside the reverberating gong.

Around them arched windowless walls of polished stone adorned with silken hangings and fragile, lacy carvings of ivory and teak. Lacquered tables about the room bore oil lamps, their flames mercifully screened to cast a shadowy light.

"Where . . . and what . . . is this place?" Straining to sit upright, Conan succeeded only in rolling onto his side amid the spongy cushions. His head felt as woozy as his body did feeble. "Curse you, where am I? And where is Juma?"

A steady tug of pain warned of dangerous weakness in his leg; yet the feeling was faint somehow, unnaturally mild. Leaning against a silken bolster, he raised tingling fingertips to his neck. Dry encrustations surrounded a long slit in the skin, yet there was no sensation. "You have drugged me," he said thickly, restraining his voice lest the cut burst open to gush forth his lifeblood.

"Do not worry; the lotus is wearing off." The firm, Venji-accented voice came from one who had entered the room unseen—a swaggering officer, commandingly large and robust for a yellow-skinned southerner. He affected a Turanian-style military tunic and turban, both cut of an unlikely bright blue fabric made more costly with gold thread and ornament. His smile flashed thin and white between his sleek mustache and goatee.

"You will forgive my lackey Sool for not announcing me by name, Sergeant." He waved a hand at the torturer, whose thick middle was doubled over in a deep bow to his master. "I am Phang Loon, Lord of Venjipur."

Conan hauled himself up straighter where he sat, aware of the indignity and vulnerability of wallowing among cushions. "You are no Venji," he grated, eyeing the warlord guardedly.

"By ancestry no, thank the gods—any more than you are a Turanian." Phang Loon's smile was tighter even than his servant's, betraying a dangerous dislike for the remark and its maker. "By birth, however, I am of Venjipur." Smoothly he seated himself on a lacquered stool at the edge of Conan's sea of cushions. "My race sailed west from Khitai when the overblown Venji empire was collapsing of its own weight. We have prospered here ever since—by conquest, by commerce and deft diplomacy, or by whatever means necessary. Now our dominance enters a new phase." Crossing his ankles beneath his seat, the warlord smiled complacently. "Your leader Yildiz is wise to recognize my fitness to rule Venjipur. Others, like your General Abolhassan, have placed even higher faith in me."

Conan shifted his cramped position, trying to move his sound leg beneath him inconspicuously. "If my employer declares you his satrap because of your skill at piracy and drug-pandering, I have no objection." Unable to avoid stretching his wounded thigh, he stifled a grunt at the steadily returning pain. "I do not know this Abolhassan; but if he is Yildiz's general, I am subject to his command. What I want to know is, where am I? Why am I here, and where is my friend?"

With an air of taxed patience, Phang Loon arose from his seat to stride a few paces across the polished flagstone floor. "Simple questions, Sergeant, simply answered—since you obviously mean to test the limits of my charity. We now enjoy the comfort of my palace on the Gulf of Tarqheba, well outside the city's squalor. Of this friend of yours I have temporarily lost track; but be assured, I have instructed my agents to scour the taverns and brothels for him so that he too can relish my hospitality." Phang Loon pivoted back to Conan, smiling less graciously than before. "As for you, Sergeant: You were brought here by secret order of your highest staff officers. They feel that your usefulness to the Turanian army has ended—perhaps because of your wound, your miserable lack of breeding, or some past indiscretion . . . or perhaps through no fault of your own." The warlord shook his head tolerantly. "Because, you know, the loftiest commanders must daily weigh considerations their petty subordinates could never understand.''

Clasping his hands behind his back, Phang Loon turned and strutted a few more steps, his northern-style cavalry boots tapping a precise cadence on the polished flags. He stopped again and turned, making a garish silhouette against the brazen face of the gong. ''Normally, such an order would result in death—the sad waste of a minion who might, but for his damning knowledge or offense, have served some further use.'' He shook his head in disapproval.

''Luckily, we here in the East are not so wasteful as in your northern lands. Ancestral knowledge brought from my family's Khitan home, combined with the availability here in Venjipur of rare mystic substances, provides us with a means of scouring the human soul and removing any taint of resentment or disloyalty. Why do you think I have tolerated your insolence so far? Because I have an infallible way of reorienting your deepest needs and desires to my loyal service.'' The warlord pivoted back to Conan with easy confidence. ''Infallible in that, for those few who are not cured by my methods, death remains a cure.''

Conan's sudden effort to heave himself up onto his feet served only to betray his weakness; a spasm of pain and unresponsiveness in his leg left him teetering on his knees before his captor, spitting curses.

''Devils gnaw you, Satrap! Go on, unleash your torturous servant on me if you dare! Crom knows, I have seen him pinch and scorch enough hapless victims. But I warn you—''

''No, Sergeant, torture is not an issue here.'' Phang Loon loitered just outside the range of his captive's most desperate possible lunge, wearing a look of wry amusement. ''Do not call down your heathen gods on me, nor your own futile rage." The sleek rooster of a man turned to depart, with Sool hulking close behind him. "I offer you only . . . the freedom of my house. Enjoy it at your leisure, and know that I am ever watchful, ever in control of what may befall you. But as for pain, fear it not."

The warlord, in apparent afterthought, turned back to wave an arm at a low table at the center of the room, arrayed with small enameled boxes, unguent jars, and a smoking censer. "As a good host, I offer you respite from pain, the renewal of that ease you have already enjoyed for some hours. Or else—grapple with your wounds and your past sins unaided. The choice is yours."

With those words, Phang Loon and his servant disappeared through a heavy, jade-inlaid door. The portal boomed shut after them, its closure followed immediately by the thud of a bolt. Conan knelt alone in scented silence.

Muttering profanities, he braced himself to rise to his feet. But his curses became a grunt of agony as his scarred leg again collapsed beneath him, sending him sprawling among the cushions. Fiercely he nerved himself to ignore the pain, which thrummed increasingly now, even when he did not use the limb. He dragged himself forward on his hands and one bruised knee toward the nearest goal the room offered, the cluttered table.

Reaching it, cursing breathlessly in resentment and shame, he drew himself up onto its edge. There he rested, his useless limb extended stiffly before him. Recovering his breath, he scanned his surroundings from this new vantage.

Of windows there were none; in spite of its luxuriance, the room surely lay in the depths of a sizeable castle. For ventilation, he could see only narrow vertical

slits between the fitted, polished stones high up under
the vaulted ceiling; these might also allow for observation of the room from without. The lush appointments
included rugs, padded stools, a silk-draped sleeping-
couch, and a glazed chamber-pot, the latter looking too
delicate to provide a usable edge if shattered. Conan's
eye found nothing which could be swung as a weapon;
even the short, round-headed gong hammers had been
taken away by Phang Loon's servant. The only thing he
saw of interest was another door in the room's far wall.

Conan, in his weakened state, had no wish to try the
strength of the stone portal used by the warlord; it had
looked and sounded massive enough to daunt him even
in his full strength and health. But this smaller panel,
made of brassbound wood, might be easy to pry or
batter open.

The problem at the moment was how to make his way
through it and beyond. Although the deep scars of his
wound had not reopened, tearing pains in his thigh told
of inner damage; any attempt to put weight on the limb
brought sweat to his forehead and a fevered curse to his
lips. Meanwhile, all his other pangs seemed to be
growing worse; the gash at his throat burned uncomfortably now, oozing slippery fluid, while his whole
body felt leaden with bruises and other miseries of his
fights and nocturnal transport. Even the damp tropic
heat, which he thought he had grown used to, oppressed
him; as he sagged against the table, the sluggish air
seemed close and cloying. The only hint of relief lay in
the thin thread of smoke that curled up from the
incense burner at his side.

Lotus fumes they were. He bethought himself of what
Phang Loon had said: Here, in the jars and coffers
arrayed on the tabletop, lay an end to pain, yes, and a
invitation to bliss. Feeling the unfamiliar craving take
shape in his innards, he was surprised at its intensity.

The drug could not have been in his system more than a few hours. But then, no telling how swiftly the various essences and quintessences refined by skillful Venji chemists could take hold. Whatever dose the warlord's men had given him, it must have been powerful. He knew that if the tides of misery continued to surge and suck in his veins, he might come to learn that he was already a cringing slave to the lotus.

In any event, his course now was clear. Taking up a beaded glass jar and unsealing its cap, Conan sniffed at the waxy-looking pink salve inside. Its subtle perfume made bright-hued pinpricks of exhilaration flash inside his skull. He blinked, feeling his nostrils flare wide open with reaction. Experimentally, he gathered a dollop of the soft ointment on a fingertip and applied it to his neck. Tracing the length of his dagger-slash, he felt warmth and well-being spread rapidly upward and downward from the wound. Next he raised the skirt of his Imperial tunic and dabbed the unguent on the still-tender scars of his thigh. He smeared it too along the swollen thews at the front of his leg, where the pain had tugged worst as he crawled.

Within a few breaths he had to force himself to stop and recap the jar, hands atremble with pleasure. He placed the container carefully, fumblingly, in the belly pouch of his tunic. By that time, his vision swam in pale, floral-colored afterimages, his breath welling in his chest like warm mulled wine. He scarcely wished to move, discovering worlds of fascination in the artful shapes and soft-lit hues of the room around him. Along with this new, boundless well-being came strength; and some part of his mind still signaled faint urgency, which the drug transformed into sprightly, reckless energy. He pushed himself up from the table, aware that his leg remained numb and unresponsive. Yet standing on it no longer brought pain; reminding himself to brace the limb straight and stiff beneath him, Conan was able to stilt across the room in nearly unbroken strides to the smaller door. When he reached it and palmed the latch, he found that it was not locked; the panel yielded silently to his touch.

The freedom of my house, Phang Loon had said. Well, whatever trial lay beyond the door, he would never be more ready to face it than now. Shoving the portal wide and clutching the jamb for support, the Cimmerian stepped through.

The room beyond was much like the first, though darker and less well-kept. Three or four lamps guttered low in corners, revealing the fact that some of the furniture and ornaments were broken or overturned. The place looked littered too, and the air bore a musty smell distasteful even to Conan's lotus-perfumed nostrils. Again no windows; but he thought he saw another door in the far wall, visible through long, sagging rents in an embroidered screen. After glancing around to be sure no peril was near, Conan stepped forward for a better view.

Behind him sounded a thud, which was the signal for a cacophony. Conan spun awkwardly on his numb leg to see that the entry door had slammed shut. The cause of this he searched dazedly for in the dim light, and finally saw: a forest monkey attired in glittering ornaments, capering at the top of the sill. No, there were two of the creatures. No four . . . no, a dozen and more, the fact borne to him all too clearly by their spreading, derisive chorus of chatters and shrieks. Spiderlike, they scampered up and down the walls, even, impossibly, through the air overhead.

The room, Conan realized, was traversed from wall to wall by thin wires, stretched just out of reach but serving as ideal perches and runways for the agile apes. They swung and cavorted along them, but with less playful energy and more purpose, seemingly, than their tree-dwelling brothers: for each of these monkeys was outfitted in a small gold helmet and breastplate, and from each tiny waist swung a gleaming finger-long crescent of steel. These were monkey-warriors, Conan saw; the slamming of the door behind him had been the first stroke of an ambush. As he watched, three of the fighters lowered themselves nimbly down the wall beside the door, turned to him, and advanced, unhooking their doll-sized scimitars and fanning out widely as they came.

Kicking would have been the best defense against these grounded arboreans, but Conan knew it was beyond the power of his wounded leg. He caught himself starting to back away from them; then realizing the indignity of it, he shifted his balance and hobbled stiffly forward. Weaponless, he bent to seize the centermost monkey, but the beast was elusive, sidestepping and slashing his arm viciously with its razored sword. As Conan lunged after the tiny warrior, its companions closed in from either side to hack and scrape at him with their own short, sharp blades. Finally, Conan laid hold of the first creature's middle and snatched it up, intending to hurl it against the wall. But the beast kept fighting, snarling at him with its little hairy devil-face, flicking its gleaming sword at his eyes and finally sinking its small, sharp fangs into his wrist.

Then at once a heavy, screeching, clinging weight struck Conan's shoulders—a whole horde of armored monkeys, dropping onto him in unison from the overhead wires. The floor attack had been nothing more than a ploy to distract him from this aerial maneuver, he realized in furious panic. Now he spun and staggered madly, thrusting and shaking off the hairy vermin while trying vainly to keep his face and loins clear of their needle-like fangs and tiny, gouging blades.

Seizing one squawking creature by the neck, he flailed wildly with it, flagellating his own back and managing to drive off most of the clinging assassins. He gave up his rush for the entry door and staggered back into the center of the room, away from the thickest swarm of shrieking, dangling attackers. Flinging aside the limp corpse of his monkey-flail, he tore and battered savagely at the two or three jabbering fiends who still clung to his neck and trunk. But other vermin were quick to pursue him; the overhead wires were strung low enough that, swinging down by leg, arm, or tail, the monkeys could deliver flying saber-slashes to his head and shoulders, and even use his reeling body as a springboard for return leaps. The sluggishness of Conan's leg made it too dangerous to stoop low; he feared falling prone, to be overrun or dragged about the floor by his teeming foes.

There came at last the moment when no more of the beasts clung to him, and the flying attacks subsided. Conan could not tell whether he was badly hurt, for he sensed no pain, only the tickle of blood flowing from many small wounds. His leg was rotten timber beneath him; he dragged it hurriedly across the floor, taking care not to slip in pools of monkey blood and offal. He was vaguely certain that the hairy fiends were regrouping overhead for another attack. And with the thought came the event, but in an unexpected form.

The creatures converged from all sides, swinging beneath the wires in a swiftly closing circle. This time the knives did not slash, dangling harmlessly at their owners' waists. Instead, as the dozens of tiny manlike hands and feet found Conan, they clutched at his arms, at his hair, at the ragged bloody scruff of his tunic, and *lifted*. To his horror, he felt his sandals scuffing ineffectually on the flagstones, his weight shifting slowly upward. As more and more of the shrieking demons laid hold of him, the overhead wires sagged under his weight and theirs, enabling them to reach lower and lower on his anatomy—to his chest, his belt, the pleats of his tunic-waist. He was swung slowly horizontal, the tree-fiends drawing him relentlessly aloft to be better fought with or toyed with in their airy element.

Red wrath seized him, overwhelming even the lingering narcosis of the drug. He flailed out with all four limbs, screaming in the voice of a rabid forest ape himself, biting and rending as savagely as his tormentors and with more deadly effect. Shaken by his frenzy their hold on him faltered, then failed. Conan plummeted, twisting in air, to crash shoulder-first on a low table which collapsed partly under his weight. Around him pattered fallen or wounded monkeys, quick to scamper away from his snarling clutch.

Staggering, lurching, he hove himself to his feet. He lay hold of the broken table, lifted it and swung it wildly overhead. It reached high enough to strike the wires, grazing some monkeys and driving the rest back from its tremors. When a squad of sword-wielders flew at him, the table shielded Conan from their blades and knocked down two, who hit the floor chittering and running.

"There, you miserable tree-lice!" he raged, smiting the table against the thrumming wires like a plectrum against a harp. "Come at me now, you slinking cowards!" His adversaries responded by scolding and shrieking from a safe distance, pelting him spitefully with dung and fruit-pits.

Feeling his mad strength rapidly dissipating, Conan saw that there was no glory to be had from this fight. He turned abruptly, not giving his enemies a chance to change their minds, limped to the room's far door, and pushed against it. Seeing it swing inward, he dropped the ruin of the heavy table and passed through. Once on the other side he leaned against the panel, gasping, and pressed it shut.

The room ahead was utterly unlike the previous one: oval-shaped, fitted out lavishly as some sort of gallery or music chamber with brass gongs and bells. No threat was evident, so he sank panting to the floor.

He hardly dared take stock of the damage done by the monkey-fight. He had no will to either, because his berserk rage seemed to have used up most of the unnatural vitality lent him by the lotus balm. His body tingled with the drug-dulled pain of a hundred gashes and of new injuries to his neck and shoulder, as well as his throbbing leg. Reaching into the pocket of his shredded tunic, unstoppering the ointment jar with shaking hands, he applied the pink salve to his mangled, blood-slimed chest and neck. Less sparingly this time he dabbed it on his tortured thigh. Its effect was not so blissful as before, but the pangs did subside. His heart pumped more steadily behind the wall of his ribs, and he was able to turn dim attention to the room before him.

Lamps hung down from the ceiling, lighting the gallery brightly but to no clear purpose; the only other furnishings hung likewise from the vaultings above. Gongs they were, cymbals, and other metal chimes: a dozen or more sizeable ones spaced in a regular pattern about the room. They hung from linkages of brass chain, some supported on pivots though their centers, others held from the edges in slings or padded brackets.

No two were alike. The centermost one was also the largest, broader even than the great instrument that had awakened him in the first chamber. This one had its edge scalloped in the form of flaring, radiating flames, so that it resembled a great golden sun around which all the lesser discs floated. It had one other noteworthy feature, a long bronze clapper suspended before it, apparently controlled by a slack chain angling down from an aperture in one wall. This striker might make a serviceable cudgel, Conan thought, if it could be pried loose from instrument's harness.

Feeling no stirrings of pursuit against the door, he hauled himself to his feet and tugged at the handle. Though he had seen no sign of a latch, and heard none, it was now locked securely. Just as well, he told himself; whatever ordeal lay ahead, he would be better able to face it without any chattering pursuers from the last room. His survey of this one satisfied him that another door lay at its far end; he resolved to exit that way.

No sooner did he stride forward, however, than the great gong struck. The effect was unsettling; possibly the drug or the oval shape of the room intensified the sound, for it smote Conan's ears tangibly and shook him to the very soles of his feet. The working of the clapper-chain, whether by automata or by someone outside the room, set the heavy disc swaying; a further blaring stroke sounded, then another, each action of the chain accentuating its motion until it moved in a ponderous arc from wall to wall.

To lessen the shattering intensity of the noise Conan moved further out into the open, where the sound seemed more diffuse. Now other gongs were in motion, set swaying ever wider by action of their own supporting chains. The movements must be man-powered, Conan realized, caused by slaves working the chains from outside the room. New tones began to sound—a pair of cymbals dashed together by flexing levers, and a cracked, discordant chime tolled by a dangling, rebounding leaden ball. But most of the gongs had no clappers; they were made simply to swing more and more violently until they clashed against the stone

walls, or against one another. Conan cursed the unseen
bell-ringers—silently, since cursing aloud would have
added nothing to the growing din.

As more and more gongs began striking, the tumult in
the room swiftly became intolerable. Conan moved
through its midst with hands covering both ears. He
gauged the sounds not by their loudness, but by which
of his vital organs they seemed to pierce, and how
deeply.

He gave up the notion of catching the scalloped
sun-gong and prying loose its clapper; it was swinging
and twisting too erratically, its jagged metal flames
threatening to rip the flesh from his bones if he ventured
too close. Now there seemed small chance even of
reaching that part of the room, because the other
chimes described wider and swifter arcs, making it
unsafe to move injudiciously. Conan sidestepped one
screaming, razor-edged disc, kept spinning by a ratch-
eted chain-lever, only to feel another, heavier gong
smite his shoulder as it thrummed past at an angle. He
staggered aside, then carefully timed a rush to get out
from between them; but on the next swing they collided,
making a brain-splitting clangor and sending both wildly spinning. Mercifully, it was not the razor wheel but
the blunt chime that struck him again, knocking him
sprawling.

The floor offered no protection; by some fiendish
geometry of the chains, the height of the gongs' sweeps
varied. The instruments sometimes clattered or scraped
across the flags, scything even into the remotest angles
of floor and wall. Worse, the swinging chains tangled
with the lamps overhead, sending them careening in
long, flaring arcs. Besides raining down hot oil, their
motions made it nearly impossible to judge the speed
and direction of the gong-sweeps. The place became a

hell of thunderous sound, swooping shadows, screaming, hurtling metal, and shattering collisions. Each new
tolling warned of a deadly rush by one of the howling
gongs; but there were never any certainties. Rules and
trajectories, obscure at best, changed without warning.

Through it all Conan crept, huddling low for illusory
safety, no longer daring or caring to shield his ears.
Carefully he timed his snail-like progress, scuttling or
diving aside when the mad ballistics of the place threatened to destroy him. Reaching the room's center at last,
he sidestepped a whirling gong whose tone dropped
from a shriek to a moan as it grazed him. He heard a
strident clanging and looked around—to see the sun-
edged disc jerked sharply off its course by its rigid
clapper-chain, spinning and hurtling toward him in a
wide arc. Before he could move, it was upon him—and
past him, its polished, oscillating face brushing him on
three sides gently as a lover's embrace before it spun
away.

Vowing not to waste this god-given luck, he flung
himself forward along the scraped, battered floor
through a momentarily clear space. Panting, he advanced with redoubled pains, relying on sound as well
as sight, trying to judge the speed and direction of each
gong-stroke by the way it smote his throbbing ears and
quivered in his guts. For every three lunges forward he
gave back two, peering around desperately in the flaring, plummeting light, cowering in the meager cover of
the room's edge. Seeing at last the opportunity to dash
for his goal, he balked without knowing why; an instant
later, two careening gongs crashed together before him,
lacerating the air where his body should have been. The
collision altered the patterns, placing him instantly at
risk; desperately he leaped to one of the reeling gongs,
grabbed its chain, and clung there, spinning giddily with

it to the far end of the room, where it dashed him breathless against the long-sought door.

Gasping, croaking, he scrabbled at the door-handle and dragged it open. Racing to avoid being demolished by a final gong-stroke, he flung himself through and collapsed on the other side.

Chapter 10

Blood and Lotus

He awoke to a silence that thundered in his ears like the mightiest cataract of the River Styx. Yet it was true silence, with no trace of the gonging and pealing he had left behind in the oval chamber. How long since that din had ceased, and how long he had lain huddled and stiff in near-darkness, his half-seen surroundings gave no hint. This room appeared to be one of dim smokes and eerie radiances; it might hold new perils, but he hardly cared.

Drawing himself up to a sitting position, he took from his pouch the jar of lotus ointment. He repeated the applications that had brought him this far, treating his neck and thigh, smearing the salve also around his ear-holes in the hope of offsetting the damage done by the clamor of the gongs. This time the balm produced no noticeable sensation; his mind remained slack and jaded, with barely enough will to drive his nerveless body forward. Yet when he crawled to his feet, he found that his leg would again haltingly support him. He limped ahead, not bothering to stop and try the door at his back.

The limits of the room were invisible in smoky gloom. The fumes seemed to rise from the floor, from pans or braziers whose reddish glow faintly illumined the spreading, billowing columns. They must find some outlet in the darkness above, he reasoned, else the air of the place would be unbreathable; but even so, his nostrils tingled with the pungency of burning wood and of more aromatic substances laid over it. Not lotus, Conan judged—at least, not lotus alone.

He made for the nearest group of braziers, thinking he saw some object in their midst. As he came near, tears blurred his sight; his head clogged and grew near-opaque with fumes. Yet, by stooping through the leaning smoke-columns and fanning his hands to clear the air before his face, he was able to advance between the fires. He confronted the grotesque thing that stood limned by their glow: a body broken on a bamboo rack.

The male figure, once splendid, now lay torn and gashed by patient, exhaustive torture; no shred of costume or uniform was left to clothe his violated dignity. Death had been inflicted by a means Conan had seen used before by Hwong warriors against their Turanian captives: in preparation, a leg-thick joint of thungee thorn-tree was straightened by a soaking in brine. Lashed behind the sloping rack, it was made fast to the victim by means of a braided yoke across his chin. As the thorn limb dried slowly, resuming its natural curve, its daggery hide was forced forward into the sufferer's spine; meanwhile his head was drawn steadily backward until, with any luck, he strangled or his neck snapped.

The drying of this spiky limb had been speeded by the heat of the braziers, Conan guessed—if indeed the torture had been carried out here. Still, the end could not have been quick in coming.

Viewing the stretched, distorted corpse, Conan realized abruptly that the dark obscurity of its outline might not be due alone to the faintness of the brazier's glow. Leaning closer, he saw that the smudged, blood-crusted skin was neither yellow nor desert-dusky but of a rarer, blacker hue. From where he stood, the victim's face was invisible, bent back sharply over rim of the rack; full of foreboding, Conan shuffled stiffly around the makeshift frame. The inverted features, though swollen and distended, confirmed his deepest fear, leaving no room for doubt: The man was Juma.

Unbelievingly, Conan extended a hand to brush the skin of his dead friend's cheek. It was dusty-dry, as unnaturally warm as the brazier-smoke billowing all around.

Reeling backward, choking suddenly on bitter smoke and bitterer wrath, Conan blundered away from the horrid scene. He lurched blindly, stumbling against red-hot firetrays without noticing the pain, shambling off into darkness with scorched, streaming eyes. But the flash of murderous anger he felt was quickly drowned by despair; what could he do, alone and weaponless in the unguessed expanse of this prison?

He must, he told himself, have lain in his stupor for hours. During that time Phang Loon had seized Juma—perhaps because of Conan's own thoughtless questions—and brought him here, to suffer the most agonizing death conceivable. Unless, of course, the warlord had lied to him in the first chamber, having already trapped the Kushite, already slain him. . . .

But then, what of it? He had no means of retaliation in any case. If he cried out now, shouted his defiance to the unseen watchers who surely lurked above, what could it possibly accomplish? What would it seem but a plea for mercy, a laughable admission of weakness? Never that!

Instead Conan clenched the sorrow within his breast, determined to dull its pain and save it along with the last vestiges of his strength.

Regaining his vision, yet still disoriented in the darkness, he cast about to find his friend's body once again. Here, just ahead, was a group of smoking braziers; but were these the same ones? He doubted it; the color of their faint, vaporous flames was not reddish but yellow, and their fumes spicier, almost cloying. Yet some dim object did lurk in their midst . . . Gripped by curiosity, Conan shielded his face against heat and smoke and ventured forward.

The figure limned by the flickering yellow light was not a dead man, but a living one. Dressed in a loose-sleeved robe of embroidered gold silk, a white silken loin-wrap, delicately pointed slippers, and a loose silk cap, he reclined at ease—but on bed ill-suited to his finery: it was a grimy cot of rough bamboo, stretched with the coarsest canvas. Fumes shrouded the figure's head, seeping from a long, narrow-bowled pipe whose stem lingered near his lips; through this smaller cloud of smoke a familiar, aquiline face could be seen.

"Babrak!" With elation almost matching his despair of a moment before, Conan stepped haltingly forward. "Glad I am to see you, my friend! At least you are alive . . . did Phang Loon's men drag you here too?" Unable to kneel on his injured leg, Conan stooped down awkwardly in front of his reclining friend. "Babrak, know you: They have murdered Juma! Or given him to the Hwong to kill, it makes no difference; I'll have their living guts for it, either way! He died cruelly—his body lies over yonder, have you seen it? Babrak, fellow, are you in your senses?"

To Conan's queries the young Turanian responded only with vacuous looks and vacant, open-mouthed half smiles. His face, sheened faintly in the firelight by perspiration, wore a lax, uncharacteristic expression. His eyes had dilated to deep brown voids, eerily unfocused. His only positive act was to touch his parted lips at intervals with the pipe's ivory mouthpiece and draw between them a visible, twining torrent of gray smoke.

"Come, lad—you are drugged even more hopelessly than I! You have learned to crave lotus, in dishonor to your faith!" Hovering before his friend's cot, Conan tried to make a jest of it. "We should never have given you to that fancy tavern-trollop; like as not she was Phang Loon's aging mother!" His laugh barked hollow, lacking true spirit and eliciting no reaction from Babrak. "But never mind, lad, this stupor will pass. We will get you away from here, out of those unmanly clothes and out of the clutches of the drug, somehow! Come, help me escape this hellish place and avenge Juma!" He extended a hand to the supine youth.

Babrak's face signaled no comprehension. That the Turanian even saw his friend was evidenced by one thing and one thing only: In response to Conan's beckoning hand, the reclining one drew the pipe out of his mouth, so slowly that a trail of smoke braided visibly from its yellowed, cracked tip to his moist lips. In languid generosity he held forth the lotus pipe, offering it to Conan.

From this gesture Conan recoiled, stricken with horror. Rather than snarling in rebuke or dashing the pipe out of his friend's hand, he stumbled off between the fires. He must restrain his anger, he told himself; if he really meant to bring Babrak out of this place, it would have to be done gently. Though Crom knew, he could barely drag himself through this maze; burdened by another drugged victim, his hope of survival would be scant.

A deeper sorrow clenched his gut. True, he had

watched others fall beneath the spell of the lotus, but
never one so dear to him as Babrak! And never had he
seen any escape who lay so deep in its grip as the waif of
Tarim seemed to have sunk overnight. Surely, 'twould
be better to come back for him later at the head of an
armored troop . . . or perhaps, just take the added price
of his loss out of Phang Loon's entrails! In truth, the lad
might be deader to him now than Juma was. And he
himself might already be facing the same forlorn death.

His despair had set him wandering off in the smoky
dark, and long moments passed before he resolved to
turn and try dragging the youth bodily from his cot of
stupor. But the drifting smokes continued to play
strange tricks; the billows floating nearest did not look
like the ones he had most recently left. The transparent
flames shooting from the beds of the braziers seemed
too tall and ghostly, their color too pallidly, spectrally
blue. Conan edged nearer to find out.

The shape reposing among these sultry fires tanta-
lized his gaze. And although an eerie intuition told him
what to expect, he had to press into the domain of the
hot, choking smoke to be sure. Only then, through
blinking, tear-rimmed eyes could he affirm that Phang
Loon's third captive was his lover Sariya.

She lay on the padded satin of an exquisitely carved
and painted couch, contoured long and low for sleep
and for less passive relaxations. Her attire in the braziers' suffocating heat was well-suited to either pastime:
a glossy silk ribbon of skirt, whose disarray succeeded
in covering only her navel; a trifling shoulder-cape
which, although perfectly arranged, concealed nothing
at all; ear-bangles, chest-bangles, ankle bracelets, and a
pair of tight jeweled slippers, which appeared only to
imprison and constrict her shapely feet rather than
clothing them.

She yet lived and desired, as the lazy sinuousness of

her movements showed. Whether she lay in the grip of narcotics or of more native ecstacies was uncertain, for she languished like a harem-slave awaiting her pasha, her eyes distractedly roving the drifting vapors overhead. Her slim hands idly stroked and plucked the velvet couch and the softer velvet of her own skin, which shone lushly agleam with perspiration in the dim blue glare.

All her womanly warmth, all her loving frankness and freshness were lost in this bizarre tableau. Yet Conan's male desires were stirred; he had to remind himself to hail her with words, not stumble forward and try to address her earthier cravings with his drugged, battered body.

"Sariya! So the fiend has fetched you here as well—doubtless on my account!" His voice rasped hoarse with passion and with more debilitating emotions. "Come, girl, we will fight our way out of this place and return to our little hut. 'Tis a night of sore tragedy, but the best can yet be saved, I swear to you."

The woman heard his voice, that was plain; her self-caresses promptly ceased. Yet, instead of a thrill of recognition, her lovely face showed confusion as her almond eyes flicked aside to penetrate the drifting smoke. Her rubied, moistened lips pouted nervously, as if in apprehension. Then her eyes found the speaker and widened in a gaze of fear.

"Sariya, girl, 'tis I, Conan! Come, let us escape from here! I need your soft shoulder as my crutch."

Croaking the words hoarsely, he reached for her. Yet he clutched only emptiness as she shrank away to the far corner of her couch. Trying pathetically to cover her nakedness with slim red-nailed hands, she regarded him wild-eyed, with her painted mouth agape, her supple throat convulsing in a shrill, terrified scream.

"Girl, what is wrong? Hush, child." As he stood

unnerved, her screams continued dinning in his numb
ears, rasping painfully on the indrawings as well as the
outpourings of her heaving breath. At last they grew
monotonous, threatening to cross the border from
terror into madness; at that, Conan turned and flung
himself away past the fires, out into wider darkness.

What vile devilment ruled here? By all the gods, how
could Phang Loon so easily snatch what was dearest to
him and defile it, or crush it to nothing? Was it real, or
was it all drug-crazed illusion? How, by blessed Crom,
how could he live on after this? Better that he should
die; his soul was already dead, entombed in this cold
clay breast! Only lotus drove him on, keeping his guts
pumping, his dead limbs twitching beneath him. . . .
Before him in the darkness loomed the dim outline of
another door; he staggered forward through it without
stopping.

As the oiled portal slammed first open, then shut
behind him, he noted absently that he was in an oblong
room, yellow-lit by lamps in wall brackets and scented
foully by smoking censers in shallow alcoves. The sole
furniture of the place, its ornament and, Crom grant, its
death-snare, was a tall black frame carved in figures of
twining serpents: a full-length wardrobe mirror. Unhesitatingly Conan heaved himself up before it and peered
deep within.

Horror upon horror: the ultimate, soul-chilling evil!
For beyond the glass there slouched a foul, decrepit,
lifeless thing . . . its tunic a funeral cerement, its flesh
more tattered than the shroud's rotting fabric, the only
hint of life on its sagging bones the thriving purulence
of decay. Not only was it loathsome, unspeakable—
without a doubt it was *he* himself, as proven by the hand
he stretched forth to test the solidity of the glass barrier:
the withered, putrefying hand so faithfully reflected by

the deformed claw which the framed abomination stretched out to him!

Here, then, was why Sariya had screamed so, even to the point of losing her poor mind. Conan prayed fervently that the girl had not recognized him as himself, her lover and rescuer—because she could scarcely fail to recognize him also as a monster, a hideous perversion cloaked and enfolded by death, able to bring only death and despair to those hapless ones it embraced.

Standing before the mirror, paralyzed with self-loathing, he traced with crumbling fingers the myriad proofs of his dissolution: the countless rips and gashes in his face and scalp where slack, unhealing skin peeled away from grisly bone; the grinning scar across his neck, gnawed and eroded so monstrously by decay that his head threatened to topple forward at any moment over exposed vertebrae and lank strings of sinew; the slashed, collapsed ruin of his torso, draped loosely by leather and torn fabric like a staved-in coffin matted with cobwebs; the knotted twigs of his arms, and his blighted trunks of legs, one weak and wasted, the other bulging and sagging with the weight of corruption, ready to burst and spew forth its noxious essence. . . .

True! It was all utterly true and real to his sight and his horridly fascinated touch. Phang Loon had poisoned him; instead of soothing his wounds with a palliating drug, the warlord had befouled and polluted him from the start. Foolishly he had consented to besmear himself with decay's potent essence; he had been made to wallow in a sorcerous death that denied him true, blissful extinction. Now he was transformed, doomed to exist as a monster or as Phang Loon's slave, until this rotting, miserable corpse finally crumbled into fragments too small to twitch and suffer. . . .

"And yet I hold the cure, wretch." The voice was firm,

resounding from the room's far end, where Phang Loon stood flanked by the burly, competent Sool. "The horror you see is but a final phase of the drug, a condition which can be arrested, even reversed, by further medicament." Sool, at his lord's gesture, held forth a lotionpot considerably larger than the one Conan had been sampling from. "What confronts you is but your true nature, from which all delusion has been purged by the lotus, scoured away as if by cleansing acid! This privilege I have bestowed on you, that you may see the hollowness of self and the virtue of submission to a greater will." As the warlord spoke, he strolled forward with his servant around the side of the mirror.

"Remember, slave: your former complacence, the blindness you so crave, is something only I can restore to you. If you want peace, if you want to don once more the garment of illusion"—he swept a hand toward the level flagstones underfoot—"you need only fall to the floor and beg for it. Henceforth I rule you, and I shall provide for you. Be assured, fool, I will turn your petty hate and resentment against those who are really to blame for your miserable state: our rebel foes, and their collaborators in your own ranks. Submit to me, wretched one, and enjoy the blessings of peace."

"Warlord . . ." Speaking in a voice that seemed to bubble out of the front of its riven throat, the thing before the mirror swung around to face its tormentor. "Phang Loon . . . as you say, you have stripped me of everything. You have taken my freedom, my rank, my love, my very flesh and life." Croaking, the undead horror that had been a man shuffled slowly forward. "How much of it is true, and how much your fiendish illusion, I know not; but I know that my loss is real. You have left me only pain." The abomination shambled nearer, satrap and servant neither flinching nor falling back before it. "Pain is now all I possess; I will not let you take that from me too!"

"Very well then; you do not choose to submit." As the rotting thing loomed close within reach, Phang Loon turned away in brisk impatience. "As I told you, my method is infallible. Sool, end him!"

The servant's instant rush bore Conan over backward in his drugged, infirm state. The pain that slammed through him as he struck the floor nearly made him regret his bold pronouncements. Yet he was surprised to find his ravaged body not only holding together under the impact, but responding with willed and instinctive motions of defense. His good knee found the Venji's crotch in a thudding thrust; unfortunately, it found it heavily wrapped and padded. His forearm smote the attacker's neck and chest with a force that would have weakened a less massive opponent.

But the Venji was obviously a trained wrestler. His weight remained atop Conan, bearing down remorselessly to control and weaken his victim. His thick hands clenched like iron, gripping and throttling the neck it should have been easy for him to rend apart, head from rotting shoulders. Apparently Conan's frame retained more cohesiveness than Phang Loon's mirror had shown. A shame, Conan thought, since it was his real, un-illusory life that was ebbing now, being choked slowly out of him by Sool's relentless grip.

His numb spirit rallying briefly, Conan thrashed and strained sideways; but his strength was too depleted by drug and ordeal to avail against this taut, fit killer. Though his flesh did not tear like rotted parchment, still it pained hideously. He heaved upward to throw off the Venji's weight and felt his weak leg give way with a sickening twist. In desperation he reached out to gouge at his strangler's eyes; but the frantic clawing, he saw through his own dimming orbs, did not even disturb the fierce smile set in his killer's face.

No strength, no voice left for a final curse, no weapon . . . but wait; scrabbling, fumbling with dying fingers in the sweaty crevice between his belly and Sool's, he managed to find his pouch, and in it, the near-empty jar of ointment. Withdrawing it, he smashed it blindly on the flagstones, feeling its glass stopper fall away among shattered fragments. Then he groped upward with the thick, jagged-edged base and jammed it into the Venji's face.

Against the sweaty, muscular skin he ground and twisted it, upon the cheekbone, just at the point of the clenched smile. He kept on and on, twitching in eternity; the repetitive action was all that remained in a dwindling, blackening universe. Oblivion . . . was.

Then remotely, miraculously, the grip on his throat began to loosen. Air seeped back into his lungs, charging his blood like liquid fire. His whole body pumped, straining to draw in more breath.

Returning vision showed him his adversary's face, slackening now in an idle, pensive expression. The smile remained, but with a new, beatific aspect. Clearly there was no pain from the gashed, blood-oozing crater that gaped now in Sool's face like a third, lopsided eye. Smears of lotus ointment mingled with the Venji's blood to provide ever headier sensations, reflected in his widening pupils. The world was lost to him; when Conan pried off his thick hands and eased out from beneath his bulk, the wrestler remained stooping on all fours, gaping in wonderment at the riddle of the blank stone floor.

Phang Loon stood watching with abstracted interest, making no move to interfere, so it was easy: Step across the torturer's broad back and reach down, one hand under the shoulder and behind the sweaty neck, the other across the chest to clasp his own clenched forearm. Conan's shoulders convulsed, and the Venji's neck gave with a thick snap. The torturer flopped to the floor, drowning at last in his lotus dream.

Conan stepped clear and started for the room's far door. An oath from Phang Loon drew his attention; the warlord was moving to block his path, and so Conan veered forward to meet him in grinning anticipation. He must not have appeared entirely decrepit to his captor either; for Phang Loon faltered, groped at his belt for a sword and, finding none, retreated. He ran to a side-wall and reached high to jerk at a concealed cord. A loud chime, bell-like and shriller than any of the death-gongs, broadcast the alarm. Conan continued for the exit, knowing he could not hope to catch the nimble lordling.

The door stood half-open; lunging through, Conan found himself at last in a proper corridor that stretched away on two sides, lit yellow by wall-lamps and containing a series of doors and archways. Hearing footsteps slapping toward him from one direction, he loped away in the other and turned through the widest arch. It led into an unlighted storeroom heaped high with crates and bundles.

Even in the dimness, hobbling the length of the room, Conan recognized the contents as Turanian military stores—the ones needed, and missed so sorely of late, by his fellow-troopers. Likely these goods had been diverted by Phang Loon for his own use, or for sale on the black market. A shame, truly; if there were more time, Conan would forage among the crates for a weapon. But he lacked the strength for a search, much less for a fight; his many sore wounds were tightening painfully for want of lotus, and the undamaged parts of his body wobbled with fatigue. Though he no longer saw a shambling monstrosity when he gazed down at himself, his ragged, blood-caked form was gruesome enough in the gloom.

Now another door loomed in front of him; before he could touch it, it opened, and a body blundered through into his arms.

The servant wore the tunic of a Venji Imperial; lacking any weapon, he yet struggled desperately. Conan, overriding his own pain and weariness, stifled the smaller man's yells, crushing him against the doorjamb; whether he broke the fellow's neck or merely stunned him, he was not sure. Closing the door, he dragged the slack body along with him and dumped it behind a pile of broken baskets.

This cavernous room, damp with smells of manure and fodder, must be the stable; good, then, it communicated with the outer gate! Seeing no more guards coming in the light of the single dim lamp, Conan limped ahead across the straw-covered cobblestones. He passed stalls whose snufflings told him that they contained horses, listless and ill-sounding in the noisome heat. Coming between rows of larger, heavier-timbered stalls, he heard more ponderous shiftings inside and smelled the riper stench of elephants. He slowed lest these more intelligent creatures smell the blood that seeped wetly from his neck, or otherwise take alarm and reveal his presence.

Yet he knew that, weak and tormented as he was, he could not stagger much further. Might it not be wiser to hide in a heap of straw—and there try to bear silently the pangs and cravings he could already feel crowding in to fill the vacuum left by the lotus? Or else, he might goad one of these mighty animals in its pen and be stamped to death; better that than to let Phang Loon retake him. He doubted whether the warlord would be as charitable now about letting him die a drugged, painless death.

All at once he heard shouts behind him, along with the scraping of the storeroom door. Stumbling aside out of open view, he availed himself of the only shelter at hand—by lying down on his back and rolling under the heavy half-door to one of the elephant stalls.

As luck would have it, the pen was occupied. His roll brought up him against a titanic hind leg, stumplike and stiff-bristled in the dimness. By its owner's prompt, irritable shifting, Conan knew his presence was ill-regarded. The beast was quite obviously male, probably a war steed; now it shuffled back and sideward toward the intruder, threatening to squash him like a flea against the sturdy timber wall. Conan had no choice but to edge forward toward the monster's trunk and tusks.

After all, he reasoned, the beast was trained to obey men as well as kill them; it might not fear a lone man whom it could clearly see. With any luck, if he could keep the brute from trumpeting or crushing him, the very danger of this hiding-place might keep the guards from seeking him here.

Squeezing past the great foreleg an instant before it scraped the timber wall, Conan crept forward into the corner of the pen. The end wall was of irregular mortared stone, and he felt safer in its angle; still, he could not repress a shudder as the great, leathery mask of the face swung toward him—high, scalloped ears outflaring, bronze-pointed tusks curving wide, the massive trunk snaking down to sniff his face. Its wet, pliant tip brushed his brow and chin, then snuffled down along his trunk to his legs, searching perhaps for weapons or edible offerings. Finding none, it writhed back up and smote his shoulder roughly, insistently.

Outside, the scatter of voices spread through the stable. Running footsteps had passed the stall and could now be heard returning. Rays of a lantern flashed in beneath the stone door, and gruff Venji accents barked at one another.

"This is the stall where the noises came from."

"Yes, and look, the beast is restless!"

Restless because of your yammering, Conan felt like rasping at them. Meanwhile he crouched stone-still in the corner, letting the elephant's massive proboscis continue its search. As the long, moist finger snuffled about his chest and collar, the creature snorted and twitched its ears, seeming excited by the scent of blood from his neck.

"We must take the elephant out and search the stall!"

"Yes, fetch a goad. But use it with care, this is a dangerous beast!"

Daring to glance left and right, Conan saw no exit to the adjoining stalls. Before him, the elephant was sidling and swaying nervously; its eyes rolled back in its head, distracted by the commotion behind it. Pushed to the last limit of desperation, Conan crept out of his corner. He reached to his oozing neck and took a smear of slimy blood on his fingers. With it, on a flat stone in the wall, he drew a half-remembered pictogram, a three-lobed figure with two dangling tails, that could be formed by a single line:

Snorting, the elephant followed his motion with its eyes and raised its trunk to the stone. Its sensitive nose-finger traced the shape accurately; then, to

Conan's shock, it sucked in a great draft of air and trumpeted shatteringly.

The tearing noise shook the very fabric of the wall, driving Conan to his knees. Quivering with pain and shock, expecting to be seized and dashed against the stone, he struggled up . . . only to find the great beast kneeling, its trunk looped at one side to make a foothold for a passenger to mount. Not pausing to question, Conan lurched forward, stepped up onto the trunk with his good leg and, aided by the uprising creature's trunk, dragged himself up onto the vast, hairy back.

Fortunately the elephant wore a studded collar, which also looped around its forehead in a sort of cap. Conan seized hold and soon had need of it, as the beast reared around in its stall and butted the door. The Venji Imperial who had begun to drag it open was now trying to close and bolt it again, but did not succeed; instead he was hurled across the stable with the force of the massive gate's swing, to fetch up limply against the far row of stalls. A second guard, approaching and waving an elephant goad high as a sign of authority, quickly fell under the creature's trundling feet.

The elephant trumpeted again, moving forward and gathering speed; the next moment it passed through the half-open doors of the stable, sending one of the twin portals banging wide as it went. Behind them the place became a zoo of shrieks and crashes, its inmates lashed to frenzy by their fellow-prisoner's rebellion. Conan clung to the broad leather strap for his life; happily, in spite of the animal's frantic *musth*, its broad back provided its rider a fairly soft, level platform.

About them now lay the courtyard, aflare with torches and ascamper with men under a crescent moon. Most of the guards and servants who had been drawn by the rogue's shrieks were now able to scatter out of its path; those who could not paid in the cheap token of their lives. A few ill-aimed arrows struck near Conan, none even sticking in the animal's thick hide. The only real obstacle ahead was the castle's drawbridge.

This opened between two flanking stone towers, a broad ramp of studded timbers crossing a ditch of unknown depth. In response to the alarms, the bridge was being raised; Conan heard chains clanking and saw men bending their backs to windlasses on the tower-tops. Heavily counterweighted, the ramp was clearly massive; as it yawned near, the helpless passenger saw it rise slowly to a height from which no lumbering pachyderm could leap. Instinct made him tug back on the heavy collar; but the elephant did not come to rein as a horse would. Instead it charged onward, straight toward the impossibly steep obstacle. Conan clenched both arms beneath the leather strapping as the elephant struck the bridge.

Momentum carried them upward, the mad brute's feet thundering on the wooden planks. At either side Conan heard the agonized stretching of chains and the stripping of ratchet-pawls. Then, inexorably, the angle of the ramp began to flatten. Wails and shrieks sounded as men were batted down or flung off the tower-tops by the fast-unwinding winches. The elephant strained upward along the creaking, rattling timbers and, just as the ramp thudded to earth underfoot, lunged forward onto solid roadway. Staggering, the beast found its stride and loped forward into the night.

The courtyard behind was a chaos of shrieks and wails; of pursuit there was no sign. Ahead lay rice-fields fringed by jungle, and a white road winding away under the moon.

Chapter 11

The War of Gods and Kings

"**S**o the outlander Conan still lives!" Emperor Yildiz squirmed with elation on his embroidered sofa. "He can survive not only battles and maimings, but a three-day carouse in a southern port town! That is the best news I have heard in days."

The Lord of All Turan relaxed in his Court of Protocols, which was empty but for a handful of functionaries; he inched himself up straighter beside the harem-slave who was busy feeding him peeled grapes. Shorter than he, she had to strain her ample body against his to pop the purple globules between his lips. Yildiz, visibly enjoying her efforts, continued, "Once he is fit enough for the journey, he can be recalled to Aghrapur! I shall make a great show of declaring him a hero."

"Declare him hero . . ." General Abolhassan digested his commander's words, his frown ill-concealed beneath his healthy brown mustache. "I counsel Your Resplendency against such a move." The general's sidelong glance toward Euranthus at his side was meant to warn the eunuch which way to tend. "Why would you want to exalt a lowly trooper thus, Sire? A foreign savage, to boot?"

Yildiz turned his head aside to nip a grape morsel out of his concubine's plump, gold-nailed fingertips. Chewing, he looked back at Abolhassan. "It may not be part of your duties to notice, General, but of late our military efforts are a cause of dissatisfaction at court. Dashibt Bey's death was a blow to us all, and we could not reasonably expect to keep Ibn Uluthan's fate from being whispered of as well. I need some excuse to declare a holiday, stage a feast, and win back popular support for our aims. This could be it."

"Emperor, I beg to protest! Your subjects are not so grossly disloyal, after all." Abolhassan broached the topic with careful solicitude. "I saw you most ably defuse the stirrings of dissent among the court women, Sire, by your interviews and . . . luncheons with them. I was privileged to assist you at the first meeting when the Dame Irilya was so openly seditious. Without her—"

Yildiz laughed. "Yes, Irilya Faharazendra, that vixen! Do not think for a moment that she has ceased to badger me. She was not won over like the other wives, and is still busy undoing my careful diplomacy." Yildiz paused to receive another grape. This one the harem-wench had prepared by placing in it her own mouth, expertly biting off the bitter skin and sucking out the seeds, and then, with gentle fingers, transferring its sweet, slimy flesh to her emperor's lips.

In a moment Yildiz resumed. "Now Irilya heads something called the First Wives League, which not only cavils at imperial policy, but questions our very traditions of wife ownership! What do you think of that, my little peach blossom?" He pinched the rosy cheek of his houri, who responded with a jiggle of her fleshy bosom and a pout of pretended indignation. "Irilya holds luncheons of her own, meets with foreign envoys, invokes church law . . . a whirling dervish of a girl! Would that she were less seniorly wed, and to someone other than my richest shah!"

"Why, the woman is blatantly treasonous, Sire!" The eunuch Euranthus eagerly seized an obvious turn for the conversation. "Even among subjects as loyal as yours, such a shameless slut is bound to cause trouble. . . ."

General Abolhassan was well aware of Irilya's transgressions, having ordered a special study of her movements and meetings since his first open clash with her. So far, fortunately, her meddling had served to undermine Emperor Yildiz in ways helpful to his own plans. Abolhassan now watched carefully, anxious to steer his ruler, yet inevitably nervous lest this interview degenerate into another disgraceful orgy of fondling and stroking between Yildiz and his floozy. There was no sure safeguard against his whims.

But the younger, less expert Euranthus had put Yildiz in a mood of unwhimsical pique directed at himself. "It is not only Lady Irilya who petitions, I remind you, Master Eunuch," the emperor now admonished him. "And not merely women either. Courtiers, merchants, my rural shahs, even some of your own eunuch brethren whisper against our Venjipur campaign. And with reason!" The emperor turned his gaze upon Abolhassan. "The cost of the war grows burdensome; I find it necessary not just to increase taxes, but to levy new tithes on our land tenants. A vast expense of weapons and stores depart up the Ilbars River, not to mention the recruits—with no clear result except a glut of widows and orphans, crippled beggars, lotus addicts and pedlars, and a host of other evils! Where are the slaves, the plunder and tribute, the rich trade routes that were promised my subjects at the outset? How am I to answer their complaints? 'Tis enough, General, to make me question my own wisdom in prosecuting this war, and your efficacy in winning it!"

"My Resplendent, All-Knowing Emperor." No sooner had the damage been done than Abolhassan diligently set about repairing it. "If your concerns lead you to doubt yourself, in your abiding wisdom, Sire, then I can safely say they are misplaced. Rather, Lord, doubt the doubters—those who undermine your programs and place their own petty welfare above your clear-sighted aims." He stood straight and proud, a loyal soldier defending his emperor. "Sire, may I suggest that you are overly generous in your sufferance of all this petitioning and civil turmoil?

"Rather, I submit, the situation you describe calls for fire and steel. The scourge and the rod, nothing less, can assert the full authority of your rule and bring these intransigents into line." His dark eyes glinted righteously at Yildiz, warningly at Euranthus. "No widespread purge is needed at this stage, Sire; merely a few highly visible examples, starting with the woman Irilya."

"Abolhassan, will you never understand?" Strangely Yildiz seemed restored to equanimity, as he so often was by the general's speeches. Smiling, he rested against his sofa-arm, hugging the harem-girl closer with her painted bowl of grapes. "What I command is not a war of knives and sticks, General. I wage a broader war, one of beliefs—fought not in a jungle swamp, but on the fields of men's minds and hearts. A war of kings, and of the very gods."

Distracted momentarily, Yildiz paused; from her new, more intimate position his concubine was able to transfer grapes directly from her own lips to the emperor's, without the untidy intercession of fingers. Now she performed this trick, leaving her hands free to pursue other errands upon her lord's silk-clothed body. A moment more, and Yildiz turned back to Abolhassan, gulping contentedly.

"As I was saying, General: I need causes and heroes, ceremony and pageantry to fight my war. Such tools can be more valuable than any victory in the field, in their effect on unity and spirit here in Aghrapur. By decorating this barbarian, we promote the idea of extending our imperial sway far beyond Turan's present borders. Let me steer the court and the city rabble, General, and you marshal the troops! Then there will be recruits aplenty, and ample use for your talents on distant battlefields."

"Thy will be done, Sire." Abolhassan bowed, aware that his face burned slightly. It infuriated him to see such grossness alloyed by such dangerous statecraft . . . but he must be careful to let this imperial swine think his blush was due to modesty. "Thank you. My last caution, Resplendency, is this: When you create heroes, you also create hazards. The barbarian might speak out unwisely, or perhaps too wisely. He might gather a rebellious following or cause other trouble for us here. There is no knowing the potential of this rude foreigner."

"Precisely, General; there is no knowing." Yildiz looked up with an air of afterthought from his new pastime of nibbling his slave-girl's ear. "Why, he might even rise through the ranks to become as valuable an officer as yourself, Abolhassan. I hope the threat of competition is not what you hold against him! But if he does not serve our ends . . . well enough." The emperor shrugged airily. "One happy fact about fractious military officers: They can always be disposed of by assignment to remote frontier outposts. Another benefit of empire!" His look at his questioner had a subtly pointed nature. "Tarim bless you, sirs." He waved, dismissing his retainers.

"Health, Sire. Tarim preserve your rule." Abolhassan

turned with Euranthus and strode out into the echoing corridor. The two did not commence their murmured conversation until they were well away from the guarded door.

"Curse that purient old fool! First we use some nameless savage to distract him from the real ills and purposes of the war, and now he wants to enthrone the lout! I saw this coming." Abolhassan strode the geometric tiles briskly, making his shorter-legged companion scurry to keep abreast of him.

"I fear the emperor's plan may be sound, General," Euranthus panted. "He could yet undo our efforts and win back a following at court."

"Indeed." Abolhassan mulled silently a moment, striding along with downcast eyes. "I would say, let him bring this clod-lumper to the capital so that we can continue using him as our own catspaw. But the northern nature is unpredictable."

Bobbing down the empty corridor, Euranthus nodded in doubtful assent. "We have already tried to dispose of the barbarian once, have we not?"

"Aye. He is loose-tongued, my spies say, and now he can reveal even more about our conduct of the war. He will have to be stopped; it should be no great matter. Once Yildiz has announced the fete, the loss will serve as one more setback to him."

Euranthus nodded, smiling as best he could while hurrying along, gasping for air. "You were wise to counsel atrocious measures against the dissenters, General. That might undermine Yildiz further and turn more even courtiers against him."

Abolhassan came to an abrupt halt, glaring at the eunuch, who staggered on a few steps down the corridor before turning. "You thought I lied? The measures I advocated are no harsher than I myself would use!" He shook his head sternly, then smiled. "And yet, eunuch, perhaps you are right; even if Yildiz tried them, they would not work for him. True tyranny requires a tyrant!"

Euranthus smiled, eager to placate his brooding fellow conspirator. "True, General, he lacks the strength for that."

Abolhassan nodded, satisfied. "Haply for us. But come, our plans must go forward all the faster now."

Atop the palace in the Court of Seers, Azhar the sorcerer directed a half-dozen acolytes in the preparation of an elaborate spell. His new position as chief mage had bestowed on him not only the rank and prestige, but also the haggard look of his predecessor. The spectacle of Ibn Uluthan's death, to which he was closest witness, had made a lasting mark on him. And more recently, nightlong star-readings and daylong porings over his departed mentor's tomes and notes left him time for only brief snatches of sleep in the hot, bright afternoons. In consequence, some of the night had come to rest in his face, its purple shadows bracketing his eyes like clouds gathering over the grave of a spent sunset.

But today he directed the sorcerous preparations with determined, restless energy. This was the decisive effort; it would right the balance. All the materials had been checked, the precautionary spells recited, the astrological alignments carefully chosen. Shipyard engineers had been summoned to construct the giant arbalest which now stood ready on its cross-shaped pedestal, the steel bow cranked back in a taut curve, the varnished silk cable forming a gleaming V in the noon light, streaming down from the roughly repaired slits of the great dome overhead.

The arrow laid along the crossbow's sturdy stock was the main ingredient: hewn of toughest ash, carefully

formed, and painted with astrological runes. Its tip was
forged of tough, porous metal from a sky-fallen star. The
shaft had been blest on Tarim's holy altar before being
steeped for potency in aconite and viper's blood.

The target of the bow was the other critical
component, looming broad and massive where the
enchanted window had stood: a black millstone set in
heavy masonry, its hollow center bored out laboriously
to a size adequate for the passage of the giant projectile.
In its middle, shards of the silvery crystal left from the
window were mounted, no single one large enough to
fill the small space. But they ringed the aperture, and
in their midst sheened a gray radiance like that which
had filtered through the void onto Ibn Uluthan's
conjurations.

Azhar knew he had restored enough of the former
spell to open a loophole to Venjipur. He judged that the
heavy stonework would provide a defense against the
kind of invasion Mojurna had wrought against Ibn
Uluthan. This mystic gap, though smaller, should be
adequate for his purpose. Through it he could direct the
bow's killing force against the jeweled skull—or better,
its owner. Now it remained only to check the aim and
see whether Mojurna's sorcerous barrier had been
thrown up once again.

"Stand ready at the trigger," he told one of his
apprentices. "Do not loose the shaft until I command
it." The burnoosed man gave a reverent nod. He gripped
the hand-lever projecting upward and backward from
the base of the arrow, whose shaft was fletched with the
black pinions of giant cliff-condors.

Azhar stepped forward with his mortar full of oily ink
and his charmed pestle. These would allow him to steer
the window, in the unlikely event that the enemy's
defenses were down.

He hesitated to place his head into the deadly swath of

the great bow; but the duty was his alone. After a final, silent prayer to Tarim, he moved past the weapon and knelt before its loophole, holding the magical implements ready in his hands. Squinting against the shimmering glare, he looked into the aperture.

What he saw there, none of the onlookers could ever say. They watched him peer inside with a rapt expression, the gray light of the aether reflecting dimly on his face. A moment later the light darkened, and something shot through the opening—an immense spider, some said later, but most agreed that it was a dark, hairy hand clutching at Azhar's face. The sorcerer drew back with a cry, causing the evil thing's grip to slip down to his shoulder, then to his arm.

The demon-hand withdrew into the eye of the millstone and was not seen again; but catastrophically, it drew with it Azhar's arm. The slightly built man, in trying to break free, dashed his mortar and its oily contents to the floor. Thrash and cry out as he might, he could not get loose; instead his arm was drawn deeper into the hole. His assistants ran to his aid, seizing his other arm and hauling on it, all the while shouting and slipping in the spilled oil. In spite of their efforts, the chief mage was pulled inexorably into the millstone. First his elbow, then his shoulder disappeared into the fist-sized hole, causing lacerations to his arm and dislodging some of the embedded glass. Then, relentlessly, the wizard continued to be drawn in, his head forced back by the stone's rough embrace, his neck bending aside to the agonized accompaniment of his shrieks and the crack of ribs.

Seeing his regally turbaned head double back hideously against his spine, and hearing his screams silenced at last by strangulation or death, the others released their grip on his arms and legs. They backed away, watching with horrified fascination as his head disappeared, impossibly, into the blood-slimed hole, followed by his collapsed chest. And then his hips, folding in upon themselves with ghastly crunching sounds before the dread, inexplicable suction.

One of the gaping watchers must have murmured "Loose!" or else the still-waiting acolyte's trembling hand slipped on the lever; for the arbalest discharged its arrow, driving Azhar's vanishing shins and sandaled feet ahead of it into the foreign void.

After the weapon's twang, the stone itself split with a thunderous crack. Its fragments sagged to the floor in a mass of rubble, closing the mystic window for the last time.

Chapter 12

The Imperial Summons

From pale morning dreams Conan woke with a start. A monkey's shrill scolding, it must have been—enough to cause him a chill ever since his sojourn in Phang Loon's castle. But the play of sunbeams through the leaf-screened window of the hut, the gentle twittering of birds, and the fragrance of flowers were enough to soothe his fears gradually. He stretched, causing the broad hammock to shift beneath him and confirming, to his immense satisfaction, that his leg offered him no pain.

Sariya stirred beside him on the tightly stretched canvas, murmuring softly even though she was not fully awake. Her hip, half-draped by the filmy coverlet, made a luscious curve against the blazing-green radiance of the window, while her long black hair cascaded wantonly from her small, silk-covered pillow. After appreciating her beauty, Conan linked his fingers behind his head and lay back, enjoying the morning peace.

The room was no longer decked with cut blossoms. Sariya had adorned it with living plants gathered for diverse uses: snare-leaved and sticky-petaled blossoms for catching vexatious insects, shrubs and ferns to sweeten and enrich the air, thorny vines outside the window to discourage thieving by apes, birds, and children, and aromatic herbs valued as medicine and seasoning. The hut's main room had become a show-place, furnished with rare bits of Venji wickerwork, weaving, and earthenware, all on Conan's middling sergeant's pay. And Sariya's boar-skull talisman still adorned their roof-pole, garlanded now by jungle vines decked with multicolored blossoms.

The hammock shifted beneath him, and a delicate saffron hand slid across his chest. "Mmm, you are awake. And you are well today. . . ." Her question was really a statement, made with the gentle force of sugges-tion.

"Yes, I am well. I think I will return to my duties at the fort. But I must be careful of my wounds."

Sariya laughed softly, caressing him. "That is not what you said last night! I feared that you would shake the hut down."

"True. I am regaining my strength . . . mmm." They rolled together, bodies nesting together on the shifting canvas.

Their morning's trysting was gentle, although Conan sensed in Sariya an earnest seeking that belied her casual jests. Afterward, they wrapped themselves in bright sarongs, took woven buckets in hand, and walked forth into the jungle. Making separate detours, they met by the nearby stream at a waist-deep pond Conan had dammed off. There they bathed, sporting and splashing one another in the cool water. They returned to the hut with buckets brimming, to find a burly figure seated cross-legged in the shade of the porch.

"Juma! 'Tis long I have waited to see you!" Setting down his water buckets, Conan strode to the uprising trooper and embraced him roughly. "How have you fared, old friend?"

"Busily, with your command as well as my own to look after!" Juma grinned and held his friend away at arm's length. "But 'tis good to see you striding so boldly, Conan. Even in a woman's wrap"—the Kushite's smirk was tolerant—"you look ten times the man who came crawling from the jungle a fortnight ago."

"Aye." Conan nodded good-naturedly, setting his buckets down by the fire-ring. "The trek from the ruined shrine was hellish hard, though it would have been less than an hour's jog for a healthy man." Moving to the porch, he dropped his sarong on the matting and walked onward to the door, unabashedly naked. "Have you heard the tale? I could not make the thrice-blasted elephant carry me any farther than the ruins." He took his leather sword-breeks from inside the hut door, stepped into them, and buckled them across the flat of his belly. "I had to throw myself down from the creature's back while he nuzzled and slobbered at the ancient carvings. Lucky it is that I found my way back to the fort." Returning to the fireplace, he settled down on a stone beside the ashes.

"To find you here, after ransacking the taverns and brothels of Tarqheba and giving you up for dead . . . !" Juma shook his head, squinting in dubiety. "Still, Conan, I would think your story of the elephant as mad as your other ravings of those first days, if I did not know that one of the beasts had saved you before."

"No, his account is to be believed." Sariya, coming from the garden with an armful of melons and tubers, laid them on a flat stone and began washing them from a bucket. "The long-nosed ones' friendship with mankind is based on mutual respect. They have their gods and customs, and were themselves worshiped by hu-

mans in Venjipur's past centuries. Sometimes they aid
one who honors the ancient faith, as you have seen."

"My mate is steeped in the ancient mysteries," Conan
said. He began tenting tinder and dry twigs together
from separate covered baskets to build a fire. "If I did
not know her so . . . personally, I would think her a
sorceress."

"She must have some magic about her, to have
brought you back from gasping death two times now."
Juma looked from his host to his hostess with simple
frankness. "Even your much-boasted barbaric fitness
could not have pulled you through those scrapes all by
itself."

Sariya did not meet Juma's gaze, but spoke with a
veiled smile. "My training as priestess of Sigtona was to
care for the sick with medicinal herbs, as well as prayers
and rituals." She knelt beside Conan as he struck the
flint and cupped his hands to blow the faint spark to life.
"But my talents would have meant little without you and
Babrak to guard Conan and restrain him during his
fevers."

Juma nodded. "Aye, 'twas worse than the last time.
Even bound hand and foot, your lover was no kitten in
his fits of lotus-craving!" He shook his head in grim
recollection. "But your herb concoctions helped to
soothe him even then, Sariya. If he is truly free of
the drug, then he is living, breathing proof of your
wizardry!"

Conan, alerted by their talk, had been scanning the
surroundings of the hut as he stoked the flames to
crackling vigor. Now he arose and walked near Juma,
reaching up to the ragged thatching. "Did you bring
this?" he asked, taking down a small, leaf-wrapped
packet that dangled from the eaves.

"No, I did not. Is it one of Sariya's fetishes?"

Conan shook his head, unwrapping the dry, papery

leaves. He sniffed their contents cautiously, his nostrils flaring at their pungency. Frowning, he strode to the fire and threw the packet in, stepping away briskly to avoid the pale smoke that went feathering skyward.

"Lotus," he told Juma, walking over to take a seat beside him. "Left for me by a well-wisher—Phang Loon's agent, no doubt. I find such presents about the place frequently. But no matter." He shrugged, his face shaded by some faint cloud of memory. "I will catch the scoundrel someday." He smiled and reached around to clap a hand on Juma's broad back. "'Tis as good to see you well, old friend, as to be well myself! Tell me, what is the news from the fort?"

Juma kept silent a moment. He watched Sariya's knife flash, as, kneeling gracefully before a plank, she sectioned the tubers. Then he spoke. "You are the news, Conan. But I did not want to tell you until I was certain you were fit to hear it. You have been recalled to Aghrapur." He continued watching Sariya, whose knife paused in midair. "Not for punishment, though; and not permanently, I am told. The dispatch says they want to proclaim you a hero and pin a bauble to your turban in a public ceremony. The order is signed by Staff General Abolhassan, issued in the name of the emperor himself."

"Proclaim me hero . . . Yildiz himself." Conan sat inert a moment, watching the middle distance. Then he stirred where he sat, restlessly. Then he swung back his arm and dealt Juma a clap on the shoulder that sent the big man rocking forward, choking and sputtering.

"A hero, by Crom! Now I will have some say around here!" Conan swung to his feet with an effortlessness that remembered no spear-wound. "Now I will hound Phang Loon to the gallows, and keep the weak-livered Jefar Sharif from playing hob with our war! I will advance to the rank of Staff General myself! Hmm,

Abolhassan, I have heard that name before . . . but no matter! Sariya, I will keep you in noble style and dress you in costlier, scantier garb!'' He strode to meet her uprising form and clasp her in a smothering embrace. "This is a great day for us all!"

"A day of peril, you mean." Still clearing his throat, Juma arose to lean against a bamboo pillar. In response to the others' surprised looks, he frowned more sternly. "In my view, Conan, 'twould be hard to imagine a greater catastrophe befalling you! Now you are exposed, and exposure in war means danger." The burly black grimaced with unease that would have been difficult to feign. "Bethink yourself, Conan—'twould be safer to lead the point of a light infantry phalanx against archers, cavalry, and fire-throwing elephants. But above all, since you may not be able to squirm out of it, this threat calls for caution—if your wild northern nature includes such a trait!"

"Juma, why rave so?" Conan moved toward his friend, drawing Sariya along at his side in an enfolding arm. "Who am I supposed to be in such pallid fear of, anyway?"

"Why, the very ones you named before! Jefar Sharif, whom you nearly strangled, the warlord Phang Loon, the garrotes, and a dozen others right up to the emperor himself! Is there any Turanian you have not given cause to crave seeing your guts shredded? Can you not understand that for all these enemies, and for as many more imagined rivals, this proud distinction, this great honor our emperor seeks to bestow on you, ahem . . ." Juma leaned against the pillar, gagging momentarily on his own bitter sarcasm, before he resumed. "Why, it lends urgency and purpose to all their old grudges! They must act swiftly to destroy you, before you unleash your newly empowered wrath on them!" The Kushite thrust himself from the pillar, striding the porch in agitation.

"Worse, it takes you away from your friends on a long, hazardous journey to hostile territory, the treacherous capital! And it leaves Sariya here in jeopardy. . . ."

"Nay, she will travel with me! Won't you, love . . . ?" Conan looked to the woman he clasped at his side, his speech trailing off at the sorrowful look she turned up to him.

"Oh, Conan, this is a great opportunity for you! You must not let me hold you back—but I cannot leave my duties here. There are sick villagers who need my care for weeks to come, and more needs that will arise later."

"Aye, I know," Conan sighed. "And your church school—as before, when I wanted you to come with me to the city."

"Yes, I must go on teaching the children."

"So that they can teach their parents, no doubt! Sometimes I wonder what it is that you teach them." He shook his head, loosening his grip on her shoulders. "The two of you surely know how to turn a triumph into a sorrow." He looked to Juma, who was sunk too deep in thought to heed his reproach. "But Sariya, will you be safe here without me?"

"Yes." Gravely, the girl kissed Conan's shoulder, then knelt to resume her meal preparation. "As before, I can stay with families in the village. They will watch out for me—hide me, if need be. But the rebels have not attacked near here lately."

"Nay." Conan moved heavily back to his place on the porch and sat down. "Nor have my enemies. But take care, girl; remember, the ancient shaman Mojurna tried to kill you once! Juma or Babrak can help watch over you if I go north alone." He turned to the Kushite. "And what of Babrak? I have not seen him in days." He tried to lighten their glum mood with a smile. "Is he still silent about his adventures in the city?"

"Aye. The code of Tarim forbids him to boast of his

exploits with the softer sex." Juma grinned back heartily. "But he still looks as smug as the fox who ate the
pheasant; the tavern matron must have been kind to
him."

Continuing to speak in this light-hearted vein, they
dined on the juicy yellow flesh of the melons and a
spiced, sweet mash of boiled roots. Juma pitched in
alongside host and hostess, content to eat a second
breakfast and stay on as bodyguard. After belching
politely, Conan donned his tunic, turban, and weapons.
Making a tearless parting with Sariya, he went to Fort
Sikander.

He chose the main gate and the most frequented
ways, striding with aggressive confidence in the day's
mounting heat. After Juma's warnings, he was keenly
aware of the looks every eye flashed at him—some
friendly, a few of the watchers even stopping him to
exchange pleasantries. But the majority eyed his passing
with mute surprise, or with more veiled feelings. As he
passed the black, yawning tent-mouths, he fancied he
could hear the feverish murmur of odds being laid for
and against his survival.

Rounding the end of the palm-fringed staff barrack,
he nodded a half salute to the guards, stepped up into
the shade of the porch, and waited. A grunt from
Captain Murad summoned him inside. He saw that Jefar
Sharif was also seated in the dimness, busy having his
cavalry boots polished by a kneeling lackey.

"Reporting for duty, sir!" He kept his tone blunt,
avoiding any courtly flourishes, while praying to the god
of fools that the sullen Sharif would keep his mouth
closed. "I am fit for action."

"Good, Sergeant." The captain's voice was equally
restrained. "We have fresh orders for you. You can take
charge of the assigned troops at once, and march by
noon."

Conan felt his throat clenching, yet he had to speak. "So . . . so soon, Captain? Aghrapur is many leagues away, it will take me time to prepare. . . ."

"Aghrapur!" Jefar Sharif's voice rang out from the corner of the room in wry amusement. "Nay, that order is not passed down yet. When it is, I will be pleased to accompany you north to the capital as your superior officer! But not just now; the order your captain refers to is a battle command."

"Aye, Sergeant." Gray-turbaned Murad finished scribbling on a stub of parchment and pushed it across his map-table, as if the Cimmerian could read it. "Our scouts have located an enemy camp at the base of the Durba Hills, here!" The captain kept his eyes on his stubby finger as it point at the stained, tattered map, refusing to look up and meet Conan's gaze. "A probative assault is ordered. You will command two companies of heavy foot."

"Aye, barbarian!" Jefar's laugh scratched in Conan's already buzzing ears. "Here is a chance for you to earn the title of hero!"

Chapter 13

The Suicide Command

Battle surged along the jungle ridge, breaking in a shouting, red-foaming tide against low promontories of clanking shields. On all sides arrows flocked through air like swooping seabirds, while green, drooping fronds and flower-vines thrashed and toppled like sea-wrack, driven relentlessly by weapon-strokes and swirling attacks.

"Reform the square! You, trooper, move up and fill that gap! We must hold our formation at all costs—and keep advancing!"

Conan's shouts, already grating out hoarsely, were in this instance wasted; for the trooper he harangued tumbled to earth, plucking at an arrow lodged in the unarmored flesh of his calf. His commander muttered an oath; the rebel bowmen were loosing their arching shafts high overhead, or straight downward from the trees. They might spell the Turanians' end, Conan knew, unless the armored troop somehow managed to seize higher ground.

The Cimmerian himself strode forward to fill the embroiled gap, not bothering to pick up the fallen soldier or his shield. He drew and swung his yataghan swiftly to hack off a spearpoint that probed inside the marching square; then he slashed the arm of its owner, and the face of another knife-wielding Hwong who pressed dangerously close. Abruptly the shield-walls on either side of him closed once more against the yelling crowd of rebels, and Conan was swallowed back inside the scant breathing-space of the square formation.

"Keep up the advance, Turanians! Close ranks behind," his voice grated doggedly above the battle-din. "Ahead are ruins, where we can hold off these monkeys until the tolling of Set's black doom! Steady, men, and forward!"

Fluidity was an advantage of the moving formation, even among the obstructing tree-boles and jungle shrubs; another boon was the chance of escaping the most concentrated arrow-fire. Conan tried not to dwell on the sole disadvantage of movement: the brutal choice it called for, whether to drag their wounded with them or leave them behind, mercifully slain as time permitted.

"Conan, what of our reinforcements?" Babrak jostled up behind his sergeant, keeping his eye on the rear of the formation, which was his own newly designated command. "If we march too far through this jungle, will they be able to find us?"

"Reinforcements! Two hundred Venji Imperials . . . !" Conan's laugh was bitter, his voice low to keep from spreading bad morale. "Even if our courier reaches them, I would be surprised to see them come running to our aid. Methinks whoever assigned us such a paltry reserve was the same fool who under-reckoned the number of our foes by forty score!" He stepped forward, swinging his sword to cut down a fallen rebel who appeared to be stirring and groping for a weapon underfoot; after wiping his blade clean on the man's bright green sash, he veered back to Babrak's side. "Nay, if we survive, 'twill be by our own grit and discipline! Then I shall have a word to say about it to our commanders." His voice abruptly swelled above the yells and moans to a raw shout, a battle cry to cover his own gloom. "Fight on, Turanians! Know you, each man of you is worth ten of these howling rebels!"

His cry raised but scattered, breathless shouts in answer. True, an armored infantryman, fighting shoulder-to-shoulder in line, might account for ten naked attackers and more. But as every veteran trooper knew, once their formation broke up into a disorganized retreat through the forest, their armor would slow them fatally, making them easy prey for their jungle-swift foes. So they braved the sleets of arrows and the yelling hordes, hacking their way onward along the crest toward the brushy jumble of stones and tents that had been pointed out from the hilltop as their objective.

"Ahead, sir, lies the gate of the ruined town!" Babrak muttered in his commander's ear. "See there, the wall is but a brushy hillock! Thank Tarim they have not repaired the defenses! But who is that, standing atop the broken tower?"

Conan followed Babrak's pointing finger, shading his eyes to pinpoint a figure stooping beneath a long cloak bright with colored feathers. Leaning on a tall stave, whose upper end terminated in a familiar, glinting sphere, the ancient-seeming one glared down at the battle a long moment before yielding to the insistent tugs of two half-visible rebels behind him. Then he shuffled down out of sight beyond the gap-toothed battlement.

"Mojurna! So this is where the devil has been lurking!" Conan clutched Babrak's shoulder, loosening his grip only after his friend's face registered real pain. "That was the old witch-man himself, high priest of all

the Hwong; I have seen him before this! We must storm
the camp without delay!"

"Aye, Sergeant—if you say so." Though disciplined
enough not to show undue fear, the junior officer
pressed close to offer his counsel. "Know you, Conan,
there is a risk in breaking our square amidst a superior
enemy."

"A risk indeed, old friend; we must weigh it against
the chance of winning this war with a single
swordstroke!" Conan wasted no more time in delibera-
tion. "Our best strength must go to the fore—you fight
on my left, Babrak!" Raising his bloody yataghan high,
he forced his rasping voice once again to a husky
bellow. "Turanians, form a wedge! Follow me to take the
camp! A year's extra pay to the man who slays the
warlock Mojurna!"

Conan's shouts raised a furor among the embattled
troops. Drawing fearful looks from some, blood-lusting
shouts from others, the giant northerner strode swiftly
to the center of the reforming line. "Kill Mojurna,
troopers! Let no rebel live! For Tarim and Yildiz . . .
charge!"

A threshing, slaying machine was then set in motion
through the jungle. Swords hacked through flesh and
foliage, spears plowed up their moist red tilth, and
shields breasted the lashing jungle to part its green
waves like the prow of a racing war-galley. The line
chanted now as it moved—a deep, throaty song older
than Tarim or the land of Turan itself, primal as a
heartbeat, setting a savage rhythm for step and thrust,
slash and shield-stroke. The Turanians' line moved
faster than before, fast enough to keep the press of
enemies ahead of them off balance and retreating,
briskly enough to outrun attacks on their vulnerable
rear and the worst of the arrowfire.

Conan, striding at the center of the human wedge,

fought like an enraged demon. His sword slashed and thrust in a mad, blinding frenzy, stitching death across the ranks of faceless mortality that pressed up before him. Its remorseless metal trailed screams and bright ribbons of gore in the air as it dashed through unprotected enemy flesh and bone.

Some few rebels, especially the green-jerkined peasants, were thrust helplessly to the fore of the battle by the mere pressure of the milling ranks behind. Not guessing the steel-clad savagery of their adversaries until too late, and never even raising their blades against Conan and his hewing slaughter-mates, they died in terror, trying to push and claw back out of harm's way.

Other rebels, in particular the lean, wiry Hwong hunters, chewed lotus leaves to increase their willingness to face pain. Their bolo knives were sharp and lovingly familiar, tied to their wrists even in sleep; and their very adornment was for death—for the multicolored cords binding their sinewy elbows, shoulders, and thighs served as tourniquets. Ready to be shrugged instantly tighter in battle, the constricting cords diminished pain and blood loss from weapon-strokes, letting their wearers fight on with wounds that would have turned other men into helpless, mewling casualties.

To these fierce warriors, Conan often found it necessary to deliver two, three, and more death-blows in quick succession, lashing out with sword in one hand and long, needle-pointed dagger in the other. He hewed away limbs and vitals deftly and ruthlessly, leaving the fallen tribesmen thrashing and jabbering underfoot. Even so, they clutched at discarded weapons or at the boots of the striding Turanians, unwilling to admit the fact of their own dismemberment.

Conan's bloodletting fury was well-matched by the gruesome efficiency of his fellow troops; even Babrak at his side plied spear and shield with a frenzy seldom

seen. On both wings of the flying wedge, Turanians
strove valiantly to keep pace with their leaders' swift,
bloody progress along the jungle trail. But these troops,
fighting through denser growth with defenders pressing
in from side and rear, could scarcely keep the same
pace. The advancing wedge inevitably deepened and
narrowed into an elongated spear-blade. The raging
Cimmerian made its flashing, gouging tip, but it was
from the trailing ends that the casualties were taken:
armored troopers gradually outflanked or drawn off in a
separate combat with fleet-footed skirmishers. One after another, inevitably, they turned to defend their own
backs and those of their comrades—sometimes with
too great success. Once they let themselves be cut off
from the fast-striding line, their deaths followed swiftly.

Yet the momentum of the heavy phalanx carried the
survivors in among the ruins. The last fringe of rebels,
faltering at the sight of the blood-caked marauders,
scattered before their onslaught.

"Hold the gate," came Conan's voice, croaking between heaving gasps, "and search yon mounds and
tents! Mojurna is old and slow; he must be somewhere
within."

Reeling with exhaustion, letting his weapons dangle
low to rest his throbbing shoulders, the Cimmerian led
the way down the vine-hung lane beyond the broken
gate. Babrak panted at his side; though both men
staggered visibly, the rebels flitted back before them;
few sought to defend the low, brushy mounds of weathered stone as the Turanians moved in to occupy them.

"Conan . . . what of Mojurna's magic?" Babrak's
voice too was broken and gasping. "Will he use some
fiendish spell to turn the battle against us?"

"No, I think not." Conan lifted the now-ponderous
weight of his sword and swung it once again to lay open
the green fabric of a lean-to pitched against a crumbling

earth. Beyond him, a handful of battle-weary Turanians closed in, arriving too late to help. The rebels gave Babrak's corpse a last kick, then turned to face their live enemies.

The harvest Conan's blade wrought among them was ripe and red. His howling, tormented fury burned hot enough to sear away any remnant of pain or fatigue. Even so, as he smote and slew, one question scorched his brain, unquenched by blood or wrathful tears: had he been ensorcelled or slyly deceived, or was the wizened, smiling Mojurna really an aged woman?

Night stalked the jungle, crouching like a panther above its frightened prey. The few, rare sounds were hurried scuffs of footsteps, low hails or muttered curses, and the occasional meaty thud of weapon-strokes. Only a faint glimmer of moonlight penetrated the forest canopy, barely enough to reveal the glint of steel or the shiver of a glossy leaf marking the passage of something deadly.

"Troopers, to me! Here, by the water—we go downstream!" Moving three silent paces from where he had spoken, Conan waited, listening warily to the nearby footfalls to judge their intent. The ones he heard behind him sounded friendly, heavy with armor and fatigue; Hwong moved with faint rustlings that would scarcely be audible over the gurgling of the brook.

"Hsst, men! Stay close together, and beware of rebels in our midst! The land levels out here." Even as he spoke, Conan heard the swish of a weapon swung against some real or imagined lurker on their flank. A moment later, a coughing moan told him someone had died, probably one of their own; the sound was followed by rapid steps and swishing blows as others struck blindly at the attacker.

Conan heard the men's murmurs and curses as they

resumed plodding; his own heart flagged with dismay. A dozen or so survivors, perhaps; surely not more than a score left of the twelvescore he had started with. That meant two hundred deaths like Babrak's—and for what purpose? He himself had let the battle go to waste! His hand tightened spasmodically on the hilt of his sheathed sword.

"Who comes? Halt, and speak up!"

The hail, accompanied as it was by a flurry of skirmish-sounds and a Hwong war-whoop somewhere in the rear, caused some fugitives to freeze, and others to blunder into them in the dark. But the voice spoke Turanian familiarly, which reassured them all.

"Are you friend or foe?" Conan craned his neck, trying to fix the sources of the various sounds. "Be warned, we are pursued!"

"Turanians, be sure you kill only rebels!" The voice was muffled, as if turned away; then it came more strongly. "Sergeant, lead your troops to the sound of my voice."

"Aye, watch for us! We are here by the stream!" Groping forward through the brushy gloom, Conan saw flickers of distant torches and heard the shouts of fresh troopers setting out after rebels. His own men jostled and panted close behind him, eager to avoid last-minute death when rescue was in sight. A moment later they faced the sudden, blinding beacon of an unveiled dark-lamp.

"Where are the rest? Is this all?" The gruff voice showed concern as it moved nearer. "Conan, your Venji reserve returned to the fort claiming they could not find you, but I did not believe the dogs! So we came hither, found the rebels, and followed them; we have been killing stray ones for an hour now."

Conan turned to watch the blood-caked, ghastly faces of his men as they staggered into the light. He felt his voice growling deep in his chest. "We were sore outmanned; the officers must have meant us to die! Someone will pay for this."

"Whom do you mean, Sergeant?" The gray figure, visible as he set down his light, was Captain Murad, flanked by two veteran troopers. In his free hand he held a blooded yataghan. "If you mean Jefar Sharif, Conan, then let me warn you, it goes much higher than that."

Conan, helping a wounded trooper climb over a log, regarded the captain grimly. "It was you I meant, Murad—had you not come to aid us. And know, blackguard, you should have come sooner than this!" His pale, blood-smudged stare wavered away from the elder officer. "But thanks for the warning; I will heed it."

Murad nodded, looking sour and rueful in the lamp's steady light. "There is evil afoot in Venjipur, too much evil for one man to mend."

"Aye, sir." The wounded soldier at Conan's side spoke up unexpectedly, clutching at his sergeant's arm. His pale, hollow-eyed face looked close to the brink of death. "But promise one thing, Conan—that when you go to Aghrapur, you will tell them what it is really like here!"

Chapter 14

Heroes and Traitors

"Curse the benighted Turanian army!" Conan shifted wearily on his bench in the jolting wagon. "Why must the quartermasters assign us sickly horses and a creaking wain, instead of elephants? Two or three long-noses would carry us in good comfort. They'd hardly mind these few paltry wares." The Cimmerian gestured behind to the wagon's cargo: a potted dwarf tree, a few bundles of wicker furniture, and some chests of provisions and assorted rarities, most sent northward as gifts for the emperor and his courtiers in Aghrapur. "This Turanian passion for horses in tropic climes must be a physical thing, like a Kothian's love of sheep!"

"Ah, well," Juma replied from beside him, "as they say, the expeditionary legion sucks hind teat on a gelded mule!" He shook his head stoically. "Only lately, at great cost in lives, have our fighting officers learned an elephant's value in battle. It may take years for their usefulness to get through the thick skulls of the supply staff. Count yourself lucky that they haven't given you an ostrich to ride through this foreign waste."

Juma's gesture swept wide enough to take in the

populous, irrigated valley about them. The main road north from Venjipur followed the broadest river fork, meandering between curtain-like jungle ridges toward the lofty Colchian Mountains and oft-snowy Kasmar Pass.

Beyond the peaks lay high, arid hinterlands of Turan and Iranistan; the travelers' way would be grueling until they left their wagon and dray team in the hill fort of Tamrish. There they would board riverboats for a descent down the swift-flowing Ilbars River, to the very dock of the royal palace in Aghrapur.

As yet, however, the riders had not left the Venji heartland. Their road was little more than a grassy dike between flooded rice-swamps, wherein the flow of the stream was dammed again and again, re-used a thousand times before seeping its way wearily to the Gulf of Tarqheba. Each field was tended patiently by a half-dozen or more peasants: men, women, and children stooping bare-legged to their toil beneath wide straw hats. Arising in turn to watch the wagon as it trundled past, they made no obeisance, nor waved any encouragement to their conquerors and protectors; they merely watched in silent resignation.

"Ah, well, we will soon be clear of all this!" Conan swung his gaze over the slouched shoulders of their Venji driver and the sway-backs of his wagon team along the road ahead—to Jefar Sharif, astride his white charger in the midst of the four-horse cavalry guard. "Not every so-called fighting officer is quick of wit either," Conan observed. Glowering darkly to where jungle slopes pressed down near the road, he added, "Soon we shall escape these endless farm fields and prying eyes, and enter remote, desolate country."

"You will fight him, then . . . ?" Juma began, only to be silenced by Conan's abrupt gesture, as the Cimmeri-

an inclined a meaningful nod toward the hunched form
of the wagon-driver on the bench in front of them. The
shaven-headed Venji had professed to understand, beyond his unintelligible native dialect, only pidgin trade-
talk; nevertheless, Conan was understandably reluctant
to blurt secrets out before him in Turanian, the one
language he held in common with Juma.

"This driver of ours," the Cimmerian proclaimed at
last, "is not a man, but a stinking heap of elephant-flops!
The elephant negligently dropped him in his mother's
lap—whereupon she, being an imbecile, thought him a
human child and raised him up thus!"

The driver never looked back; his hunched shoulders
did not stir, nor did the wrinkles on the back of his bald
dome even twitch. It was evident to both passengers that
he did not understand Turanian.

"You will challenge Jefar Sharif, then?" Juma glanced
warily to the backs of the cavalry riding ahead. "What of
his horse-guard?"

"Yes, I will challenge him, the moment there are no
more watching peasants to bear the tale. When he
refuses, as you know he will, I will shame him and then
kill him anyway." Conan patted his sheathed sword,
which was propped on the bench beside him. "The
guards are seasoned jungle hands; they will allow a fair
duel. If not, I leave them to you."

"A thousand thanks for your faith in me!" Juma
glanced up at the jungled hillside, which encroached
ever nearer the river channel and the road. "You are
sure, then, it was Jefar Sharif who ordered the fatal
mission?"

"Aye. He suborned false scout reports, acting on
secret orders from some staff officer named Abolhassan.
Captain Murad is a whipped old dog, I know, but he was
once a good officer; he would not knowingly throw away

Turanian lives." Conan shook his head, scowling in grim perplexity. "It would seem, truly, that the sole aim of the mission was to have me killed!"

Juma nodded, unsurprised. "Remember, I warned you of the danger of playing hero. Now they are letting me accompany you to the capital; perhaps it means that I too am marked for death."

"Likely so, the both of us! Mayhap 'tis best that Sariya chose not to come." Conan's scowl deepened, unpleasant to behold. "Even so, I will ensure that my friendship is healthier for you than it was for Babrak."

Juma's melancholy silence showed respect for the dead, but after a time he resumed speech. "What puzzled me about it all was the presence of the priest Mojurna so far down-country. Are you sure it was he that you saw?" The Kushite frowned. "When last we found him, it was at a remote shrine in enemy territory; and even then, he had come down but briefly from the hills for some unholy ritual. What murky business brought him so near Fort Sikander this time? I wonder."

Conan sat pensive a moment. "Juma, I must tell you, I learned something about Mojurna . . . that is, I cannot be sure I learned it . . . but I thought it was so at the time. It made me waste my chance to strike a fatal blow, the one I had risked . . . everything for—"

"There, now, Conan," Juma broke in solicitously and a little uncomfortably, "you are bound to be confused! I have seen men mazed by wizards many times before in my native Kush. There is no shame in it, though it may take months for the spell to lift entirely. But say, by Otumbe—who approaches?"

A flurry of splashes had arisen in a swamp paddy beside the road, a field strangely devoid of peasant laborers. From behind a fringe of jungle trees, a rank of horsemen advanced—seven riders, clad in Venji armor of an antique kind rarely seen except in curio stalls.

Above the centermost warrior fluttered the black and yellow tiger-striped banner of the Venji resistance. The mounts, hock-deep in water, kicked up a foaming, spraying tide that approached across the paddy like a supernatural ocean wave. But as the wagon-riders watched, the body of horsemen split up—three to engage the cavalry, who had halted some fifty paces ahead, and four veering back toward the wagon.

"Tarim strike me a eunuch if these be rebels!" Conan said, unsheathing his sword. "I have never yet seen a Venji rebel who could afford more armor than a rice-pot helmet, much less a rebel straddling a horse!" As he spoke, he worked the empty sheath into the belt of his tunic and tied it in place. "See how they split their force; these weary nags and this potted tree must be highly valued prizes to them! Nay, teamster, do not lash your sluggish jades, stop the wagon! Angle it across the road, here, and make it hard for them to gallop past. Good, now hold the team quiet!" Conan had switched to the rough Venji patois to command the driver. The latter, having obeyed him, sank down to the wagon bed, there to cower beneath the plank seat.

Swiftly the attackers were upon them. Juma and Conan leaped to the threatened side of the wagon, the Kushite wielding a long-staved ax he had procured from beneath the bench, Conan swinging his sword. There rang forth at once the din of a farrier's shop as clanging metal strokes, shouts, whinnies, and the stamping of hooves surged about the wagon.

The riders veered by in quick succession, crossing weapons smartly with the defenders, yet suffering some disadvantage due to the height and stability of the wagon platform. The first attacker was knocked half out of his saddle by an ax-stroke from Juma, the second was fended off and belabored by Conan's lashing blade. One marauder leaped aboard the plank bed of the wagon, only to be knocked back over the side by chiming, concerted blows from both defenders. The mounted standard-bearer, obviously the leader, hung back from the fight at first, rallying his troops to fresh efforts with arm-waving and gruff shouts.

But the attackers' second pass fared even worse, leaving one man prone and motionless in the field, one dragging himself painfully up the embankment, and a third trying to stay astride a weakened, bleeding horse while engaging in an ax-duel with Juma. The leader wheeled his mount on the far side of the roadway, having failed to skewer the agile Cimmerian in a lance-charge straight past the wagon.

Yet Conan, massaging his well-exercised sword arm, did not wait for the lancer's next pass. Sheathing his sword and striding back along the bed of the wagon, he leaped from its edge straight onto the back of one of the riderless cavalry mounts waiting in the field.

He felt the animal start and stagger under his robust weight and then rear high, pawing the air with a whinnying scream of protest. Conan lashed the reins fiercely and dug his rough boot-heels into the animal's ribs, urging the stallion forward and downward. Reluctantly the beast complied, whickering as it leaped up the embankment. This placed the wagon's bulk between Conan and the spearman, gaining him time to get the animal under control.

"Juma, I know yon flag-carrier," he shouted to his friend, who was still locked in a murderous grapple with the man on the bleeding horse. "I go to face him down while you finish here."

The Kushite, busy dragging his foe from the saddle, would have been hard-pressed to answer, and the Venji wagoneer cowered useless in his place beneath the seat. But it hardly mattered, for Conan had already urged his steed around the wagon toward the fourth rider—who, in turn, lowered his bannered lance. He spurred his mount forward to spear his challenger.

The horsemen met in a mud-splashing flurry of hooves and weapons, too swift and turbulent to be seen clearly. But one stroke must have told, for amid the jabbing of blades and the glinting arcs of spray, the flag-bearing tip of the cavalry lance fluttered down into the mire, shorn off by a powerful blow. At this, the armored man suddenly broke off combat, spurring his horse in a wide curve back toward the jungle. The unarmored rider, screeching out a savage war-whoop, was quick to wheel his mount in pursuit.

The remaining three harriers of the original seven did not follow; though still in the saddle, they were occupied with the wagon's cavalry guard further up the road. The Turanians, maneuvering under Jefar Sharif's strident commands, engaged the putative rebels in a series of drillyard cavalry passes. These clashes were rendered picturesque, if comically slow and ineffective, by the muddy field and the high-spraying arcs of water.

Meanwhile Conan, crouching low against his laboring horse's spine, ate flying mud; he spat it from his mouth and shook it out of his eyes with every plunge of his galloping steed. His horse, less burdened because of its rider's lack of armor, slowly overtook the fleeing horse and rider; the only question was whether steed or man could see to find their quarry in the spume of foul water kicked up by its flying hooves.

The racers drew together soon after the armored rider re-entered the jungle at the reedy edge of a field; his mount was slowed by the sudden upward slope, enabling the pursuer to close. Conan's horse thundered alongside, forcing the other steed to edge away in its headlong flight. The shift took the fleeing animal too close beneath an ancient tree; a leaf-screened limb knocked its passenger from the saddle onto the weedy earth, where he struck with a brazen clank of armor. His riderless steed galloped off into the forest; Conan, meanwhile, reined in sharply, forcing his animal to halt a dozen paces further on.

Leaping down from the horse's back, he ran to the fallen rider. The man's crested helm had been knocked from his head by the collision; he lay gasping on the ground, groping vainly for his sword, which had been knocked out of its sheath. His face, though bloodied and disfigured by a mashed nose, bore a familiar cast; the slope of his eyes, as they narrowed on Conan's looming shape, was definitely Khitan.

"Well, Warlord, I expected to see you again." The Cimmerian's sword was raised upright as he halted over his enemy. "I would go through the nicety of a duel with you, if there were time . . . but there is not. My apologies." His sword slashed down, cleaving the suddenly wide-eyed face and the skull behind it.

Leaving the body twitching its last, Conan returned to his winded horse and swung himself up onto its back. No sooner had he done so than a splashing sound drew near and ceased, to be supplanted by the swish of jungle fronds and scuff of hooves through forest litter. Conan urged his horse forward to meet the approaching rider, a wary-looking Jefar Sharif.

"Ah, Conan, so you have survived." The Turanian officer's face creased in a smile to hide his initial look of crestfallen surprise. "A creditable feat, fighting on a stolen horse against an armored foe." The sharif cast his gaze around the jungle foliage. "Where is the rebel leader—he escaped you, I take it? A shame, since my men are busy killing the last of his cohorts. There will be none left for questioning . . . Tarim!" His banter ceased as his searching eyes found the armored body lying prone among the weeds.

"Nay, Sharif, he did not escape." Holding his sword

down out of sight by his side, Conan sidled his mount ahead through the brush. "I do not think there is any need to tell you who it is, since you and he planned this ambush and my death! But that is the least of your treachery."

"What mean you, Sergeant? We fight on the same side . . ." Jefar's pretense ended abruptly with the scrape of his drawn sword, as Conan raised his ready weapon. "Curse you to hell, barbarian!" Yet the sharif, instead of meeting his subordinate officer's rush, wheeled his mount around toward the rice field.

The horse, winded and listless in the heat, did not turn quickly; in a trice Conan was upon its rider. Instead of smiting the sharif's armored, lavender-cloaked back, the Cimmerian launched himself atop the lordling and bore him bodily from the saddle. The two plunged into a red-flowered bush and rolled there in a savage, thrashing fight, sinking from view in the greenery. The plant's pendulous blossoms continued shaking in a spastic frenzy which dwindled gradually to stillness.

At length the bush shivered once again, its twigs cracking with the burden of shifting weight. From it Conan arose, holding Jefar Sharif's red-streaked dagger in one hand. Breathing heavily, he flung the knife away into the forest and stepped from the bush. Then he turned to face another flurry of hoof-splashes approaching from the nearby field.

It was Juma, hugging another of the attackers' un-manned horses between his black, blood-streaked knees. He reined the animal roughly to a stop and took in the scene, glancing knowingly from Conan to the purple-clad body crumpled in the brush. "Our beloved sharif . . . killed cruelly by rebels, no doubt."

"Aye," Conan breathed wearily. "But fear not, I have already avenged his death on their leader, who lies yonder." Stooping to recover his sword, he pointed with it into the trampled undergrowth. "It was Phang Loon, as I guessed—though none, I am happy to say, will recognize him now." He turned and strode off to collect the riderless horses from among the trees.

Juma tugged his mount around to face the other three troopers who now cantered up from the rice field. They reined in and raised their mud-splashed visors, regarding the scene with looks ranging from astonishment to suspicion.

The Kushite addressed them in gruff tones. "Good work, men; I see that the rebels are all slain. Jefar Sharif's heroic death leaves me, as senior sergeant, in command. All that remains is to strip the bodies and continue our trek to Aghrapur!"

Chapter 15

The Triumph

In trackless reaches of the Colchian Mountains the
Ilbars River had its source, brewed of snowmelt on
lofty, jagged peaks and of rain-squalls on the broader
slopes. Down barren ravines and chasms the number-
less torrents flowed, lapped along their courses by goat
and bear, lizard and panther. Hence onward the waters
wound their way, through broader ponds and streams
where sheep sucked, and steel-eyed hillmen reined their
horses to drink, through silver-blue forests and braided,
gleaming cataracts.

Where the tributaries joined to form the mighty
Ilbars, the land stretched level in fertile valley and
steppe. Here the river rolled slowly and deliberately,
finding the leisure and the unopposable will to meander
through lush meadowlands. Along its broad, smooth
artery coursed the lifeblood of an empire: trade, plunder, and migration, flowing past thriving cities from
walled Samara through caravan-rich Akif, to Aghrapur
itself, the pulsing, glittering heart of Turan.

The river swarmed with many types of craft: fishing-boats, coracles, reed rafts, and oared galleys, even tall-masted galleons ghosting upstream under shallow sail from the weedy mains of the Vilayet. One of the strangest vessels, square and cumbersome-looking as it poled clear of Akif's busy dock, was a low-sided, boxy-cabined raft, built of sturdy planed timbers which would have floated high in the water even if they had not been roughly joined and caulked with pine-gum and oakum.

The unwieldy barge traveled a one-way journey downriver from Tamrish in the wooded hills. Such craft were fated to be broken up when they reached the capital, their timbers planed as roof-beams for the city's burgeoning tenements, or perhaps as stout keels for more weatherly ships.

Though slow and ungainly, the barge scattered the less massive boats or jostled them aside as it wallowed out into the main river channel. Across its deck, amid curses and the thumping of poles wielded more as weapons than as navigational tools, one specially nota-ble figure flitted: a slim, perfumed, resplendent eunuch of the royal palace, looking decidedly out of place on the raft's broad stern—for the aft deck resembled a barnyard in its assortment of lowing animals and crops baled and basketed for the city markets. In those rough surroundings, the official's silk robes and effete bearing drew stares and murmured comments, muted only because of the presence of a large, oiled, capable-looking slave close behind the functionary, bearing the various sacks and baskets of his equipage.

The eunuch was engaged in a search, plainly. He moved haltingly along the raft's low bulwark, some-times venturing a question to the rustic passengers seated there, sometimes only wrinkling his nose in impatient disdain and passing onward. At one place, near the chained muzzle of a fly-swarming, cud-chewing bullock, he received an answer to his query. The animal's rag-turbaned owner sucked thoughtfully on his toothless gums, then pointed further aft. There, a handful of steersmen plied broad-bladed oars, directing the motion of the keel-less craft and keeping its stern from swinging around to become its bow.

"Conan?" The eunuch, lifting his robe daintily to protect it from water and other substances washing the rough deck, minced toward the stern bulwark. "Is Sergeant Conan of the Expeditionary Guard among you, sailors?" Flanked closely by his burly slave, the functionary stopped a safe distance away to regard the line of ragged idlers.

The steersmen received him with snorts and scornful smiles, their white teeth gleaming in rough, sun-darkened faces. A few spat contemptuously—yet the largest one of all remained sober-faced. This was a turbanless rogue, lank and black of hair, clad in the shredded, scarcely recognizable remnant of an expeditionary tunic. Handing his thick oar to another worthy, he stepped forward and replied in a barbaric accent.

"I am Conan, late of Venjipur. This is my brother officer, Sergeant Juma." He waved one hand to the hulking, half-uniformed black who sat on a crate beside him, tilting to his lips an earthenware flask of some upstream vintage. "Are you the Emperor Yildiz's delegate?"

The question brought hoots and guffaws from the other steersmen. But their amusement soon gave way to raised eyebrows and murmurs of astonishment. For promptly, at a nod from his master, the slave opened one of his baskets and released a white carrier pigeon. The bird fluttered tentatively upward, then flapped away into the low sun to eastward. The eunuch regally ignored the event, addressing the steersman with a deep, brisk bow.

"Greetings; I am Sempronius, First Assistant Secretary of the Imperial Chancery. I was told that you were aboard this . . . vessel, but I did not expect to find you riding . . . back here." The eunuch was a slender, fine-featured man dressed all in silk, from turban to vest, to pantaloons and pointed slippers. He moved with an energetic, supercilious air, his glance around the crowded deck hinting at boundless distaste for the raft and the rowdy-looking group he confronted. After speaking, he raised a lavender-scented kerchief to his finely sculptured nose to mask the stench of the cows and other livestock.

"Aye, well," Conan answered him plainly, "we took regular passage as your dispatch advised. But strong hands were needed to help navigate the rapids, and fight off river pirates." Stepping away from the stern transom, Conan reached down to haul Juma to his feet. The Kushite hove up wistfully, surrendering his sloshing jug to one of the steersmen. He waved the others a drunken farewell as he and Conan followed Sempronius forward. "Our traps and the gifts for the emperor are stowed yonder." The Cimmerian pointed to the roof of the squat, boxy cabin, where perishable cargo had been lashed to keep it dry.

"Gifts—from the southern lands?" Sempronius eyed the bales and bundles heaped on the upper deck as he approached the cabin, licking his thin lips with interest. "Did you bring along anything good . . . lotus, say, or hemp?"

"Nay," Conan replied absently, with hardly a glance aside to Juma. "We brought a potted jungle tree for Yildiz, as well as some wickerwork and assorted smaller gifts."

"Oh." Sempronius swiftly lost interest in the cargo. "Well, my task is to prepare you for the public triumph and banquet, and to introduce you to His Resplendency and the court"—he turned around to eye them dubiously—"both of you, I suppose, since you make an impressive pair. Though we need a native Turanian officer to round out the group and inspire fellow feeling in the crowd."

"One did start the journey with us." Juma, speaking in drink-slurred Turanian, joined the conversation for the first time. "Unfortunately, he died in a rebel attack the first day. Poor Jefar Sharif!" he concluded with a maudlin, overdone sigh.

"No matter." Sempronius shrugged in profound unconcern. "The dead are of no use to us. It would hardly serve our purpose to parade heroic corpses before the mob. General Abolhassan can appoint some good-looking Turanian to play the role, or else fill it himself." Already moving as if he owned the raft, among passengers who parted respectfully before him, the eunuch conducted them around the cabin and onto the less crowded foredeck. "We will have much to occupy us, what with the reception, the palace tour, and your decoration." As he spoke, Sempronius signaled his voiceless slave to set down his baggage in a vacant place along the raft's bulwark. The servant immediately began opening parcels.

"Tell me," Conan asked with some interest, "will we get to see the emperor's pearl-lined baths? I have heard much about them, and of the skill of the masseuses employed there—"

"You will need to bathe sooner than that! I will have my slave rub you down with scented oil." Sempronius turned back to Conan, holding a piece of iridescent silk that might have been intended as raiment. "When we were astern with the cattle, I did not notice it so much"—the eunuch wrinkled his nose primly—"but frankly, Sergeant, you smell."

"Smell, do I?" Conan shot an angry glance aside at

Juma. "Hardly more than yourself, foppish gelding, with your stinking pomade and courtly fragrance! In the jungle, indulgences of that sort would get you quickly tracked and killed." He bunched a heavy fist, flourishing it before his detractor's face; the eunuch and his slave only edged closer together, confronting him stubbornly. "If your nose were mashed flat against your pretty face, I do not think my smell would bother you so much!" Conan glanced again at Juma, who, beneath the dull passiveness of intoxication, looked vaguely concerned.

"But—ah, well, what matters it? No need for an oil-rub by a scented steer!" Abruptly, Conan relaxed his belligerent posture. Shaking off the miserable rag of his vest and stepping out of his torn breeks, he strode up onto the bulwark, then over the side of the raft into the water, splashing the startled watchers with the spray of his plunge.

Swimming was not really necessary, since the river current rolled at the same resolute speed as the raft. An occasional kick was enough to keep Conan alongside, bobbing and cavorting in the water. Beyond him the nearer riverbank rolled by, bushy with reeds and screened by a few low-hanging trees. Amused passengers offered to watch out for crocodiles; they shouted many spirited warnings, most of them unjustified. Meanwhile, passing sailboats steered close to the barge to see the cause of the commotion.

Before long Juma too had stripped and leaped in. Shedding most of his winy stupor in the brisk morning coolness of the water, he proved that he too possessed the rare knack of swimming. Whilst the two ruffians sported and strove to drown each other, Sempronius leaned overside and emptied a gleaming blue glass jug over their heads, anointing them with soapy, perfumed oil.

Their frolicking went on a considerable time before

the chancery assistant persuaded both men to climb back on board, remain there long enough to dry off, and don some of his silken finery. When this was accomplished, the two had a decidedly gaudy, imposing look. Yet Sempronius's costly silver-gray version of the standard expeditionary tunic contrasted strangely with the wearers' unshorn heads and bestubbled, jungle-scorched faces. To remedy this, the eunuch bound their wet scalps in supple violet turbans. He then made each man in turn submit to the gleaming razor of his mute, solemn slave.

With their faces freshly shaven and oiled, the two looked merely splendid. Iron-trim bodies and bright, sharp gazes lent both a dashing, aristocratic appearance. Their fellow passengers, mostly farmers and merchants, watched every step of the transformation and applauded its result; afterward they dispersed politely as dates and palm wine were produced from one of the baskets to reward the troopers' obedience.

The only real disagreement was over the veterans' battered, disreputable jungle knives, which they would not surrender. The sweat-grimed shagreen hilts, Sempronius insisted, jutted too obscenely from the pleated sashes of the bright new outfits. To settle the matter, he finally had to barter the weapons for his own and his servant's gemmed, gold-hilted daggers; these, on careful inspection, the warriors found to be of equal keenness to the mute slave's steel razor.

The mighty Ilbars straightened its course to eastward, rolling now at a swifter rate toward the capital and the sea. The croplands on either bank showed the change, looking steadily tamer and more populated. Yet progress was still too slow for Sempronius, who grew more and more restless as the sun approached its zenith. "Where is that boat?" he muttered distractedly to the others. "'Twould be an ill omen if my pigeon were

downed by a hawk! The rabble would hardly care for
that, nor would the emperor."

But at last a gilded canoe appeared, gliding upstream
through shady shallows on the river's southern bank. It
raced smoothly under the expert paddles of eight kneeling oarsmen, their pace set by a red-turbanned drum-
mer seated astern. In graceful response to the hails of
the eunuch, who waved imperiously from the raft's
bulwark, the canoe circled out amidstream. No sooner
had the rowers sculled to a halt alongside, than
Sempronius was stepping aboard and beckoning to his
charges. "Come, we must not be late! You," he told his
slave, "bring down that quaint tree! But stay aboard the
raft yourself and see to the rest of the baggage!" The
man turned silently away to comply.

In moments the canoe raced ahead with Conan and
Juma in its waist, waving farewell to their cheering
admirers. The potted tree had been placed in the bows
for balance; the three passengers squatted amidships on
polished benches set athwart the wooden hull. The
speed of the oarsmen redoubled that of the river, as was
apparent whenever the craft angled near the bank.
There reeds, trees, and rude cottages flashed by at a
breathtaking rate, faster than the fastest courser could
gallop.

Yet for the most part they stayed out in midstream.
The oarsmen effortlessly skirted larger, slower ships
that were likewise availing themselves of the swiftest
currents. Small, maneuverable vessels kept a careful
distance, respecting the gold Imperial plaque affixed
below the eagle-headed prow of the canoe.

Once only, Conan laid a hand on the shoulder of one
of the paddlers, offering to relieve the man and try out
his own skill. But the naked rower, scarcely breaking
stroke, glanced back haughtily; he shook his head in
obvious resentment at the interruption. So Conan

squatted idle with the others, sipping syrupy palm wine, a new flask of which Sempronius had produced. Lulled by the oars' liquid whisper, the throb of the hardwood drum, and the low chant the rowers occasionally hummed to match its rhythm, they sat watching the passing scenery.

In an amazingly short time, the eastern sky had begun to color with the coppery haze of ten thousand city smokes; simultaneously, more buildings and stone quays began to appear on either bank. River traffic increased, yet posed no hindrance to the expert crew—particularly since the river broadened here. More islands lay in its midst, some surmounted by walled, domed villas of the high-ranking rich. On the now-swampy southern bank, communities of small, decaying boats abounded, the leaky dwellings of poor riverfolk.

Then, looming above the graceful droop of willows, Conan spied the city wall of Aghrapur. Crenellated and curving, it stretched away southward, its slim, minaretted towers piercing the smoke-tinted haze at stately intervals.

To Conan's surprise, the canoe landed before the city wall, at a broad stone quay abristle with masts. 'Twas a thriving port, clearly, for the pier abutted a stone plaza ringed with custom-houses and merchants' stalls. Yet the bustle of the place, as the Cimmerian could not help noticing, seemed particularly intense this afternoon; at first, though lulled by wine, he experienced mild alarm, imagining that a siege was underway. But as Sempronius led him and Juma through milling crowds of cavalry troopers and their prancing, brightly harnessed mounts, he realized that a parade was forming up.

"Make way! Move aside, there, I bring the heroes!" Sempronius's commands were officious and sharp, delivered in the high-pitched voice his boyhood mutilation had left him. "Where, under the gods, is the chariot of honor? Spatulus, you miserable eunuch, who commands this mess? Ah, yonder is the general! Hail, great sir, we are arrived! The triumph can now proceed."

Conan was dragged before a tall, black-turbaned officer, whose eye passed over him briefly and incuriously. By the time he heard the name "Abolhassan" muttered somewhere nearby and realized who the man was, Conan's rumored enemy had turned away to mount a gold-trimmed chariot. Meanwhile, Sempronius led him and Juma up to a broad, low, rectangular box decked with embroidered pillows. The enclosure was obviously meant to be sat in.

"What is it, a raft?" Conan asked of no one in particular, letting himself be ushered inside and deposited on a pillow. "Or is it a howdah?" he asked Juma as the Kushite climbed in opposite him. "If it is one, how do we get up on the elephant's back?"

Sempronius, afire with his official duties, hurried off without answering; Conan's curiosity was satisfied only when four pairs of silk-shirted slaves marched up. Each pair bore a long, polished pole, all four of which they fitted under brackets in the sides of the platform, two transversely and two lengthwise. Suddenly, seemingly without effort, the box was borne up to shoulder height: a plush, open-topped sedan carriage.

Conan did not feel exactly comfortable at being trundled aloft thus, like a trussed pig on its way to a feast. On the other hand, the motion of the ride was even smoother than an elephant jaunt, the litter-bearers seeming to maneuver every bit as skillfully as the rowers of the royal canoe. Striding between cavalry and infantry columns, they crossed the busy courtyard to arrive at the road. There, the city's eastern gate loomed open before them, its entry festooned with flower chains and bunting.

An interminable wait ensued, with the bearers stooping in stylized, ready submissiveness like well-trained dogs around the grounded litter. But finally a trumpet salute blared ahead, and drums rattled an answer. The litter was borne aloft and the march began.

"I do not see the need for this armored escort," Conan observed to Juma, "when the canoe could have taken us straight to the dock of the Imperial Palace."

"You think all this is for our benefit?" The Kushite, though drunker and more complacent than Conan, was not too drunk to smile cynically. "Butchering far-off enemies is only one of the uses they have for us, you will come to learn. Our greatest service to the empire, possibly our last and fatal one, still lies ahead!"

Meanwhile the litter, moving near the front of the procession, passed through the city gate. For Conan it was an odd feeling to travel supine, gazing up at the slits and loopholes of the overarching gatehouse and the sharp metal teeth of the cullises. Trumpets blared from the battlements, whence, instead of stones and hot oil, flowers rained down on the marchers.

Arriving at the plaza inside the gate, the litter drew up smartly, the whole column halting likewise before and behind it. A gray-bearded city official in a gleaming gold turban stepped up onto a platform to place garlands over both the passengers' necks. Then, to the heroes' surprise, a pair of lush-hipped harem-maids in diaphanous, flowing costumes clambered into the litter, there to wriggle down cozily in place beside the passengers. The watching crowd, consisting of little more than a backing-up of the normal gate traffic plus a few market idlers, whistled and hooted appreciatively as the procession moved on.

"Well, maidens, you are a welcome reward for weary soldiers!" Conan squirmed close against his plump, pleasing wench, patting her soft olive flank as she turned to wave to the cheering onlookers. The litter was moving along smoothly once again, its bearers apparently not overburdened by the added weight of the women; the only noticable differences were a bit more sluggishness starting out, and some additional sway on the turns.

"Nay, sir, behave yourself! We are meant only as adornments for your journey, like your flower wreaths!" The harem maid turned her pert, carefully painted smile on Conan and lifted his hand from her thigh. "Pray do not disarrange my gown so."

"Do not worry yourself about it, child." Conan clasped an arm about her dimpled shoulders. "If you are chilled in this scanty garb, I'll cover you and keep you warm."

"Nay, sir, not here!" she answered primly. "Just wave to the crowd and enjoy yourself." Disengaging his hand from her soft skin, she raised it above his head and waggled it high in a limp salute. "There will be ample time for sport later, at the palace."

Juma was evidently meeting similar, skillful rebuffs from his squirming companion. By calling their attention to the onlookers outside the litter, the wenches could unerringly dampen the men's ardor, Conan realized. While giving the appearance of passionate wantons, the houris actually directed all their seductive charms to the crowd, with little more than polite professionality left over for their seatmates. Discouraged at last, Conan contented himself just sitting up among the cushions in what he hoped was a dignified posture, watching his surroundings race by.

The procession moved down a broad, straight avenue of high-walled estates, with ample room along either side for onlookers. These were few, estate slaves mainly, stretched beside the road in two narrow, broken lines; but the procession seemed well-equipped to attract more. Led by a phalanx of brightly clothed, fez-hatted heralds whose incessant trumpet-blasts echoed sourly down the street, the column promptly widened to a quadruple rank of drummers; Conan could see their tassles and drumsticks bouncing in the air far ahead.

Behind them came threescore crack garrison infantry, followed by their arrogant commander: General Abolhassan, standing alone at the reins of a splendid four-horse chariot. Its black-and-gilt colors matched those of the stallion team, whose glossy ebon backs were set off by gilded harness. Conan, watching the general's own black-robed, gold-plated back as the officer postured before the crowd, could not help feeling a twinge of jealousy. He observed how much more the hero Abolhassan contrived to look than himself, plumped in an unmanly litter, foppishly dressed, armorless, and blithely ignored by a pair of crowd-teasing harlots.

Yet things could have been much worse. Behind the general's chariot, and just ahead of Conan's striding sedan, trooped another necessary part of this mock military triumph: a gaggle of prisoners, limping along in their rags and their bare, whip-striped skins, burdened with shackles especially weighted to make the wearers look weak and miserable. Hyrkanians they were, grimy and straggle-haired, doubtless captured in some imperial skirmish far to the eastward. Not of Venjipur, and not even dressed like Venji rebels, they had nothing to do with Conan and, quite likely, little to do with Abolhassan. But the ignorant city folk would hardly know this; they needed some object on which to pour out their contempt. As the luckless prisoners passed, lashed forward by mounted Turanian overseers, the watching crowd hissed and reviled them. Some pelted the captives with stones and offal too, as universal Hyborian custom dictated.

Behind the captives came a happy change of mood: Conan and Juma, the heroes of Venjipur—a doughty-looking pair, even if they were obviously foreign. So, after all, were many of the city's merchants, soldiers, and valued slaves. In any case, the crowd's sympathetic interest was caught instantly by the smiling, waving concubines, who leaned far over the sides of the litter to display their buxom charms. Thus attended, and obviously bashful and ill-at-ease because of it, the two giant westerners, one fair and the other jet-black, were greeted with good-natured applause, even cheers.

Just beyond the litter, pulled by a single donkey, trundled a cart containing the potted Venji tree. Pathetic as it was, this exhibit furnished the sole authentic touch of Venjipur and of the war blazing in its jungle depths. To the watchers, no doubt, it seemed but a first, faint token of the vast wealth that would pour northward to reward the Turanian Empire's military prowess.

Furthermore, behind and around it galloped a rousing demonstration of that prowess: trick cavalry riders. They trotted and wheeled their nimble horses from side to side across the avenue, standing up in the saddle, leaping from horse to horse and performing acrobatics atop, alongside, and beneath their running mounts. All these riders wore Turanian military tunics; they were somewhat smaller and more elegant, perhaps, than any cavalry the empire would have thrust into the forefront of a battle, as were their steeds. But again, the unschooled crowd could scarcely tell the difference between these circus pranksters and real soldiers, or know how little their antics had to do with grim warfare. They received the act enthusiastically, applauding and strolling alongside to watch more of the daring feats.

Beyond them paced regular cavalry of the city garrison. They carried brightly bannered lances, whose waving folds blocked Conan's view of any further con-

tingents of the parade. Yet from well behind came more
trumpet blasts and drum cadences, proving that the
procession extended a good way back. And all the
tumult had its desired effect, for as the march proceeded into a district of denser, double-storied buildings, the crowds thickened, closing in along narrow
sidestreets. Turbaned, fezzed, and shaven-headed men,
women both veiled and less modestly robed, and above
all, swarms of naked, shouting children gathered in
the avenue, drawn to the spectacle this brassy tumult
heralded.

Conan, watching their reactions, sensed their less-
than-total acceptance of the display. There was a strong
cast of skepticism in those faces, even of resentment—
more, it seemed, than hardened city-dwellers' custom-
ary wariness against selling their goodwill too cheaply.
Aside from the leers of the men at the shapely women,
the winks and kisses thrown his way and Juma's by
ribald wives and tavern-girls, and the awed gape of
ragged youths at the glittering military regalia, there ran
a deeper current of discontent. Some watchers sneered
or mouthed curses, even waved fists; most showed
flagrant unconcern or sly self-interest. The Cimmerian,
his eye trained by years of thievery, spied more than one
cutpurse working the crowd to his advantage. A poly-
glot, healthy city mob after all, he decided.

As the procession moved on past taverns and open
marketplaces into a more lavish quarter of temples and
civic buildings, other forms of enterprise prevailed.
Hawkers plied the avenue, holding aloft sticks of knotted pastries and sheaves of smoked fish, trading their
wares for copper coins. Possibly the efficient eunuchs
had managed to spead word of the march in advance; or
else these vendors, like the thieves, were quick to
respond when a crowd formed. Among the various
flowers, coins, twigs, and other debris flung at the

marchers, came flying a whole smoked fish, which
smote Conan on the chest. Unsure whether it implied
adoration or disapproval, he nevertheless ate it and
found it tasty.

In this teeming temple quarter the crowds soon grew
thick enough to block the avenue, and files of infantry
and horsemen were dispatched forward along the flanks
of the procession to clear the way. Abolhassan, who gave
the order, showed no inclination to slow the march, so
the troops hurried forth at a trot, pushing back spectators with brisk efficiency.

Yet Conan hardly expected, as a vast, minaretted
temple of Tarim loomed on one side, to see a flock of
black-clad mourners, men and women alike, pouring
out of its open archway to beset the passing troops.
These petitioners, wailing loudly and wringing their
clenched hands in the air, met the procession just ahead
of the general's chariot. Their cries of "Give us back our
sons!" and "Where are our children?" apparently were
meant to bemoan offspring of theirs who had been
impressed or killed in the imperial wars.

The troopers were quick to close ranks, but unable to
head off all the bereaved, so fighting erupted. Stray
mourners were thrown to the cobbles by footsoldiers or
clubbed down by horsemen's spear-butts. In the melee,
the Hyrkanian prisoners also tried to scuttle away; these
were dealt with more bloodily, and some confusion
between the two sorts of victims unavoidably occurred.
Yet the march continued too swiftly past the scenes of
conflict for Conan to form any clear idea whether he
should leap from his seat and take part. The litter-
bearers bore their burden smoothly forward, not even
swerving or breaking step when they had to clamber
over writhing, bleeding bodies.

After that, the mood of the onlookers grew distinctly
hostile; word of the skirmish was spread through the

crowd by indignant shouts, easily outrunning the pace
of the march. With the Hyrkanian prisoners absent, the
clods and offal intended for them now pelted the troops
instead—this despite the fact that the hurlers were
beaten with sheathed swords whenever they could be
caught. In its disapproval, strangely, the crowd pressed
closer than ever it had in good fellowship. The trium-
phal parade threatened soon to become an armed
excursion, its trumpets blaring in warning rather than
festivity, its bannered lances couched in deadly earnest.

Yet of what happened next, there was no warning; it
came as the marchers wound into a neighborhood of
tall tenements inside the old city wall, with the very
towers and domes of the palace looming not far ahead.
The first unusual thing Conan noticed was Juma's
sudden movement, dragging his female escort down
into the litter and rolling atop her in what seemed a
sudden excess of passion. Then the pillows all around
them began to sprout short, feathered shafts, and Conan
felt the conveyance falter and sag as some of its bearers
went down. Without conscious refection, he clapped a
hand on his own seatmate's arm and rolled out of the
sedan, hauling her after him. He forced her down to
keep her concealed beneath the litter, but the slaves
kept pacing doggedly, stepping over their wounded
brethren to carry the vehicle past danger. So the harem
girl had to run stooping along the street, protesting
angrily as Conan held her in the shadow of the moving
platform.

They stopped when General Abolhassan wheeled his
chariot to a halt, brushing arrow-shafts from his own
harness. At the general's shouted order, a file of troops
went running into a decaying brick warren of dwellings,
whence he declared the volleys had been fired. Other
soldiers drafted fit-looking bystanders out of the crowd
to replace the fallen litter-slaves, whose bodies were

now dragged off in litters of their own. While Conan's harem-wench, complaining about her sore shoulder, straightened her mussed hair and garments, the Cimmerian peered into the sedan chair to see whether his friend had been hurt.

Juma, still face-down among the cushions, seemed untouched by arrows. In response to Conan's insistent pummeling he finally looked up, his rugged black features smudged with kohl and rouge. Beneath him the slave girl also seemed unharmed, if somewhat flushed and breathless.

"By Otumbe, is the ambush over already? For me it has been the best part of the ride!" The Kushite made no move to assume a more decorous posture.

"Hmmph, Juma, look here!" Conan spared no humor for his friend's reckless ardor. "This fellow Abolhassan says the arrows came from yon building, but look at the angles!" He pointed to the fletched shafts protruding from the cushions in the litter. "Any fool can see that they flew from the other side."

"Ah, well, what matters it, anyway?" Shrugging his bulky shoulders, Juma lay down close beside his escort, who nuzzled his neck with frank interest. "The assassins are long since fled."

"Perhaps." Already outdistanced by the clopping chariot team, the litter resumed moving, with Conan pacing restlessly beside it. "But I saw the arrows striking Abolhassan's chariot; if you ask me, the heads were already broken off." He snatched one of the skewered pillows from the sedan chair, holding it up to reveal the razor-pointed arrow tip protruding from the underside. "The shafts that struck near the general were not as deadly as these!"

"You think not?" Juma narrowed his eyes at the cruel brass point, then laughed. "You could be right; if so, then likely you are learning more about the ways of power, and the perils we heroes have to face."

Turning from Conan, Juma resumed cuddling his pliant harem wench. The other girl sat bored among the cushions, regarding the embracing pair a little jealously. Conan, for his part, would not climb back into the litter, but stalked watchfully alongside it. The march went faster now, with the troops ruthlessly clearing the road ahead. The few remaining onlookers stood in doorways, windows and alleys, watching solemn-faced as the procession threaded its way toward the imperial palace and safety.

Chapter 16

Court of Protocols

From the broad, bustling stableyard of the Imperial Palace, Conan and Juma were conducted to a well-guarded door of the vast edifice. There they met Sempronius, who must have traveled ahead of the parade either by boat or carriage. He ushered them past the scowling, motionless guards into a long corridor of arabesque tiles.

"Your reception feast lies ahead, in the Court of Protocols," the eunuch announced, striding before them with officious quickness. "No special ceremony is planned, because His Resplendency will not be present until tomorrow. You need only mingle with the crowd and try to make a favorable impression. Watch your manners, eat and drink as the courtiers do, and you will be well received."

"In sooth," Conan muttered, "I shall eat and drink most carefully to avoid taking poison! Our fine reception so far has included an ambush, did you know? Or did you arrange that too, Sempronius?"

"Nay, nay, Sergeant! 'Twas a regrettable mischance, for which I apologize—and a terrible blow to our

emperor's plans for this festive day." Slowing his pace
and lowering his voice, Sempronius turned a worried
look back at them. "Rumors of rebellion and conspiracy
have been rife for some time—but who would have
thought the malcontents would go so far?" He shook his
finely sculptured head in dismay, making the tassel of
his fez wag limply. "The emperor has already been
apprised, I assure you. In leniency, His Graciousness
has decided not to sound a general alarm yet. The
decoration ceremony tomorrow is to proceed as
planned." The eunuch had paused in the hallway, his
voice sinking to an earnest whisper. "It could be the last
chance to win public support for the Venji campaign,
you know, without resorting to sterner measures. I pray
that you will help as best you can."

"I see," Conan nodded thoughtfully. "Rebels, you
say? And what of Abolhassan, do these ambushers have
some special liking for him?"

Sempronius's face closed off abruptly. "Of that I can
say nothing. Both my eunuch chief Euranthus and the
general himself have denied those seditious rumors!
They still pledge unstinting loyalty to our Resplendent
Emperor Yildiz."

"I see—eternally loyal, for the nonce." Flashing a
skeptical glance at Juma, Conan pressed Sempronius
further. "Is General Abolhassan at this banquet? Mayhap I should take it up with him directly!"

The eunuch turned and started off down the hall,
speaking sharply over his shoulder. "I do not know, but
I warn you, he would be a formidable adversary. Pray,
do not spoil the evening with more bloodshed or
insubordination!"

As they drew near the open double door with its two
frozen, red-cloaked guards, Sempronius kept silent.
Beyond the high, fluted arch lay a glittering swarm of
talking, laughing aristocrats—a world apart, seemingly,

from the turmoil of the streets. As the three entered, trumpet notes rippled from an alcove at one side, and a white-haired eunuch announced Conan and Juma's names. Guards relieved them of their sabers, to be returned later, they were told; from that moment Sempronius disappeared, and his wards were beset by sleek, fashionable courtiers.

"At last, here come the heroes! What fine, strong specimens they are!"

"Truly! Are the two of you natives of Venjipur, or some other primitive land?"

"Nay, nay, the pallid one comes from Vanaheim; it was in the dispatch! But he knows civilized speech, they claim."

"Tell us, warrior, how many men have you killed? Too many to count, I'd wager! But just in the past year, say, how many?"

"Yes, tell us! Do you kill the women and children too, or merely make them slaves?"

"What fierce-looking brutes they are! I can see why we use barbarians to enlarge our empire!"

The questions were posed with a mixture of fatuous awe and condescension, and were too numerous to be answered at once, fortunately. More fortunately, a servant distributing beakers of fine kumiss stood close at hand; the more one drank, Conan found, the longer one could postpone answering.

"You must be good men to have in a tight place. If you grow tired of slaughter in far-off lands, the slaves on my date plantation, a few days' ride north and east of here, need a firm hand. 'Tis an easy job; you need not even speak their language—in fact, our late overseer was a mute! When your term of enlistment is past, Sergeant, look me up: Craxus of Kezank-March, at your service!"

The women were the most persistent. Males seemed obliged to confront the heroes and prove themselves, but they usually sheered off judiciously before the warriors' guarded grunts and surly looks; but the females found their dour aspect enticing. To Conan's astonishment, Juma played expertly to their fascination, mingling his gruffness with tantalizing hints of war experience and personal prowess.

"Oh, Sergeant Juma, I can just imagine what it would be like to be princess of a village stormed by your troops!" A svelte matron, whose silk turban had more fabric in it than her brief, clinging gown, drew the willing Kushite down beside her on a pillowed ottoman. "You look so virile and strong! Now confess to me, you don't *always* slay the women, do you?"

Conan himself fell as prey to a leaner, hungrier courtesan, a dusky Turanian, auburn-haired from some trace of western blood. "I envy you troopers your travels to exotic lands and your adventures in strange ports! We women have to be content with homier pleasures." She sank onto the cushioned seat, clinging to the Cimmerian's horny hand with both of hers as he loomed over her. "In Venjipur, they say, rare and exciting potions are to be found. Did you bring back any such mementoes for us city-dwellers? Lotus elixirs, say, or other foreign delights?"

"No." Conan shook his head gravely. "Such potions steal the soul. I have tasted their evil power and seen too many others die or go mad from them. 'Tis foolhardy even to use them to soothe the pain of a wound, you know; some troopers learn to crave them ever more, gashing themselves over and over again for the sake of applying the balm, until they sicken and die of the creeping blood-rot."

Conan's frank speech made the woman flinch and relinquish his hand uncomfortably. Yet at the same time, the tale seemed to engage her deeper interest. She stared thoughtfully into his eyes for a few heartbeats, then whispered something to her turbaned companion, who still cooed over Juma.

"Officers," the women announced, "your appetites must be . . . simply ravenous after your long journey! Let us go and bring you drink and dainties from yonder table. You wait here; we shall return at once to hear more of your fascinating stories."

As the two bustled away through the crowd, Conan sank down on the ottoman beside his friend. "Come, Juma, let us get away from here. I cannot bear this morbid questioning; it brings back too many evil memories."

Laying his empty kumiss-jar on the tile-blazoned floor, Juma shrugged. "Just sit here and play along, Conan, and I guarantee you a soft bedmate tonight. Know you, these courtly females will love you less curtly and wearily than Venji campgirls. Unless, of course, you miss your Sariya. . . ."

Impatiently Conan shrugged his remarks aside. "Juma, how you can take your leisure so calmly with arrows drawn at our backs, and our enemies conniving against us? You, who warned me of the perils of the capital . . ."

"Did I not also say that a hero's life is a short, intense one? We have no choice now but to relax and enjoy it." Juma eased back onto the cushion, a living example of pantherine calm. "This is the best way to spin out our lives another day, by doing what is expected. Tomorrow you meet Yildiz; by then, some course of action may present itself."

"Aye, perhaps—but even the Sunrise Throne looks shaky these days. Methinks I should warn Yildiz before the night is over, or seek out the source of the threat directly!"

Juma raised his hand to Conan's arm in a cautionary gesture, his voice sinking to a stockade-whisper. "Put no

faith in Sempronius's guesses and innuendos; that eunuch is as sly as any of his brethren. Above all, do not
hint at any weakness in this Yildiz's reign, unless you are
ready to take the blame for undermining it!"

"My thanks for your counsel." Conan clasped the
Kushite's wrist, detaching his friend's grip from his
arm. "But I cannot bide here tamely now. Take both
wenches with my compliments, Juma, but be wary."
Before the courtesans had returned, he slipped away
through the crowd.

Abolhassan was nowhere to be seen—an annoyance,
since Conan was half-minded to confront him and settle
their real or rumored differences without delay. Watchfully he scanned the thronging, lofty-arched hall, from
his vantage a head above most of the idlers. He met
dozens of glances, some conveying distaste, others a
pathetic eagerness to make closer contact. He had to
sweep his gaze ruthlessly free of them all, wishing that
his height, coloring, and garish dress did not make him
so conspicuous.

Maddeningly, he felt himself unable to move smoothly through the crowd; though he would have navigated a
night jungle without stirring a twig, he could not seem
to bypass a single babbling, gesticulating courtier without colliding with him or her, and then having to
extricate himself from their voluble courtesies and
protestations. Inching past an especially raucous, close-
packed group, he found himself the target of a municipal officer with a strident, sharply pitched voice.

"Ah, here is Conan, the pride of Venjipur, soon to
receive the benison of the mighty! I have been wanting a
word or two with you, fellow." Failing to snatch Conan's
dagger-hand in his earnest grasp, he pummeled him on
the shoulder instead.

"Oof! Back off, man! Who are you?" Stepping away,
Conan made forcible room in the crowded surround-

ings; he wanted to be able to see his challenger's hands and have adequate time to react to a sudden blow or a knife-thrust.

"I? I am Omar, Captain of the Civil Horse-Guard. You may have seen me earlier today, leading a saber detachment to save you from a mob of your . . . admirers." The medium-sized, red-tunicked man smiled and added his own bray to a spate of appreciative laughter from watching courtiers. His brown-mustached face, rubicund with drink and temerity, had a pursed look about the lips, making them seem well-suited to uttering slights and slanders. "Come, let us talk man-to-man. Even though I am your senior in both rank and years, I would not let that stand between us."

"Nor would I, since civil guards have no sway over fighting officers." Standing with his hands loose at his sides, Conan courteously reminded himself not to clutch at his dagger-hilt.

"No, perhaps not. What I meant to take up with you"—Omar paused, visibly playing to the audience of watching courtiers—"was to congratulate you on your victory at . . . where was it . . . Sikander! I read the official reports, and I agree that your conduct was most valiant. A dozen-hundred enemy dead at least, allowing for double counting, and impressive losses on our own side as well, to prove your courage. Well done, soldier!" Omar beamed around at the group as if the putative credit were his own.

"Yes, truly," he finally resumed in the face of appreciative nods and murmurs, "after reviewing your conduct of the battle, there is only one small criticism I can make: Where were your cavalry, fellow?" With raised eyebrows and outspread palms, Omar invoked the judgment of the watchers. "Why, a good horse charge might have doubled the enemy dead-count, with but a fewscore more losses among our own ranks. Elephants

and so forth may be traditional down south, but there is
still no substitute for the old hack-and-trample!"

Conan, regarding his critic narrowly, nevertheless
lowered his eyes as he answered, for he felt slightly put
off by the number and intensity of the watching stares.
"If by Sikander, you mean the battle of the Elephant
Shrine—why, the cavalry was far behind us at the fort.
They never even found the fight. But that is just as well,
since I see little use for horses in jungle combat."

"Ah, but there, you see!" Omar crowed triumphantly.
"Your attitude is at fault there, Sergeant! To leave the
cavalry in the rear of battle is like setting the horse
behind the plow and lashing the yoke to your own weary
neck. Once the enemy has been put to rout and is fleeing
through level forest, that is where a horse troop can
shine, outrunning the pitiful fugitives, riding and slashing them down mercilessly! If you entertain a prejudice
against cavalry, sir, may I suggest that it is only because
you have not *tried* them."

"Crom blight your impudence, man! With my friends
being butchered all around me, I would have been
happy to see help coming, whether astride horse, camel,
or goat! But come they did not; your saddle-brothers
shirked the fight! Whether because of the torpor of their
sickly nags or their own miserable cowardice, they left
us for dead." In spite of his earlier resolve, Conan found
himself not only clutching his dagger, but sawing it
angrily in and out of its sheath.

"Sir, I am insulted! This offense to me and my
brothers in service can be redeemed only by blood!"
Omar's demeanor had changed abruptly; he spoke low
now, standing pike-straight, his eyes flashing righteously
around at the company. Conan, sizing him up as rangy
and trim in spite of a slight swag-belly, decided he might
be a capable fighter.

"I would invite you into the stableyard now," the

glaring captain went on, "except that I see you are not prepared." Glancing down at Conan's gem-crusted knife, he slapped his own long, straight scabbard. "Therefore, may I suggest the municipal barracks at midnight, where swords are plentiful."

The silence of the nearby onlookers was eerie against the continued babble and clink of the party in the room at large. Conan, flushed and irritated, did not bother to restrain his voice, and so drew more shocked stares. "Damn you, rogue, I will be happy to meet you this midnight—provided it means I do not have to bear more of your insolence now! Fry in Tarim's deepest hell!" he concluded, turning and shoving away through the crowd.

The buzz of voices behind him, though intense, was still not loud enough to divert the attention of the entire broad hall; and so Conan found refuge in the crowd around the banquet table. This hollow square of trestles, cluttered with food of all descriptions, was besieged on every side by hungry guests. Some of the viands were dispensed by bloused, pantalooned servants moving within the enclosure and by bolder menials who made forays among the revelers.

Conan shouldered his way to a table, plucking up handfuls of grapes and raspberries to cram into his mouth. Looking diagonally across the festive board, he was surprised to see another figure looming tall above the loiterers—Abolhassan, still caped and armored from the parade, accepting a smoking skewer of fruit and meat from a cringing servant.

Well enough, then, Conan told himself; the strident Captain Omar might yet be denied his quarry, if his antagonist and his general fell to blows first. Muttering gruff pardons and warnings to those he pushed past, he began working his way around the table toward his goal.

Halfway there, an even more striking figure intercepted him. She was tall and lavishly built, short-caped and kilted in a costume as splendid as any of the courtiers' gowns, if slightly mannish in cut. More conspicuous than her dress was her pale blond hair, which flowed like a banner in the wake of her brisk movements. She was further distinguished by an entourage: three or four courtly women, more typically Turanian in their dusky looks. Nevertheless they seemed to share the alert, directed gleam that played in their leader's eye.

"Might you be Conan, the hero of Venjipur?" Her voice, in keeping with her appearance, was bold enough to draw the attention of those nearby. "Are you the valiant officer soon to be decorated by the emperor, in honor of your prowess in his southern campaign?"

"Aye." Meeting her eye, Conan savored the appealing flash of daring. "That I am."

"Good, then; let me be the first to decorate you!" With scarcely a pause she took up a silver trencher from the table and slung its contents onto Conan, spattering his face and his silken garb with pink, creamy sauce dotted by unidentifiable lumps. "That for all you warmakers and child-butchers, who march our brothers and sons off to distant battles, and who squander the wealth of our land in cruel, vainglorious war!"

When she had finished, her stridency echoed in a silence more resounding than any uproar. The entire room turned to regard the towering, besmirched hero; the sudden rustle of their attentiveness was punctuated only by gasps and cries of astonishment. It was left for Conan to answer—which he did by taking up a wooden vat of oiled, spicy fruit pieces. "This," he proclaimed, "is for sleek Turanian wives who fatten on trade and tribute from abroad, but scorn its procurers!" So saying, he emptied the vessel in the general direction of his assailant.

The pale-haired woman, quick on her sandaled feet,

sidestepped the slimy torrent; only one shapely, darting leg and the hem of her skirt were besmeared. Instead, a pair of innocent eunuchs behind her caught the cataract's full force. These two, angrily spluttering and expostulating, shook themselves free of the oily fruit as best they could. Then, instead of assaulting Conan with blades or fists, they laid greedy hold of bread, sausages, melon chunks, and other assorted viands and began hurling them at him.

Promptly the pale-haired maid rejoined the fray, exuberantly calling on her followers to do the same. The Cimmerian, oversized and practically immobilized by the press of the crowd, made an easy target; nevertheless, many of their projectiles flew high and wide. Invariably these struck others in the throng, who in turn joined Conan, laying hold of more foodstuffs or snatching them out of the air to return the treacherous bombardment. In no time the entire throng near the feast-table was embattled, and the room became a flying banquet of fruit, loaves, cutlets, stuffed squab, cheeses, and pastries, with dollops of sauce and pudding of all sorts.

In spite of the melee's rapid spread, Conan's attention remained fixed on its blond, brazen initiator; yet the heavy barrage of condiments raining down at the heart of the fray made her difficult to reach. Breaking free of grasping, flailing throwers, he made a headlong lunge, only to slip in a welter of spilled chowder and fall to his knees. His long-haired adversary's next offering of stuffed shrimp, still nested within a heavy faience bowl, struck him above the eye with an impact that set his brain reeling. Several thundering pulsebeats sounded in his skull before he found the equilibrium to stagger once again to his feet. He plunged into the crowd after his vanished quarry, who had clearly been headed for the door.

Some distance from the table, standing calm amid the howls and taunts, two warriors conversed: General Abolhassan and the cavalry captain, Omar. The latter was unscathed by the rain of edibles; but the general, using a finely embroidered silk kerchief, carefully mopped pale green liquid from the lapel of his elegant black cape. His mustached lip was pursed in a fastidious, unpleasant expression.

"The vixen Irilya has gone far enough," he observed icily. "A brilliant fiasco this, most destructive to the emperor's order; but here ends her usefulness to our plan. The army is now on the brink of revolt and the court is far past caring, as this disgraceful scene shows." He gestured around the banquet, which had rapidly assumed an orgiastic air of abandon, with some few pairs of drunken revelers rolling in combat or in open lust on the food-littered floor. "In the next stage, Irilya would only pose a danger. Pass the word to have her brought to me."

Omar smiled understandingly. "You plan to interrogate her—and perhaps celebrate the eve of our coup? I would not mind putting such a lively maid to the question myself!" Abruptly, glancing up and seeing Abolhassan's dark look, he grew prim-faced. "I will have her sent here as you command. And of course, I will deal with the barbarian."

"Aye, slay him as publicly as possible. But first, humiliate him further." Abolhassan's scowl twisted into a grudging smile at the notion. "That should not be difficult for an expert wag and duellist such as yourself. If he does not show up for the fight, spread the news of his cowardice abroad and leave him to me. In either event it will end Yildiz's laughable attempt to create a hero." The general pivoted on Omar, who clicked his heels and nodded a salute. "To tomorrow, then, and mutiny!"

Chapter 17

Night Pursuits

Down filigreed corridors, across jade floors and lapis-lazuli terraces, Conan pursued the fleet-footed Irilya. It had not taken long for her attempted departure to become a chase at full speed. The lower level of the palace's spacious west wing was laid open for festivity that night, so the red-liveried guards posted along the halls stood stiffly immobile as the two darted past them.

The race was close and fast, with the female's slender build and lithe, horsy legs challenging Conan's hard-hewn fitness. The only true advantage he enjoyed was the pursuer's age-old privilege of seeing the course unfold clearly before him, and of cutting corners to avoid the costly delay of uncertainty.

Yet it was not until both runners sped through a yawning archway, out into a moonlit garden of hedges and geometric ponds, that Conan drew near enough to hear the steady pant of Irilya's breaths and smell her musky, overheated scent as she ran. His heart surged strong within his chest, and to his senses the night air tasted cool as wine; he knew he could keep up the pace.

He ran with the steady sureness of a leopard on the track of a supple, tender gazelle.

The mazelike garden might serve either as a refuge or a trap. Irilya, hearing her pursuer's steps thudding near, sought to elude him by making a sudden, sidelong dash down an aisle between rectangular fountains. This created an opportunity Conan was quick to seize: veering swiftly as his prey, he launched himself into air above the corner of the nearer fountain. Completed, this leap cut the last few paces off Irilya's lead, enabling Conan to catch her shoulder in his extended arm. Predictably, though, it left him little room to stop; so, skidding across the narrow tile apron between the fountains, he plunged into the farther one. His quarry was borne along with him, to fall atop him in a spraying flurry of tangled limbs.

Splashes and curses resounded for a few moments, drawing no particular attention in the deserted garden. The turmoil gradually subsided, giving way to a forlorn, steady dripping. Hunter and hunted faced each other knee-deep and motionless, separated by a single, curving length of steel: a dagger gripped in Irilya's taut, wet hand.

"Enough, wench; back off!" Conan declared self-righteously. "If I wished to fence with you, why, I have a weapon of my own. But I am a forgiving sort!" The Cimmerian shook his now-turbanless head, sending drops of water scattering from his soggy mane like a wet mongrel shaking itself. "I consider that I have repaid your earlier affront with this dousing—which we both needed, in any case, to wash off the remains of this night's banquet! Now take that pig-skewer out of my face!"

"I may, barbarian"—Irilya lowered her blade and prepared to give ground, or rather pond, to him—"if you will give more thought to whom you call wench!"

All at once an arc of water sprayed up as Conan's foot swung wide, sweeping his adversary's legs from beneath her. Both figures went down in a new flurry of splashes, resolved forcibly this time in a tight clinch. Then a wet impact sounded, and the combatants broke apart. Steel shone once again, making a gleaming hyphen to their sundering.

"Off me, you raping, murdering brigand! Next time the damage will be permanent!" Irilya's blade flickered meaningfully at waist level.

"All right, by Crom! I only sought a kiss, as honest recompense!" Conan's voice sounded slightly impaired, and his step faltered a little as he squared off against the maiden. "Methought you were enjoying it too, until you struck me a foul blow!"

"I enjoyed the blow more," she said, turning away. Unhurriedly she waded to the edge of the pond and climbed out. "I save my kisses for real men, not for the marching, slaughtering minions of General Abolhassan!" Sheathing her dagger and taking her pale hair in handfuls, she wrung and twisted it, letting its moon-silvered brightness pour in long rivulets down to the rippled surface of the pond.

"Abolhassan? I am no friend of his." Conan bent to splash his tunic with water and slough away the last traces of pudding and chowder. "I have reason to question his loyalty to the realm."

"Loyalty!" Irilya's laugh was clear and bell-like. "What is loyalty in Aghrapur? Mere self-promotion! Doubtless you envy Abolhassan, and mean to take his place and become a worse tyrant! I have pled causes before the emperor often enough to know that there is no real difference between power-seeking males . . . or power-seeking eunuchs, for that matter!"

"When I plead my case, Yildiz will listen." Conan, having finished his ablutions, was now wringing his shirttails into the fountain. "He would be a fool to ignore a general who appropriates military stores to his own secret uses, and who stages false assassinations in the capital."

Irilya laughed again. "Tell Yildiz what you will, at your own peril; he and Abolhassan are thick as thieves. But do not pretend for my sake that you are some high-minded reformer!"

Though scornful, the maid could not help being beautiful as she bent to press water out of her skirt with a knife-edged hand. She continued speaking without looking directly at Conan. "You dance to the emperor's tune, and promote his pet wars; you are part and parcel of a corrupt order soon to be overturned. Your safest chance would be to leave our city—but why do I even bother to tell you this? Good riddance!" Straightening, looking only vaguely disheveled in the crescent moon's radiance, she strode off along the causeway in the direction of the palace's soft-lit arches.

"Wait, do not leave!" Conan called, wading after her to the pond's margin. "I need to hear more about your cause, and of the situation here in Aghrapur."

"Oh, really?" Irilya did not slow her determined pace. "And why should I pour out secrets to you, my political enemy? Why waste time with you at all?"

"Why?" Conan followed her along the fountain's edge. "Perhaps because worse enemies wait in the offing."

"What—you mean, those?" Turning the corner of the fountain walkway, Irilya paused to regard three shadowy figures moving toward them from the direction of the palace. "Why, they are only banquet guests made curious by our struggles—or my friends from court, come to see to my welfare!" She drew breath for a shout. "Hello, sisters, is it you?"

Her cry echoed starkly in the silent courtyard, unanswered. The three dim, turbaned shapes seemed to be moving in concert, having fanned out to cover a wide area of the garden. More menacingly, when Irilya strode boldly across the central plaza toward an empty path skirting more ponds, all three hurried sideward to cut off her route of escape.

" 'Twould seem they are the agents of some enemy of yours," warned Conan, who had hauled his dripping bulk out of the pool behind her. "But go, confront them if you want; I will back you."

Whether Irilya had greater mistrust of the three shapes slouching ahead of her or the one hulking behind, she strode forward, staying well clear of Conan. Her aspect was one of boldness, her hand visibly clutching the dagger stuck in the waistband of her skirt. "Here, you three, identify yourselves! And give a lady some protection against this rogue who pursues me."

Her words were disregarded, coaxing forth no reply; and there was nothing friendly in the way the three mufti-clad men converged on her, two of them reaching to take hold of her arms, the third turning to head off the approaching Cimmerian. "Stay clear," he murmured gruffly. "This is no business of yours."

His face wore a surprised look as Conan's hand shot out and grasped his neck. When, an instant later, the northerner's other hand rapped a dagger-hilt against his temple, his expression slackened from one of strangulation to one of oblivion, and he dropped senseless to earth.

Irilya was fending off one of the other two men with her dagger; the third, shifting his attention from her to Conan, stiffened before a stroke of the Cimmerian's malleted fist and toppled over backward. His body splashed into a fountain, where he drifted motionless.

By then, Irilya had the third attacker whimpering from a dagger-slash to his arm; nursing it, he turned and scuttled off toward the palace. Conan started after him—until, looking back, he realized that Irilya was pelting away in the other direction. Cursing, he abandoned the one pursuit and took up the other.

"What, no thanks for me?" he called, drawing near her jouncing shanks and damp, flapping garments. "Where are you bound now?"

"Leave me alone, will you?" she tossed back over her shoulder. When he continued to gain on her, she added, "If you keep company with me, I want no more of your vile attentions. I warn you—try anything, and one of us will die!" Rounding a hedge onto a broad walkway leading to the outer wall, she slowed her pace to swift walk.

"Whatever you may think of Imperial troopers, I am not a wholesale ravisher of women and killer of babes." Conan drew up beside her, keeping a decorous distance. "Who were those men?"

"I recognized them as palace agents," she breathed heavily. "I have seen them watching me before, but now things must have come to a more desperate pass. They want me silenced, it seems, and my husband's rank will no longer protect me."

"Your husband?" Conan blurted out, his mind suddenly overwhelmed by imponderable complications.

"Nay, he is far from here, with no great concern over me and no lack of foreign women to occupy him." She patted her damp skirt as she walked, straightening it where it clung to her striding thighs. "But I . . . ! I am now an outlaw, unsafe even in my own manor house, I would venture. Yet I do not care; I welcome it, if it means that the crisis is finally at hand!"

She cut off her speech as they neared the outer gate. Its portals stood wide, flanked by two frozen-faced pairs of guards; these let the couple pass without question. Outside, in the cobbled city street, beggars and indigents loitered; they eyed the departing pair but did not crowd forward to beseech them, whether because of their wet, bedraggled looks or because of Conan's dangerous size and more dangerous scowl.

When once again they drew clear of listening ears, he spoke. "I seem to have come to the capital at a time of political upheaval."

Irilya laughed bitterly. "Aye! If this rotten, despised regime lasts another day, 'twill be by special dispensation of all-seeing Tarim himself. Or herself!" She turned aside, forcing Conan to follow her along a cobbled residential lane that trended uphill, away from the lights of the palace.

"You do not fear the horrors of civil war, then?" Conan pressed her.

"Can it be worse than the horror of civil tyranny? When sharifs and satraps impress our young into foreign wars and kidnap innocent subjects off the streets?" Irilya spoke in a practiced way, speeding her steps to keep slightly ahead of Conan. "Noble rank has allowed me and my few friends at court to be the sole voices of protest—until now. Now at last I say, down with the established order! Any change will surely be a change for the better."

"But you have never seen true anarchy." Conan gestured to the blank-walled dwellings on either side, lit by moonglow dimly suffused across the hazy sky. "These houses all burned, their tenants beggared or slain, the cry of havoc loose in the town . . ."

"Nay, Sergeant, we need never fear real anarchy here, except perhaps from such as yourself! Turan is a civilized land, the will of her people alloyed together as one." Irilya shook her gradually drying hair, spreading it across her shoulders like a mantle of silver threads. "The citizens crave only wise, peaceable rule; their hearts will tell them what to do when the time comes.

Most of the city garrison is already on our side, so any violence and turmoil will be but temporary, toward a nobler end. Understand: Things must get worse before they can get better!"

"Hmm, I know nothing of that." Conan shook his head doubtfully, his natural skepticism softened by satisfaction at having drawn this splendid creature into earnest conversation. "Remember, girl, players like Abolhassan do not wager their high-ranking necks for nothing! I would guess that he plans to gain much from any reshuffling, perhaps a throne!"

"But do you not see, the general is discredited, as is Yildiz himself! They cannot win the support of the people—any more than they can win their puny war in Venjipur, which drags on year after year. Their best hope there, the sorcerous power of the Court of Seers, has been thwarted and stalemated; that is open knowledge! Even with the aid of mighty heroes like you"—here her voice skipped on the rough edge of laughter—"they are powerless, and the court and the people know it!"

"Mayhap so, mayhap not," Conan demurred carefully. "But might it not be that the southern war is only a blind? 'Tis whispered among my troopers that most of the provisions meant for Venjipur are taken as graft, or set aside for use here in Turan, against Yildiz himself—"

"A good thing, then!" Irilya said abruptly. "I never imagined they were put to such a worthwhile end! Death to all these fools and tyrants!" She laughed then in earnest, glancing aside lingeringly at him for the first time. "Strange to hear myself say it! Once I was a woman of peace, seeking nothing but an end to this mad war. But since those days I have garnered so much frustration and pain, and seen so many evils. . . ."

"I can sympathize with you, Irilya!" Debating silently

whether to put an arm about her shoulders, Conan decided only to risk patting her lithe back. "After killing so many in Venjipur, I find many here in the capital who are far more in need of killing!"

They had emerged at the top of the hill, where had been decreed a treeless park surrounding a graceful, domed temple. To eastward and southward city lights glimmered. On the northern side, moving beacons of ships traced the Ilbars River's winding course, with the torches and fire-urns of the palace providing a grandiose centerpiece. The mild air of Persian night, warm and jasmine-scented, was fast restoring the walkers' hair and garments to comfortable dryness.

"You know, Conan," Irilya declared, turning to him more charitably than she had yet done, "as I said before, your wisest course would be to leave this place and hie back to your northern wastes. But if you are ambitious, as I suspect, and not too slavish a dog of your imperial masters, there is another avenue open to you. You could join us rebels, turn your fighting skills to our cause, even use your quaint status here to become a leader! Of course, you would have to place your own will second to that of the people."

"Irilya, it sounds as if your cause has too many leaders already."

"Nay, but it could be most opportune! Think on it." She clasped his upper arm in her respectably sized hands, applying gentle force to silence him. "The rebels are set to strike any day now—tomorrow, if chance permits. And tomorrow, if all goes as planned, you will be on a dais, as close to the emperor as I am now to you. Abolhassan will also be nearby, doubtless. If, when Yildiz reaches up to pin his medal on your turban, you would but draw your dagger and plunge it into his breast, thus . . . !" Her swift, sudden motion had enough of reality in it to make Conan flinch aside from her flashing blade. "Then, for justice's sake, you might kill Abolhassan too." Stabbing the night air, she grinned up at him, looking as wild beneath her blond tresses as any Aesir warrior-maid.

Yet the creeping chill he felt was of the here and now. "Nay, girl," he protested, "you do not know what you are asking! Abolhassan is my enemy—only Abolhassan! Why? Do not ask me; my bones tell me so!" Stubbornly he lashed his damp black hair across his shoulders.

"Tomorrow, when I receive my decoration, I will denounce him before Yildiz and tell the truth about the war in Venjipur, as I have promised my fellow troopers I would. I will explain it all—and mayhap kill the general, if time permits. Explaining may not have worked for you, but it will work for me, I swear! It must work!"

He found that, in his zeal, he had been gripping her shoulders forcibly and shaking her; now she pried herself loose and turned away, angrily rubbing the sore spots. "Very well, then, Sergeant! It appears that we have nothing in common, so we may as well part. I can make my way alone from here."

"No, wait, Irilya!" Shaking his pounding head again to clear it, Conan strode after her. "I have an appointment at the city barracks at midnight. Can you show me the way?"

She turned back to regard him coolly. "What a coincidence; that is where I am bound. I will take you there—if I can trust you not to betray my friends!"

Chapter 18

Night Pairings

In Aghrapur's central district the day's bustle had subsided, as had the stamp and scuffle of marching feet. The crowds were abed and the blood-runnels long since dried, yet there remained furtive traces of life. Foreign merchants mumbled over campfires smoldering redly before their stalls, and idlers lounged in the porticoes of brokerages, singing ballads and passing around slack wineskins. Elsewhere about the plaza, small bands of restless youths roved, excited by the day's events, angry and uncertain about what might ensue.

As Conan escorted Irilya across the littered cobblestones, he saw her wave and call out more than once, greeting familiar faces, bandying catch-phrases or bits of news, but never names. "Hail, brother! Make ready for the morrow! Citizen, have you heard, the port guards refused to charge the crowd—they stand with us! Strength to our cause!"

As the spike-topped wall of the civil barrack loomed ahead, loiterers grew scarce and Irilya became more discreet. But to Conan's surprise, as soon as they drew nigh the postern gate, she strode straight up to it and knocked boldly. A light winked in the peephole, and the portal opened inward. She entered to the sound of murmured greetings, with Conan crowding in close behind her.

"You see, these are soldiers faithful to the people's will. And my escort, here"—Irilya introduced Conan to three troopers who wore looks of mingled suspicion and recognition—"is an officer pledged to secrecy, who may yet learn the merit of our cause."

"Well enough, sister, if you vouch for him. Now come—the captain has heard our demands, and is about to render his answer!"

The troopers, leaving one of their number posted at the door, led the visitors to the archway of an inner chamber. It was overflowing with garrison troops strangely alert and ready-looking for this time of night; the armored crowd extended out into the hallway, blocking the entry. From within the room, a firm voice could be heard addressing them.

". . . I have read your petition and I agree that, after this day's slaughter, such a thing must not be repeated. I am prepared, therefore, to review any future orders of my superiors in the light of what I consider to be the public good—my stipulation being, of course, that you men will continue to obey me personally and unquestioningly. But I promise to heed the spirit of your protest; never again will the civil guard be turned against innocent citizens, in the service of an unrighteous cause!"

The shouts and cheers that greeted this statement demonstrated the troopers' renewed commitment to their leader. Promptly they were hushed as the speaker continued, "Many forces have been at odds during the recent, troublous days. Tomorrow bodes to be specially turbulent, in view of the ceremonies and public meetings planned. Therefore, I order that all troops remain armed and mobilized from this hour forward."

This speech was greeted with more cheers, and Irilya clasped Conan's shoulder excitedly. "Did you hear, he is with us, and tomorrow is the day!"

But the Cimmerian, brows knit in suspicion, pressed forward through the crowd of grinning, departing troopers. Shoving into the doorway, he gained a look at the speaker lounging on the edge of table on the far side of the briefing-room. It was, as he had guessed, Captain Omar.

Glancing up unsurprised at Conan, the captain calmly finished addressing a turbaned functionary beside him. "I have passed the order; now make sure the mounts are fed and readied by dawn. Before I take my place in the staff room, there is an errand I must attend to. Go, and I will meet you there shortly."

As his flunky hurried from the room, Omar's voice shifted to a more courtly, insinuating tone. "Well, barbarian, my suppositions about your cowardice were too hasty, perhaps." He glanced around with arch humor to the few who remained in the place. "Being late to a fight, after all, is not quite so dishonorable as shirking it entirely. Trooper, lend our guest your sword!"

The guards and civilians looked from him to the Cimmerian sharply, showing by their abrupt, retreating movements that they knew or guessed what was afoot. The soldier whom Omar had commanded drew his yataghan, handed it hilt-first to Conan, and hurriedly stepped aside. The Cimmerian slashed the sword before him, finding it to be of standard infantry balance, reliable enough, perhaps.

"I do not understand, Sergeant," Irilya demanded at his elbow. "You have already met Captain Omar, then? What is the matter?"

Ignoring her, Conan strode among benches toward the lamplit head of the room. Omar had drawn his own sword and now held it ready before him. "More honorable if we met at lance-point, perhaps—but this will teach you that a cavalry officer is no coward, afoot or in the saddle!" So saying, he lunged, sending his point darting at Conan's throat. His entire body arched behind the thrust, which Conan needed all the strength and quickness of his arm to deflect and send clanging past his ear; from that instant, he knew he faced a deadly opponent. Omar's swift, tidy grace left no opportunity for a riposte. The two blades slithered together twice again, each smoothly neutralizing the other's murderous tendings; then the fencers stepped apart to breathe.

"Conan, what are you trying to do?" Irilya, instead of keeping clear of the fight, complained shrilly at the Cimmerian's back. "Captain Omar is an ally of ours, a friend of the cause! We cannot afford to lose him in some childish brawl—come, end this fracas at once!" Suddenly, to his alarm, the Cimmerian felt her hands clutching at his elbow, tugging his sword-arm back out of action. Omar, quick to see the opening, danced forward, his blade raised in a slash well aimed to take off that same arm at the shoulder.

By an impossible duck-and-twist, Conan stepped forward into the stroke. Simultaneously, levering his weapon up with both hands, he deflected the hard-swung sword and sent it skating a hairsbreadth from his shoulder. Shaking off the still-protesting Irilya with a snarl, he spun to parry two more swift cuts. As Omar stalked him further, the Cimmerian froze in a defensive crouch, striving to regain his former, icy calm; he knew he could not allow himself the luxury of anger against this enemy.

"Sergeant, cease this duel, or I will kill you myself!"
Wild-eyed, Irilya had drawn her dagger. Conan edged
away from her, his eyes darting uneasily between his
two foes.

But to his gut-churning surprise, the captain's next
stroke was sideward, toward Irilya. The flat of his blade
lashed forth deftly, striking the woman's cheek with an
audible slap; from it she staggered back, fingering the
pale welt where the steel had crossed her delicate skin.

"Madam," Omar proclaimed then to the whole company, "need I inform you that this is an affair of honor?
Your importunings on my behalf are unwelcome—nay,
insulting, and so I suggest that you leave here. In fact,
messengers, our confederate—the highly placed one
who cannot be named—has requested to see the Lady
Irilya tonight. You two may as well take her to the
palace . . . at once!"

Before Irilya could turn and bolt, the two turbaned
aides Omar had commanded stepped forward, seized
her arms, and marched her toward the door. The
troopers in the room stood watching uncertainly. They
were cowed by the spectacle of the duel, no doubt, and
by their captain's capable, steel-edged authority.

But Conan could restrain himself no longer; growling
curses, he sprang to attack the hypocritical Omar. His
sword volleyed blows, chiming and grating against the
captain's infallibly raised steel, slashing and flailing at
his foe in savage, murderous cuts.

The Turanian's blade countered the strokes by a
seemingly magical omnipresence. Weaving a web of
invulnerability in vacant air, the swordsman unfailingly
met the hazards from each new angle. Elegantly the
captain paced, sidestepped, retreated, conserving
strength in the face of his attacker's angry, profligate
efforts. The wave of every attack must peak, as expert

fencers knew—and afterward topple and dissipate, in a seethe of vulnerability a clever fighter knew how to exploit.

The climax came as Conan's whistling brand drove downward in a mighty overhand stroke. Omar, penned between table and wall, could not evade it; only a brute parry was possible. The two blades met overhead with a clash that could have shattered one or both; instead, they locked in air, grating and grinding together in a pointless stalemate. No fine fencing here, and no elegant resolution possible, either; just brute effort . . . until Conan disengaged his sword and turned easily away, leaving the jeweled hilt of his dagger protruding from Omar's belly.

As the captain crumpled, the watching troopers rushed forward to his side. Conan strode to the doorway, pausing only to tell them, "You may keep the dagger, since it is lodged in your commander's ribs. Would that I could use it to carve the lies out of his gullet, the way pearls are cut from an oyster! But I must go now and undo a small part of his mischief!"

Conan overtook Irilya and her captors in a deserted lane a short distance from the barrack. The three were already engaged in a scuffle; one of the men came stumbling back, propelled by a kick, to fall on the Cimmerian's all-too-ready sword. Conan, once he had shaken off the writhing body, sprang to Irilya's side—only to find the second man already kneeling before her, choking on the dagger she had stuck in his throat.

The woman, trembling with reaction, clutched Conan's arm tearfully to steady herself. After long, panting moments she addressed him, rough-voiced. "Captain Omar is dead, then?"

"Aye, or soon to be! He was no true friend of your rebels; more likely a pawn of our common foe."

"Perhaps." Irilya sighed raggedly, letting Conan lead her away from the reeking, trickling bodies. "With so many plots and deceits afoot this night, how can we be sure of anything? It all seems so wild . . . maybe chaos will descend tomorrow, after all!"

"Who can say? We are not gods." Conan clasped her shoulder. "'Tis hard even to know whether a single mortal can make a difference."

After walking some distance, keeping to dim, deserted lanes, they came to a broad, softly splashing public fountain. To Conan's surprise, Irilya let go his arm, stepped across the sculpted rim, and waded into the moon-silvered water.

Turning, she smiled at him for the first time, alluringly. "We are both soiled again, this time with evildoers' blood." Undoing her gown at the neck, she let it slip from her creamy shoulders into thigh-deep water, then stepped out of its floating folds. "We would be wise to wash it off," she said, stretching her ivory arms to him. "Come, hero, let me cleanse you!"

"What say you, eunuch? Captain Omar, dead?" General Abolhassan paced his chamber, his black cape and turban casting a lurid shadow on the room's scarlet hangings. "Strange to say, the consummate duellist, outdone by jungle savagery! Somehow I did not expect it." The bemused shake of the warrior's head made the gems in his turban glint in the lamplight. "The captain's death will be an inconvenience to us; see that he is replaced by a trustworthy subordinate." The general wheeled, fixing his gaze on his visitor. "What of the barbarian, was he scathed?"

"Nay, sir." Euranthus stood before the general, obviously uneasy at being the bearer of ill tidings. "By report of my spies, he was last seen naked in a public fountain, coupling with the woman Irilya."

Abolhassan's face darkened and he spun away, striding another dozen paces in his spurred, clinking boots. "I see," he finally answered on his return, wearing a forced, unpleasant smile. "Perhaps it is a boon that my enemies consort together, making it easier for me to watch them. But remember, as soon as the girl is alone, I want her taken!"

"Yes, General." The young eunuch chief stood not quite at attention, his hands nervously clasping and unclasping behind his back. "And the barbarian. . . ?"

"Just make sure that he attends his ceremony; this puts me in mind of a new plan of action." Turning and stalking the floor like any commander on the eve of his greatest battle, Abolhassan dictated briskly to his minister.

"Tomorrow, when our emperor fulfills his fatuous dream of proclaiming a hero, I will be standing beside them both to present the golden bauble. I once regarded that menial task as beneath me, but now I see its value: 'Twill be a simple matter to slay Yildiz, then cry out that the assassin was Conan and skewer him as well! None will know the difference, or dare to tell it; in any case, those at the forefront of the assembly will in the main be our friends." He came to a jingling halt before his guest. "Well, Euranthus, what think you?"

The slim youth stood frozen, his eyes widening to take in the enormity of the deed. "A daring plan, Lord Abolhassan! 'Tis brilliant!"

The general grinned as broadly as any man would ever see him do. "Aye, eunuch, and a sound one! This way, we shall have no need of civil upheavals or ultimata, and no humiliating dependence on the rabble. 'Tis my foolproof path to kingship! Now we need only work out the details. . . ."

Chapter 19

Reward of Valor

During the hours before dawn, through the efforts of the invisible, industrious horde of slaves and eunuchs ever waiting to work the Resplendent Emperor's will, the Court of Protocols underwent another transformation. Spent bodies and foodstuffs were removed from its floor, the spattered tiles and inlays were scrubbed and polished, banners and bunting strung high from the room's carved vaultings, and silk cushions set forth to pamper the seats of Aghrapur's mighty. Lastly, around the chamber's high walls and broad, lofty dome, the vents and lancet windows were opened, letting golden sunrays stream in to illumine the splendors of the place for the gathering celebrants.

These worthies straggled in throughout the morning, displaying a trepid uncertainty that ill matched the lavish preparations on their behalf. Some were haggard from the previous night's debauch; others looked oddly wary and doubtful whether they ought to be present. Uneasy at mutterings of discontent and rebellion, they weighed the risk of a public appearance in such parlous times against the greater risk of non-appearance, a too-conspicuous absence from a ceremony ordained by the omnipotent Emperor Yildiz.

Afraid of missing the event, in compromise, they came late. What they failed to realize was that, as always at these lofty functions, lateness was a measure and a privilege of rank, with the highest functionaries arriving much later, and the emperor last of all.

As the guests trickled in they sat on pews or cushions carefully chosen, with reference to the seating of rival factions, the emperor's probable line of sight, and the exits. Primly each noble tidied his robes and retainers around him, conversing in discreet murmurs, genteely ignoring the servants. As the morning advanced these nonentities glided forth with trays of drink and foodstuffs unappetizingly like those which had flown about the courtiers' ears the previous evening.

Yet in one quarter of the spacious court, food and drink were briskly in demand. In that small corner, in a railed box close alongside the dais reserved for the more public phases of state business, there reigned a mood contrary to the prevalent atmosphere of bored resolution. There sat Conan with Irilya, now obviously and unabashedly his intimate. These two were among the earliest arrivals, certainly the noisiest. Around them flitted servants attending to their needs, bowing and smirking politely at their jests and antics; around them too flitted the eunuch Sempronius.

"I am glad to see you enjoying yourself here at court, Sergeant, and that you have found yourself an . . . admirer." With an air of dubiety, Sempronius eyed Irilya's abandoned posture as she lay against the sprawling Conan, both arms and one leg tangled among his own disheveled limbs. "I hope you will appreciate, too, the solemnity and dignity of this event, as Aghrapur and her immortal emperor honor a hero."

"Aye, in sooth, I do appreciate it," Conan rumbled

good-naturedly, meanwhile twining the fingers of one hand through his lover's blond tresses and making her purr in contentment. "'Tis truly a hero's welcome, one that any of my brother troopers would crave! I thank you for it heartily, gelding!" He adjusted his posture on the low-backed couch, drawing Irilya closer. "Now, you mentioned something about finding us new tunics to replace these damp, shredded ones?"

"Yes, to be sure! That would improve your appearance, and perhaps make it less necessary for you to . . . huddle together for warmth. I will see to it at once!" Officiously the eunuch turned away, sending servants scattering left and right before him.

When Sempronius had gone, Irilya drew herself up at Conan's side. With a languorous sigh she watched him drain his silver beaker of kumiss and replace it on a lacquered tray for refilling by attentive slaves.

"He is right, you know," she murmured in his ear. "Though we delight in one another, and though I cannot keep my hands from you"—this she demonstrated with a gesture rendered invisible by the rumpled pleats of his tunic—"we must remember the seriousness of the day and the perils that range around us." Coolly her glance swept the gallery, the servants, the still-arriving courtiers, and the guards standing rigid by the archways. "I credit your good faith in wanting to warn Yildiz, Conan, though likely your plan will not work. In any event, we must not become too drunk or too lovestruck to seize the moment—or at least, save ourselves."

"Aye, Irilya, you are right; I will drink only kvass henceforth." Conan waved accordingly, dismissing one pair of servants and beckoning another. Then he looked around to her with a smile. "But I warn you, I cannot vouch for my friend Juma, yonder; judging by his bleary look, he may require the strongest liquor."

As Irilya took in the black warrior, he approached the box, not in fact seeming even slightly fatigued. On either hand clung his two courtly escorts of the previous evening, both looking distinctly contented, even radiant. Juma, after stepping over the wooden railing of the box, assisted the women across, with much patting and giggling. Irilya accepted the three with equanimity, and so they seated themselves beside the couple on the curving, upholstered couch.

Their arrival renewed the festive atmosphere of the booth and drew more stares from idle watchers elsewhere in the hall—especially when Sempronius arrived with new garments for Conan and Irilya to try on. They did so with hilarity, screened from general view by a silk canopy held upright by servants. Afterward the small party set the slaves scurrying even faster for food and drink, while exchanging droll anecdotes of the previous night's food battle.

"Tell me then, Juma," Irilya asked the Kushite, "does Conan have a woman in Venjipur?" Her sudden question brought giggles from the other females, instant silence from the men.

"Truly, milady," Juma answered with hardly a stumble, "there is no shortage of women in Venjipur! Camp followers, tavern girls, peasant daughters whose kisses can be had for a brass arrowpoint. But Conan, as you know, is a man of rectitude, a steadfast warrior who would not squander himself on such—"

"Yes, I have a Venji woman," Conan said, interrupting his friend with a frank look at Irilya. "Her name is Sariya; I rescued her from death in a pagan rite."

"You keep her safe, then?"

"Yes, we live together in a bamboo hut. Sariya is a wise, able girl, schooled far beyond my own meager learning . . . but I confess, at times I do not know her heart."

Irilya's answering gaze was quiet and deep, her bearing steady. Juma and his companions quickly raised a distraction, pointing to new activity at the front of the dais.

But this was of slight importance, just another of the innumerable false starts which attend such gatherings. Four male slaves carried in a litter containing the Venji potted tree; having set it down on the dais, they slid the earthenware pot clear, took up their litter, and departed. It was not, after all, a final prelude to the ceremony; the tree was left there by itself, looking slightly ridiculous. Its potbellied trunk and glossy, bedraggled leaves drew a few disparaging comments from the assembly.

Nevertheless, this bit of preparation kindled expectations and seemed to reawaken everyone's doubts and fears regarding the gathering. Talk in the slowly filling chamber murmured low and earnest. Conan confided his own intentions and misgivings to Juma, and both men surreptitiously checked the readiness of their gold-hilted ceremonial sabers. They watched the arrival of more lofty court personages, some of whom Irilya named to them or waved greetings to from afar.

With more forebodings, they saw the arrival of a special contingent of twenty Imperial Honor Guards, whom General Abolhassan marched in a file before the dais and stationed there, rigidly outward-facing. The general, tall and imposing in his black uniform, did not greet Conan's party, nor even glance their way. But he spent much time elsewhere in the gallery, clasping shoulders and whispering in the ears of petty functionaries and potentates alike.

Conan saw much around him to unease his spirit: the taut, wary looks on the most noble faces; the fact that the eunuchs, almost equaling the guards in number, went armed with long daggers; and the sudden, awkward restraint of their guide Sempronius, evident only after his private conversation with the chief eunuch he called Euranthus. The Cimmerian had sensed that his attendant's frequent, noisy pronouncements of loyalty to the emperor did not sit well with his fellows; now, abruptly, these protestations ceased. The eunuch uncharacteristically left off fretting over his heroic charges and stood well apart from them.

Abruptly, an exultation of trumpets thrilled the room. In the hush that ensued came the shuffling of boots and the rattling of scabbards; then in through the tall central door strode Emperor Yildiz. Resplendent as his imperial title implied, he nevertheless looked squat and plump between General Abolhassan and another towering, gray-turbaned officer. Behind them, fetchingly caped and pantalooned, trooped two smiling harem maids whose height and robustness also tended to dwarf their emperor; obviously, Yildiz did not select his attendants for scantness of size or physique.

The two officers parted from their emperor on the dais, marching away to either side as Yildiz proceeded toward the front. His pair of houris followed, to sink down adoringly at either hand. Seating themselves on the floor, they left their resplendent lord standing as the foremost, loftiest object before the crowd, taller even than the potted Venji tree.

"Loyal subjects," Yildiz began in a grandiloquent, surprisingly resonant voice, "I have decreed these feast days and commanded your presence here to honor a hero! Nay, more than just a single hero, a whole host of them: the brave, able Turanian sons and converts who fight for our Imperial cause in far-off Venjipur and elsewhere along our restless borders.

"Doubt not that they are heroes, each and every one; for they spread the light of empire to obscure corners of the map. They broaden our sources of trade and tribute, helping to make Aghrapur the principal city of the known world! They kindle the bright dawn of civilization amid the murky night of barbarism. Above all, remember, they fight a religious war, for a holy cause—the struggle of our enlightened, all-embracing Turanian faith against ancient and primitive idols, of whose evil rites and manifestations you have heard. In doing so, these heroes face perils, even death—but remember, in the words of the Prophet Tarim, the death of the body can mean the birth of the soul into righteousness!

"They fight for Tarim, and for our greatness; nevertheless, there are those among my subjects who bridle and fret at the burden of this holy war. They mourn the loss or removal of their beloved sons; they cry and rail against the inexorable force of destiny, as all bereaved kin must. To them I offer this reminder, again in Tarim's immortal words, that a man is judged by the worth of his enemies as well as by that of his friends. Of what merit, I ask you, is a man without foes, or an empire without wars?

"For all of you, I intended this day of heroes to be a renewal of spirit, a fresh inspiration toward our Imperial cause. I hope that my subjects will begin to ask less of their empire and more of themselves, in advancing our mutual destiny. And now"—at the casual gesture of his hand, a servant hurried forward bearing a gold goblet on a golden tray—"for those of you who have drink ready to hand, I commend a toast!" He raised his cup to the crowd in salute, across the rigid backs and red-swaddled heads of the line of guards. "To Conan, the hero, and Juma"—Yildiz pivoted where he stood, doffing his drink toward the box containing the two foreigners—"and to all the heroes who serve our empire, in Venjipur and other far climes!"

He sipped sparingly from the goblet, or pretended to, certainly mindful of the risk of poison. "And after the

toast, a libation"—glancing around the patterned floor
of the dais, immaculate beneath the dimpled knees of
his harem maids, Yildiz quickly settled on the pot of the
jungle plant as the only handy receptacle—"to our
mighty god, and to the soil of Venjipur that cradles this
tree, which we now declare to be part of our own land.
Hail, Tarim!" So saying, he emptied his goblet over the
tree's roots, then tossed the cup aside on the dais.

All across the gallery the toast was reciprocated,
though not the libation, except by a few who
unintentionally splattered their draughts as they raised
them high. Conan heard his name and Juma's given
back in a scattered murmur by scores of throats; in all,
the crowd's reaction to their emperor's speech seemed
tolerant. Yildiz, in his personable, plain-spoken way,
had evidently won over some of his listeners and
soothed others' fears of civil turmoil. In the babble of
comment exchanged by the audience, Conan sensed for
the first time a note of acceptance and relief.

"And now," His Resplendency was saying, "if the
heroes will come forward so that we may honor them in
person . . ." Signaled by Sempronius, Conan and Juma
arose and stepped to the gate of their railed enclosure.
"The good General Abolhassan bears tokens of our
favor—but what is this, a miracle?"

Conan had been watching the scowling general
march forward, aglitter with gold trim and weaponry,
holding before him a tasseled pillow to which a pair of
gleaming trinkets were pinned. But Yildiz's sudden
exclamation diverted the Cimmerian's attention; looking to the center of the dais, he saw with surprise an
odd, unnatural agitation in the leaves of the potted
jungle tree. It moved squirmingly, shudderingly, its
limbs and glossy foliage shifting in a restlessness no
earthly wind could have induced. An agony of sudden
growth it seemed to be, massive and impossibly acceler-

ated; in the time it took Conan's jaw to sag in wonder, the tree nearly doubled its height and width, jostling and overshadowing Yildiz and his concubines as it swelled greedily into the sunrays streaming down from the overhead vents.

The growth looked eerily natural, except for its uncanny speed; Conan could see branches extruding at the ends like blind, questing worms, and baby-green foliage exploding from fresh buds along the way. Yet there was a devious directionality to it; as the Cimmerian watched, frozen in his tracks, long shoots propagated out and downward from the thickening shoulders of the tree's main limbs. Widening in a parody of long, grasping fingers, these branches managed to seize sudden hold of Emperor Yildiz and one of his quailing concubines. It happened impossibly fast, before the gaping monarch could even flinch; the second maiden escaped only by throwing herself flat on the floor. Squirming and wriggling, using all her skills as a harem-dancer, she managed to evade the fronds and tendrils that groped forth to ensnare her.

The clutching growth was lightning-swift and deceptive; in the space of a single, startled breath, Yildiz and his houri were hoisted clear of the floor to hang helpless, struggling in the tree's twining grip. New tendrils snaked forth to enfold their necks and faces; yet once they had been snared, the darting urgency of the first growth was gone—transferred outward, it seemed; for the tree still grew on all sides, expanding ever faster.

So it went; one moment the wild-eyed harem wench was clawing past Conan, to pelt away on bare feet; the next, nearly all the guards along the front of the dais were entangled with grasping branches, their weapons half-drawn, their orders and military decorum forgotten in a clawing struggle for survival. That same moment Abolhassan threw aside his spangled pillow and drew his saber, to hack furiously at fast-spreading limbs; Conan, for reasons he scarcely paused to examine, found himself advancing with sword drawn, stalking toward the tree's center and its slowly strangling victims.

By the time he had taken two steps he was embattled, greedy tendrils snaking down at him from the ever-thickening mass overhead. He hacked them off with the skill of an old jungle hand, plying his gold-hilted sword like an oversized brush knife. Yet the silent, insidious creepers also snaked down behind him, entwining his neck and shoulders in their rough, leafy clutch before he could twist free. Their grip was surprisingly tight, and Conan soon felt the reach of his sword-arm dangerously hampered. Struggling vainly against the tough, constricting foliage, he watched supple vines race the length of his extended sword-arm, there to branch upward toward new fronds threading down from above.

Of a sudden, a blade flickered near the corner of his eye, and heavy chopping noises sounded about his ears, together with gasps and curses.

"Blast this weed, 'tis an abomination under Ito, a sending of the fierce jungle itself!" Juma's gruff voice panted in his ear.

Feeling the tight, dragging restraint on his body suddenly loosen, Conan tore free, muttering half-choked thanks at the Kushite.

To his surprise, as he shook off the last of the clinging fronds, he blundered up against Irilya; she stood close beside Juma, slashing at the tree's leafy overburden with a hook-headed pike she must have retrieved from one of the dangling guards.

"Woman, what are you doing here?" Conan demanded of her, even as he raised his sword to prune back new, probing tendrils of the demon tree.

"What? Why, rescuing you, you thankless clout!" Her

bill-hook slashed perilously close to his face as it chopped down an insinuating frond. "Why, where should I be?"

"You . . . uh . . ." Conan was about to order her off to safety, but a glance around the hall showed him that safety did not exist.

Everywhere, even among the frenzied crowds clawing toward the archways, the devilish fronds and creepers plucked and insinuated themselves freely. From its puny original size the tree had burgeoned impossibly wide, filling the entire Court of Protocols; its height beneath the spacious dome was unguessable, except by the leaf-filtered dimness of jungle light trickling down from above. Many of the onlookers, especially those in favored places on or near the dais, already depended from the tree's crooked limbs, furiously battling or slowly strangling. Vine-swathed, they resembled frantic insects wrapped in spider-silk or strange, writhing fruit.

Whether such a death was worse than a fatal trampling in the exits, Conan was no judge. So, slashing tirelessly at the menacing vines, he turned to Irilya and Juma. "Come, stay together then, and follow me! We will fell this sorcerous tree like a worm-eaten forest snag!"

The task did not promise to be an easy one, for the tree's trunk had grown almost in proportion to its girth. Its planting-pot had long since shattered to fragments; now the massive overhead limbs radiated from a knotty labyrinth above a rough, pot-bellied trunk. Thick, gnarled roots plunged downward into the very stones of the palace, clenching its foundation like talons and forcing up long ridges of inlaid tile that mapped their tortuous windings beneath the floor. Hard as thick-knotted cables, the roots seemed almost to pulsate with the strength of their grip on the stony substrate.

"Ah well, at least we jungle hands are better at hewing

shrubbery than city or desert troops!" So saying, Conan protected the others' backs as they slashed at the tough vines enwrapping Yildiz and his houri, suspended close before the trunk. Soon the latter's faces hung visible once again, blue and fish-mouthed with strangulation, yet thirstily gasping in air.

Then Conan and Juma attacked the trunk of the tree, swinging sharp-bladed axes dropped by the ill-fated household guards. They alternated strokes in swift, expert rhythm, hacking through the tough outer bark and its oozing green underlayer, then deep into the tree's damp, pale flesh. In unspoken agreement they concentrated on the widest part of the trunk: the swollen, sinister belly. From its gravid fullness they sent thick chunks of wood flying with tireless blows. They trusted to Irilya to chop and slash away encroaching vines with her bill-hook, which she plied at their backs with desperate energy.

"Watch beneath—beware the roots!" Conan heard Juma grunt between ax-strokes.

He looked down to see the tree, in diligent self-defense, sending up pale, hairy tendrils from beneath the shattered floor-tiles. These grew swiftly, threading snakily up over the men's ankles. Yet Conan scarcely shifted his footing as Irilya desperately alternated her chopping above and below, slicing perilously close to his feet with her halberd. Instead, in silent accord with Juma, he leaned harder into his ax-strokes, hewing rhythmically at the great trunk, whose bulbous belly now echoed thuddingly with each blow.

"Hollow, by Crom!" Conan exclaimed, prying out blackened splinters of wood from the heart of the trunk with a twist of his ax. "And, faugh, smell that stench! Can it be rotten already?"

"Look, there is treasure within!" Kneeling before the splintered cavern their axes had opened, Juma pointed to gems glittering from the interior darkness like winking eyes.

"No, do not reach inside!" Irilya, shoving the Kushite's hand away, thrust her hooked weapon into the fecund aperture and probed there, raking forth the sizeable lump of riches it contained.

"Why, 'tis a human skull, thick with silver and gems!" Juma exclaimed. He started to reach for it, but jerked back his hand as Conan's ax hurtled down. The blow smashed the sinister ornament into flying fragments of silver, gem, and bone.

"'Twas the emblem of Mojurna, leader of the Hwong rebels," Conan said to the others' questioning stares as he disentangled his ankles from the suddenly brittle rootlets. "I should have guessed that this accursed tree was Mojurna's, sent to wreak vengeance on the Emperor Yildiz and the whole court!"

At mention of the emperor, they turned back to him where he hung enwrapped with his concubine. Both were semiconscious, their labored breaths constricted as in a python's hug, yet still alive; it was Juma who drew his dagger and undertook the task of cutting them free and easing them to the floor.

With the smashing of the jeweled skull, the hellish vitality of the jungle plant seemed to depart. Now Conan and Irilya saw leaves withering before their eyes, fluttering to the floor in what must soon become a deep carpet. Branches in far-flung corners of the court groaned and sagged low, laden heavily with their mortal harvest. The last humans free to move had fled the room some time before; for most of those in its toils, the tree's death had come too late.

Conan and Irilya roved the place, cutting loose the lucky few—the guard-captain who had been saved by his helmet and breastplate, the courtesan fortunate enough to have donned heavy neck-clasps that morning.

As they went, Irilya pointed out many illustrious faces empurpled by choking death: diverse eunuchs, including both Sempronius and Euranthus, the fanatic high priest Tammuraz, a young, foppish aristocrat named Philander, and countless others known to her. General Abolhassan they found in a tangle of braid and armor not far from the tree's trunk, dangling head downward, his tongue protruding almost as blackly as the loops of his disarrayed turban.

By the time they returned to the emperor's side, he breathed steadily, his gaze slowly refocusing under Juma's careful ministrations. He even ventured dry, rasping speech.

"What a horror! Our pageant ruined . . ." Yildiz rolled his eyes and lolled his bald-topped head weakly aside. "What of my little turtledove, is she all right?" His Resplendency squinted closely at the fleshy, heaving bosom of his houri. "Tarim bless her, she lives! But many have died, I fear."

"Most of the court, Sire." Irilya stooped low over him. Conan knelt close beside her, unsure of her intentions, and watchful lest her hand creep to her dagger. "'Tis a day of great sorrow for our city," she continued. To Conan's surprise, he caught the gleam of tears in her eyes. "But the worst menace is past. We can survive all this, Sire, and your rule can be sustained peacefully, if only Your Resplendency will end our foreign campaigns and concentrate on improving things here at home."

"Aye, Emperor," Conan added gruffly. "Among the dead are those who plotted against you; now you can revamp your court. As for the war in Venjipur—well, that can still be won, but it must be run differently. The present command system is rotten with greed and misrule—"

As Conan had feared earlier, Irilya's hand flew to her dagger, forcing him to clutch her wrist and restrain her.

But her lunge and her tearful glare of hatred, he found with surprise, were directed not at Yildiz but at himself. After a tense moment, their standoff was interrupted by an anguished croak from beneath.

"Venjipur! Tell me not of Venjipur," the emperor moaned, waving a hand at the vast, wilting tree of death above them. "Was not this horrid doom another curse of their vile witchcraft, meant to strike me down in the peaceful heart of my empire? Venjipur! Oh, how I rue ever hearing the wretched name, and curse the greedy whim that made me wish to rule it! I relent—do you hear, O gods, I want no more of it!"

The survivors knelt distraught, staring at one another as their ruler's oaths rasped out across the court. Meanwhile, from the entryways sounded thumps and hails as the outer world overcame its fear and ventured to return.

Chapter 20

Return to Venjipur

"**T**here is smoke on the wind from the gulf." Sitting beside Conan in the swaying howdah, Juma stated aloud what had been evident to both men for some time. "'Tis not the season for burning rice husks, so there must fighting along the river delta. See, even our elephant knows something is amiss!"

The Kushite nodded toward the huge animal's trunk, which curved aloft cobra-like, sampling the breeze in various aspects. In this matter of tasting the air, their lumbering steed was privileged to be at front of the column, free of the dust and stink of the four more elephants and five hundred border infantry tramping close behind.

To Juma's observation Conan made no answer, merely flaring his own nostrils and thoughtfully scanning the hazy expanse of farm fields and jungle ridges ahead. This return to a land he despised as he would death itself, but which he had nevertheless found himself yearning for in recent weeks, stirred up poignant, indefinable feelings in his breast. Part of his emotion

271

was the desire for his lover Sariya; yet he knew there was also more than that, and less.

"Ha!" Juma observed to nobody in particular. "Even I underestimated the perils of playing the hero game, it would seem. Now we are saddled with the job of calling off this war and extricating the Imperial legions, all with the aid of a mere token force! Do you think old Mojurna and his Hwong tribesmen will feel charitably inclined and let us all go home in peace?"

After a moment the Kushite, tolerant of Conan's silent moods, barked another laugh and continued the one-sided conversation. "But then, after all, who could have refused Yildiz's offer? His decree, rather: a field promotion for you to the rank of captain, and guaranteed berths for both of us in the Imperial Honor Guard once we return—if we return! And that will hardly be the limit of your success with His Resplendency, I think, if you do nothing to foul it up!"

Turning his gaze aside to Conan's cross-kneed, pensive form, the Kushite frowned a little petulantly. "I could confess to having some jealousy over that; why should he choose to promote you, the junior of us two, after it was I who cut him down from the devil-tree and nursed him back to life?" Juma shook his head resignedly. "You are his pet, it would seem, Conan; welcome to the privilege, and good luck surviving it!" He sighed mightily. "But 'tis no matter—once we deliver his Imperial proclamation and return to Aghrapur, life will be pullets and gravy for both of us."

Juma rattled on good-naturedly, patting the scroll-case lying in the fighting-box before both of them. The ornate metal tube contained Yildiz's decree that the war would cease and the Turanian forces be withdrawn. As his friend touched the case, Conan also did so protectively; turning to face his friend, he opened his mouth to speak at last. But just then there came a shout from their elephant-driver and they turned to see their mount's bat-winged ears fluttering in warning. Squinting ahead, they spied horsemen approaching on the road.

The riders were some two hundred troops, Turanian by their costume, weary and ragged astride mud-spattered mounts. They reined in gratefully just ahead of the halted infantry column, although their faces were too grim to show much rejoicing at the friendly rein-forcements. Conan recognized their commander and called down to him from the howdah. "Greetings, Shahdib, what news?"

"The worst, Conan—Captain, I mean," he amended, eying his questioner's gold-medalled turban with respect. "The rebels are up in arms, more of them than we have seen before. The city of Venjipur fell in a single day! The smaller outposts have all been wiped out, and the forts are heavily besieged. Yesterday we escaped the fall of Karapur—"

"What of Sikander?" Conan asked abruptly.

"Sikander has been embattled for days. If it still exists, 'tis by a miracle; in any case it cannot hold for long." The officer cast his head down as he shook it, seeming reluctant to meet Conan's eyes. "The main rebel activity has been in that area; we dared not try to relieve the fort—"

"Then dare to do it now," Conan told him, waving a signal to his infantry officers. "Fort Sikander is where we are going."

The column started forward with a weary scuffing and stamping, the horse troops reluctantly turning their mounts to march at the fore.

"Otumbe's lightnings!" Juma muttered grimly at Conan's side. "Affairs have come to a sorry pass since we left! You are right, we have no choice but to venture into the tiger's jaws, and try to save what few of our friends have not yet been chewed up and swallowed. I hope the rebels will accept our withdrawal; peace is our only hope."

"Perhaps." Conan sat cross-legged once again, watching the smoky valley unrolling ahead. "On the other hand, our force is a seasoned one, and may grow larger with stragglers from other battles. Revolutions have triumphed before in a single day, only to go down in defeat the next."

"Conan, you would not dare to defy the emperor?" Juma glanced at Conan's hand, which held the scroll-case containing the imperial decree. In his massive grip, with its flaring, bronze-capped ends, it resembled, more than any peace treaty, a sceptre of royal rank.

"Would Yildiz complain if Venjipur were handed to him on a platter?" Conan's face, stern and a little haggard-eyed, flashed his friend an icy look. "This war has been poorly waged from the start; you and I can correct that. As for the rebels—if they have harmed Sariya, I will not feel much inclined to offer them peace!"

The road to Sikander was strangely free of armed resistance. In places the muddy track streamed with refugees, and with larger groups of Venjis who seemed purposeful and organized. Possibly these bands were rebels, yet they yielded the road to Conan's troop and made no threatening gesture; in any case they were too numerous to attack, so the troopers passed them by. The distinction between rebels and friendly peasants had always been a chancy one at best.

Later, even when the scarred palisades of Fort Sikander loomed in sight, the rebels did not contest the road. Conan marched his column past the site of his cottage, which now existed only as a litter of charred timbers beneath felled forest trunks. The village outside the fort likewise had been burned, its rubble converted to makeshift offensive bastions facing the gate. Conan had his men take up positions there as he and Juma ambled their elephant up to the main approach. The gate stood half-open, with Venjis and weaponless Turanian troopers milling before it.

Conan recognized some of the men by the half-closed portal: one-eared Orvad and a handful of Conan's other fellow-troopers, who saluted him with guarded nods and smiles; yet he noticed that all the faces along the rampart were Venji, and none too trusting. Ordering his elephant halted, he swung down its precipitous flank and confronted the familiar, gray-haired senior officer.

"Murad, what has happened here? Has Fort Sikander fallen, then?"

The Captain's gray eyes met Conan's only briefly, and with brooding suspicion. "Ask your girlfriend!" he replied, shrugging.

"Why? Is she within?" Conan shot a quizzical glance at Juma, who stood by his side seeming equally puzzled. They both looked up then to see the fort's double-valved gate swinging the rest of the way open before them. Within, before a wooden altar heaped high with palm fronds and flowers, stood an assembly of brightly clad Venjis: chieftains, priests, Hwong warriors and maidens, with a remarkable-looking female standing at the fore.

She was taller than any of the others, wrapped in a white robe belted with spangled snakeskin. Garlands of jungle flowers draped her hair, and from her neck dangled charms that looked more mystical in purpose than ornamental. One of her beringed hands gripped a tall wooden stave topped with a bulky emblem: the skull of a forest pig, its razored tusks entwined with flower-vines. Ruby pinpoints twinkled from the eyeholes, and small bits of silver and gemstone had been inlaid elsewhere about it. Remembering the talisman from the roof-pole of his ruined hut, Conan's eyes traveled back down the staff to recognize its owner.

"Sariya, girl, 'tis you! Are you a captive? But no matter, I see they have not mistreated you!" Conan strode forward, extending an arm to embrace her. "It warms my heart to see find you here."

"No, do not touch me," the woman replied with a remote, regal air. Though she remained steadfastly facing him, two frightened-looking Venji maidens, one on either hand, edged forward as if to protect her. "I am now priestess, and yours no longer, Conan of Hyboria! For know you, Venjipur has but one Priestess! Our time together is past."

"Sariya, what . . . ?" Conan halted in his tracks, speechless with amazement, scanning the stiff faces and ceremonial dress of the tribesfolk and elders arrayed behind his stately lover. Abruptly his hand closed on his sword-hilt. "If this is something they mean to force on you, Sariya . . . ! Some new enchantment of Mojurna's—"

"Mojurna is dead, Captain." Her words foreclosed coldly on his. "When her magic died she could not live on for long—for Mojurna was a woman, as you have learned." Raising her free hand, she gestured aside her to the flowered altar; it was a pyre, Conan realized. In its midst, lying amid fronds and blossoms, he spied the wizened face and shriveled breasts of an ancient crone.

"And now," Sariya was saying, "the time has come for me to take her place . . . the role I was trained for, yes, and conceived for . . ."

"Sariya, when I first saw you, Mojurna wanted to kill you!" It was Conan's turn to interrupt, pointing angrily at the funeral bier. "Or else sacrifice you alive to a deathless demon! That vile old witch—"

"Yes, 'tis true, she would have broken with our age-old custom." Sariya's voice rang firm, clearly intended for other listeners besides Conan. "For Mojurna was a harsh priestess, strong-willed and ruthless when commanding her followers in battle. Perhaps she thought the war would never end, or that I was too weak to win it. For my own part, I still hope someday to be priestess over a land at peace." Her lustrous almond-shaped eyes scanned the watchers with remote, inhuman calm. "She sought to steal my youth and, with the goddess Sigtona's help, prolong her own life. If she was fanatic, even maddened at the end by the awful burdens she bore, still I must forgive her—knowing that she was my mother."

To this horror there was no possible reply. Conan stood slackly before the gate, reeling with the magnitude of it all as from a hammer-blow to his brain. Juma moved up beside him and laid an arm across his shoulders to steady him. Meanwhile Sariya spoke gravely on.

"Whatever the cruelty of her methods, they have led us near victory—though none knows what the morrow may bring. My own way was more subtle, yet it was chosen just as carefully for the good of our land. I defied Mojurna, led my own faction among the faithful, and spread my beliefs. No other Venji than I could have resisted her magic or shielded the heretics. For my own protection in a violent time, I clung to one who was invincible in battle, a natural leader. I counseled him, healed his wounds and strengthened him further." For the first time, as Sariya's gaze returned to Conan, he heard the merest quaver of sentiment in her firm, level voice. "We learned the ways of the home together. And the ways of love, as every Priestess should. But those days are gone."

A long silence ensued, eerie under the smoke-yellowed sun. At last Conan, searching in his taut throat, found a ragged, grating voice. "Mojurna's magic was strong enough for your purpose, Sariya—almost too strong. Yildiz sues for peace." Reaching to his belt, he drew forth not his sword, but the tube containing the imperial decree. He stepped clear of Juma's comforting arm and held the proclamation out to Sariya.

"No surprise, I confess," the priestess answered. "Venji magic was always stronger than the smug faith of Turan." She nodded to one of her chieftains, who came forward and accepted the scroll. "I will call a halt to the various sieges and set your men free. That will lessen the suffering, but not end it; the Venjis who served your cause will have to decide whether to go with you, or risk staying. It may bring peace—if your soldiers will obey you and follow you from Venjipur, never to return."

"A more welcome order could not be given"—Conan lingered, facing Sariya—"for most of them." He searched her eyes. "For myself, I still wonder if this is truly your wish."

"Fear not, Conan." She met his gaze with utter composure. "I desire nothing more than to live out my destiny as Priestess. Be assured that after me, the line will continue." She leaned on her heavy, skull-headed staff, waving a slim hand toward the defeated Turanians. "For you and these others, there is no longer any place here."

"Well enough then, Sariya. Goodbye!" Raising a hand to her cheek, he touched her dark hair and her smooth, amber skin a final time. Then he turned to address his troops before the gate. His words, though brittle and rasping, were repeated throughout the ranks, and a cheer began to build, spreading to every throat within and without the wall.

"Send word to the embattled outposts: all expeditionaries are to ride forth and join us here. Then we head northward, dogs, and home!"

CONAN

☐	54260-6	CONAN THE CHAMPION	$3.50
☐	54261-4		Canada $4.50
☐	54228-2	CONAN THE DEFENDER	$2.95
☐	54229-0		Canada $3.50
☐	54238-X	CONAN THE DESTROYER	$2.95
☐	54239-8		Canada $3.50
☐	54258-4	CONAN THE FEARLESS	$2.95
☐	54259-2		Canada $3.95
☐	54225-8	CONAN THE INVINCIBLE	$2.95
☐	54226-6		Canada $3.50
☐	54236-3	CONAN THE MAGNIFICENT	$2.95
☐	54237-1		Canada $3.50
☐	54256-8	CONAN THE RAIDER	(Trade) $6.95
☐	54257-6		Canada $8.95
☐	54250-9	CONAN THE RENEGADE	$2.95
☐	54251-7		Canada $3.50
☐	54242-8	CONAN THE TRIUMPHANT	$2.95
☐	54243-6		Canada $3.50
☐	54231-2	CONAN THE UNCONQUERED	$2.95
☐	54232-0		Canada $3.50
☐	54252-5	CONAN THE VALOROUS	$2.95
☐	54253-3		Canada $3.95
☐	54246-0	CONAN THE VICTORIOUS	$2.95
☐	54247-9		Canada $3.50

Buy them at your local bookstore or use this handy coupon:
Clip and mail this page with your order.

Publishers Book and Audio Mailing Service
P.O. Box 120159, Staten Island, NY 10312-0004

Please send me the book(s) I have checked above. I am enclosing $_____
(please add $1.25 for the first book, and $.25 for each additional book to
cover postage and handling. Send check or money order only—no CODs.)

Name _____

Address _____

City _____ State/Zip _____

Please allow six weeks for delivery. Prices subject to change without notice.

THE BEST IN FANTASY

☐ 53147-7 DRINK THE FIRE FROM THE FLAMES $3.95
☐ 53148-5 by Scott Baker   Canada $4.95

☐ 53396-8 THE MASTER by Louise Cooper $3.50

☐ 53950-8 THE BURNING STONE by Deborah Turner Harris   Trade $7.95
☐ 53951-6   Canada $9.95

☐ 54721-7 FLIGHT IN YIKTOR by Andre Norton $2.95
☐ 54722-5   Canada $3.95

☐ 54719-5 MAGIC IN ITHKAR 4 $3.50
☐ 54720-9 edited by Andre Norton and Robert Adams Canada $4.50

☐ 55114-1 STALKING THE UNICORN by Mike Resnick $3.50
☐ 55115-X   Canada $4.50

☐ 55486-8 MADBOND by Nancy Springer $2.95
☐ 55487-6   Canada $3.95

☐ 55605-4 THE HOUNDS OF GOD by Judith Tarr $3.50
☐ 55606-2   Canada $4.50